Love You, Mean it

OTHER TITLES BY LAURA PAVLOV

The Blushing Series

You, Me, and Forever

Love You, Mean It

Rosewood River Series

Steal My Heart

My Silver Lining

Over the Moon

Crazy in Love

In a Heartbeat

Whisper Sweet Nothings

Magnolia Falls Series

Loving Romeo

Wild River

Forbidden King

Beating Heart

Finding Hayes

Cottonwood Cove Series

Into the Tide

Under the Stars

On the Shore

Before the Sunset

After the Storm

Honey Mountain Series

Always Mine

Ever Mine

Make You Mine

Simply Mine

Only Mine

The Willow Springs Series

Frayed

Tangled

Charmed

Sealed

Claimed

Montgomery Brothers Series

Legacy

Peacekeeper

Rebel

A Love You More Rock Star Romance

More Jade

More of You

More of Us

The Shine Design Series

Beautifully Damaged

Beautifully Flawed

The G. D. Taylors Series, Written with Willow Aster

Wanted Wed or Alive

The Bold and the Bullheaded

Another Motherfaker

Don't Cry Over Spilled MILF

Friends with Benefactors

Love You, Mean It

Laura Pavlov

This is a work of fiction. Names, characters, organizations, places, events, and incidents are either products of the author's imagination or are used fictitiously. Otherwise, any resemblance to actual persons, living or dead, is purely coincidental.

Published by Montlake, Seattle
www.apub.com

EU product safety contact:
Amazon Media EU S. à r.l.
38, avenue John F. Kennedy, L-1855 Luxembourg
amazonpublishing-gpsr@amazon.com

ISBN-13: 9781662525452 (paperback)
ISBN-13: 9781662525469 (digital)

Cover design by Hang Le
Cover photography by Regina Wamba of ReginaWamba.com
Cover image: © Yurii Romanchuk / Shutterstock

Printed in the United States of America

I cannot remember exactly the first time your soul
whispered to mine, but I know you woke it.
And it has never slept since.

JmStorm

CHAPTER ONE

Violet

This smoke detector was a nuisance. Could a girl not make some unhealthy pizza rolls without notifying the entire neighborhood that she was doing so?

My head was spinning as the siren blared with a fury.

I tried waving a towel at the ceiling.

I tried opening the back door to let some fresh air in, even though it was colder than a witch's tit in a brass bra outside.

So, right now, I was taking one for the team by fighting this monstrous beast on my own.

"That's it!" I shouted at the freaking smoke alarm from hell. I yanked it down from the ceiling as I balanced on a barstool in my highest heels. "You are not going to win this one!"

I stumbled back down on my four-inch stilettos, grabbed the hammer from the kitchen drawer, and cranked my neck from one side to the next as I prepared for mass destruction.

I am going to make this bastard my bitch.

"What the hell are you doing?" Charlie's voice boomed from the open doorway as he stepped inside, one brow arched with complete judgment, per usual.

"Have you ever heard of knocking, Charles?"

He took the hammer from my hand and fiddled with the smoke detector, which of course decided to turn off easily for him.

He glanced around the room, taking in the two tennis shoes I'd thrown at the ceiling, along with the empty Amazon box that I'd chucked up there as well.

And then his eyes moved to me.

His tongue swiped out along his bottom lip as his gaze moved from my face down to my feet. I glanced down, realizing that I was wearing nothing but a cropped black tee and sleep shorts that were more like panties, along with my favorite Manolo Blahniks, of course.

"Nice outfit. Heading out for tea?" His voice oozed sarcasm, but I didn't miss the way his heated gaze took me in.

I placed my hands on my hips and blew out a breath.

Charlie was sort of my landlord, although he didn't charge me rent. The home I'd just purchased from my best friend, Montana, had flooded shortly after I'd moved in. He was my contractor as well, so he'd offered me his guesthouse as a place to stay while he renovated my home.

But the man is one of the most infuriating people I've ever met.

"I'm trying to go to work. But apparently making a healthy breakfast is a crime around here."

He glanced over at my pizza rolls, sitting in a pan on the counter, and his lips twitched before he straightened his features.

"So you decided to throw some tennis shoes and an empty box at a smoke detector and put on a pair of heels?" he grumped as he took the hammer and set it back in the kitchen drawer where I'd found it.

The house was well stocked, and all I'd had to bring with me was clothing and toiletries, and of course some decorative things to make the place a little bit warmer.

"Yes, Charles. I was trying to get dressed for work, so I tossed a few items at the ceiling in hopes that I wouldn't have to climb on that wobbly barstool and yank that bastard off the ceiling."

He eyed the barstool I'd found out in the garage, which currently had a book under one leg because the other three legs were taller.

"That was supposed to go in the trash."

I shrugged. "I was working at the kitchen counter over the weekend and found it out in the garage, and it suited my needs."

"And the heels?"

What is his obsession with the heels?

I glanced down at my feet, noting that Charlie's eyes were focused more on my legs than my feet. "Duh. I couldn't reach the ceiling on the stool, so I needed a few more inches."

"You could have used a broomstick and avoided balancing on a broken barstool in a pair of deadly heels."

The only way these heels would be deadly is if I took one off and clobbered you over the head with it.

"I'm not a construction guy, Charles. I think on my feet, or shall I say, I think on my stilettos?" I held up one leg and shook it twice as I chuckled.

"I don't need a lawsuit from a tenant who isn't even paying rent," he hissed.

Was this guy for real? I risked my life turning off his stupid smoke detector, and he's giving me attitude?

"The only way I'm suing you is if being a dick is suddenly a crime." I glared at him.

He barked out a laugh, which was almost startling, seeing as the man had no sense of humor.

"I came in here to make sure you didn't burn the place down, not get a lecture on what a dick I am."

"I doubt you need a lecture to know what a dick you are," I said, using my hand to cover my laughter. I walked over to the counter and popped a pizza roll in my mouth and pointed at the pan. "Want one?"

"I'd be too afraid you were going to poison me." He turned toward the oven and bent down. "Let me check this out for you. I don't think my cousin cooked much when she stayed out here. She'd eat in the house with me and Harper most nights."

Charlie had a six-year-old daughter named Harper, and he was raising her on his own. His cousin Jordan had moved out recently, which worked out well for me, as I was in need of temporary housing.

"Well, as you can tell, I'm a real gourmet cook," I said, my voice light. My gaze moved down his muscled shoulders to where he crouched on his thick thighs as he looked inside the oven like he was trying to figure out life's biggest mystery.

He stood up and turned to face me. The man had to be a good foot taller than me. "I'm guessing it's just old. I was planning to renovate this place after she moved out, but then you went and flooded your house, so I don't see that happening anytime soon."

"Are you insinuating that I flooded my house on purpose?"

"You didn't turn your water main off when you went out of town."

This freaking guy.

"I don't know anyone who turns off their water supply when they go out of town," I said, my voice coming out much louder than I'd expected it to.

"Everyone I know turns off their water when they travel." His lips remained in a flat line, as if he was the one who was irritated with me.

"Well, you're from small-town Alaska, where a local resident is a moose with a giant set of cojones."

"You got a real thing for dicks and balls, don't you? Every time I see you, you're referencing one or the other." He walked toward the door.

"Calling someone a dick is not really referencing an actual penis. You know that, right?"

He paid me no attention and ignored the comment. "Your tile came in, if you want to stop by your house and check it before they start your primary bathroom renovation tomorrow."

"Oh. Isn't it gorgeous?" I'd chosen a beautiful blue Italian tile for the bathroom. Now that I'd been forced to renovate the house, I was going to make it my own.

"I mean, it's tile." He made no attempt to hide his sarcasm.

"Spoken like a Neanderthal." I reached for another pizza roll.

These really are the breakfast of champions.

"I'll order a new oven. If you need to cook, just come over to the house and use the oven until the new one gets here."

"Fine."

"Fine," he said as he stepped outside. "And let's not throw things at the ceiling or smash things with a hammer."

I moved closer, grabbing the door handle and forcing a smile that was obviously not genuine. "Thanks for the helpful tips. See you around, Charles."

I slammed the door as he turned to walk toward the main house, and I heard him chuckling.

I popped the pizza roll in my mouth and glanced out the window to see him walk across the yard.

He was tall and ridiculously good looking in that rugged, muscly, manly sort of way.

Which irritates me.

I made my way to the small bedroom and quickly changed for work. Luckily, I'd already done my hair and makeup, and I hurried into my closet and grabbed my boots, as it was still cold outside.

My phone rang, and I saw my best friend Montana's name light up the screen.

"Hey, Monny."

"We have a meeting in twenty minutes," she said. "Where are you?"

"I know. I'm leaving now. I had a small smoke detector issue, and a run-in with my grumpy landlord."

Loud laughter sounded from the other side of the phone, and I put her on speaker as I slipped into my favorite camel-colored dress coat.

"I don't think a man offering you a free place to live is really a landlord." She chuckled. "I just pulled in your driveway. You can hop in, and we'll head to the meeting together."

"Great. I hate driving in the snow."

"I know you do. You need a car with snow tires. But this way we can go together."

"Perfect." I grabbed my cream beanie, pulled it over my head, stepped outside, and ended the call as I hurried into her car. "We just need to stop by my house after the meeting, on our way to the office. My grumpy contractor, who also happens to be my grumpy landlord, said the new tile arrived, and I just want to check it before they move forward."

"You sure are getting your fill of Charlie lately." She smirked.

"I sure am."

And I was equal parts annoyed and entertained.

Maybe slightly more entertained than annoyed, depending on the day.

CHAPTER TWO

Charlie

"Daddy, why do you have hair in your nose?" Harper's voice woke me from sleep, and I peeked one eye open as I stretched my arms over my head. I glanced at my watch to see that it was barely six o'clock in the morning.

"Why are you up so early, Harps? I thought we agreed that we'd stay in bed a little later on Saturday mornings?"

"We did," she said, climbing up on the bed beside me. "But then I woke up because I missed you."

My fucking chest squeezed at her words.

This kid was pure sweetness.

"You missed me, huh?" I said, tucking her long waves behind her ear. "Is that why you decided to come look up my nose?"

She giggled. "I was going to tickle you, but then I saw some hair up there. And guess what, Daddy?"

"Tell me," I said, pushing to sit up, my back resting against the headboard as I yawned.

"You have hairs in your ears too." Her green eyes narrowed as she looked at me.

"Everyone has hair in their nose and their ears, baby girl," I said.

"No. I went to check. Look up there, Daddy." She climbed on my lap and tipped her head back, giving me a perfect view inside her nostrils, which made me laugh. "There aren't any hairs in there. And look in my ears too."

She gave me a nice shot of her ear next, and I scooped her up and moved to my feet. "Maybe my parents were monkeys," I said as she laughed some more.

I carried her to her bathroom and set her down on her feet, then handed her toothbrush to her and applied a dab of toothpaste. "Brush. Let me get dressed, and I'll make you some breakfast."

"You're not a monkey, Daddy. You're just a hairy man," she called out as I walked back to my bedroom and into my bathroom.

I quickly slipped on some jeans and a hoodie. I needed to get out to two jobsites today for a few hours, just to make sure the weekend crew wasn't slacking.

The large hotel that I was overseeing for my friend Myles St. James was progressing well. We'd bulldozed the Seaside Inn several months ago, and we were putting up a much larger structure in its place. I also had to get over to Violet Beaumont's house to make sure they were making progress on the bathroom and kitchen renovation. She was staying in my guesthouse, and the woman was a big thorn in my side, so the sooner I got her back in her home, the better. She'd practically burned the place down a few days ago, and I'd walked in on her in a pair of panties and high heels. The woman was a mess.

A sexy-as-sin mess.

I finished brushing my teeth and rinsed my mouth as I thought about the way she'd had her hands on her hips, ready for battle.

She was feisty and always ready to argue.

A distraction that I didn't need living in my backyard.

I strode over to the kitchen, and my little girl came out of her bedroom dressed for the jobsite: a white turtleneck, overalls, her cowboy boots, and the pink tool belt I'd gotten her for Christmas. "Saturdays are for pancakes, Daddy."

"Yes, they are," I said, grabbing the box and then whipping up some batter quickly.

My girl would eat pancakes every day of the week if I let her. But we saved them for Saturdays, and we either ate them here or went over to the Brown Bear Diner for a nice stack.

I ladled the batter into the pan before grabbing her a glass of milk and pouring myself a cup of coffee. Harper grabbed the maple syrup from the refrigerator, placed it on the table, found two napkins and some utensils, and set us up.

She'd wanted to learn how to do some chores over winter break, and she was a quick study, just like her old man. It was important to me to raise my baby girl to grow up and be self-sufficient, even if I knew that I'd take care of this little angel until I took my last breath.

She was my reason to do better.

To be better.

I plated our food, and we both sat down at the table.

"Napkin in your lap, Daddy. I saw it on a movie. We don't live on a farm, so we shouldn't act like animals."

Did I mention that my daughter is six going on thirty?

She was a bossy little thing and full of fire. And I wouldn't change a single hair on her head.

I set my paper napkin on my lap and raised a brow. "I suppose that means you should be keeping your desk area clean in your room, if you don't want to live like an animal."

She took a long sip of her drink, then set it down and looked up at me with a white milk mustache over her lip. "Those are art supplies on my desk. Artists are messy. Mrs. Wharton even told us so."

"Is that so?" I waited for her to look up at me. "Would that be the same Mrs. Wharton who talked to me at school yesterday about you missing recess for talking too much?"

She shrugged. "That lady runs a tight ship."

I tried to cover my smile, because my girl was a witty little thing, but I kept my tone serious. "Harper."

"Daddy," she mimicked.

"Listen, you want to grow up and be real smart. You don't want to have to work as hard as I do out there building things when you can be sitting at a desk in a fancy office. So stop talking and listen to Mrs. Wharton."

"I was only talking because Cooper was upset. He didn't understand the directions. No one would help him because they're all afraid of Mrs. Wharton. But he started crying, and I felt bad."

"Well, why didn't he go ask Mrs. Wharton for directions?"

"He did. And she said he should have listened the first time, so she wouldn't help him," she said over a mouthful of pancake.

"I do believe you are supposed to wait until you finish chewing before you speak, Little Miss Manners." I smirked. "And maybe Cooper should have listened the first time."

"He couldn't." She set her fork down. "He got sent to the nurse's office at recess 'cause his nose was bleeding. And Mrs. Wharton gave the directions when he wasn't there. And that's not fair, right, Daddy?"

She made a good point. She rarely got in trouble, and the few times her teacher had talked to me, my daughter had given me a reasonable explanation.

"Did he tell her that?" I asked as I sipped my coffee.

"Nope. Because she told him, 'No talking.' That's the rules. But that's not fair, and you told me if something isn't fair, I should say something."

I reached for both of our plates and headed to the sink.

"I did tell you that."

"See? I'm following the rules. I just like your rules better than Mrs. Wharton's," she said as she polished off her glass of milk and walked it over to the sink.

I roared in laughter at her comment.

Mrs. Wharton had to be pushing eighty, as she was my teacher back in the day, and she was old as dirt back then. I'm sure she didn't even remember that Cooper had left the room.

But Harper was an observer. She was always watching everyone around her and making sure they were okay.

I loaded the dishes in the dishwasher and dried off my hands. "All right. Well, you lost recess privileges. Was it worth it?"

"Cooper stopped crying. It was worth it." She smiled up at me. "Plus, I got to sit on the bench and think about my birthday party. I want to have a Pinkalicious party."

My daughter loved talking about her next birthday party. She'd start months in advance, but seeing as it was only six weeks away, it was a good time to start thinking about it.

I mean, what the fuck did I know about birthdays for little girls?

I'd never had a birthday party in my life. So, I let Harper call the shots about what she wanted.

"Come on, kiddo. Let's get your coat on and get over to the jobsite, and you can tell me all about this Pinkalicious party on the way over." I helped her slip her coat over her shoulders and zipped it up.

She ran down the hall to get her backpack with her coloring books and crayons. She knew the drill. This was how we spent our Saturdays. We worked for a few hours, and then she got to pick what we'd do in the afternoon and evening.

Once we were both in the truck and buckled, I pulled down the driveway and glanced out the windshield. The snow was falling pretty good this morning.

My daughter filled me in on her birthday party on the short drive to Violet's house. She wanted to invite everyone in her class, along with some adults she'd known for most of her life. She wanted everything to be pink. The balloons, the cake, and the sandwiches.

How the fuck does one find pink sandwiches?

But I nodded and listened as I pulled in front of Violet's house, then groaned when I saw her car parked in front of the two work trucks that were also there.

"You growl too much, Daddy," Harper said as I helped her out of the car.

"I didn't growl. I groaned."

"Both make you sound grumpy." She turned to see the car parked a few feet from us. "Yay. That's Violet's car!"

"Yep." I tried to hide my irritation because the woman kept showing up at her house to check on things, which was distracting my guys. Why the fuck do you hire a general contractor if you're going to be micromanaging everything?

"I like her," Harper said as she started running toward the house.

That makes one of us.

Once we were inside, I rolled my eyes when I saw Violet making a design on the table out of some of the tile that she'd already approved for the kitchen backsplash.

Yet here she was changing the design.

Again.

"Hi, Violet!" Harper ran over to her, and Violet stopped what she was doing and smiled down at my daughter.

"How's the cutest kid in the world doing today?" she asked.

"I'm good." Harper beamed up at her.

"What do you think of this design, Harper?" Violet asked my daughter, the six-year-old who has no design experience.

My right-hand man, Will, just stood there smiling at her like a starstruck pussy. I shot him a warning look, and he cleared his throat.

"Uh, hey, boss. Violet had an idea about changing the pattern on the subway tile to give the wall more—what is it?" Will asked her, and I rolled my eyes.

"Depth and character. I sat up last night thinking about it. Why would I want to just have the tile laid the way everyone lays it on the wall, when I could make it stand out?"

"I like it a lot," Harper said, staring at the ridiculously complicated pattern on the table.

"I'll tell you why. Because that's the whole point of subway tile. And sure, you can make a unique design, but that design has to work on the entire wall. Your kitchen backsplash area isn't that large, so only half of this is going to fit in the space beneath the cabinets, and we're going to have a ton of cuts and it's going to look like crap." I crossed my arms over my chest.

The woman was wearing me out with her constant changes.

"I see Mr. Doom and Gloom has entered the building," Violet said. "I like it. Will likes it. Harper likes it. But of course, you think it looks like crap."

You also thought it was a wise idea to balance on a barstool in high heels.

Will is thinking with his dick.

Harper is six years old and wants pink sandwiches for her birthday.

"I didn't say the design looks like crap. I said it would look like crap on the wall, because it will be cut off on every single side, and it will look like a half-done job. If you don't like the subway tiles, there are other tiles you can use that have designs that are meant for the space."

"I'm trying to avoid slowing down my timeline," she said, holding her chin up defiantly.

"Then stop distracting the crew and stop changing everything that you've already approved." I blew out a breath and told Will to get back to work on the bathroom.

"It's my house, and I should love the design."

"I couldn't agree more. That was the point of you choosing the finishes. But now everything is ordered, and we're trying to stay on track with the timeline. And you keep making changes."

"Have you ever heard the term 'It's a woman's right to change her mind'?"

"Have you ever heard the term 'Make a decision and stick with it'?" I grumped.

"No, because that's not a thing. Mine is actually a thing."

"Daddy's grumpy," Harper said, and I wanted to tell her I'd serve brown sandwiches at her party for being a traitor, but I held my tongue.

"Go sit down at the card table over there, and get your crafts out." I gave my daughter a stern look.

"*Daddy is definitely grumpy*," Violet said sarcastically.

"Do you want to live in my guesthouse forever, or would you like to get this job done?" I asked, stepping closer to her, because I was done having this conversation day after day.

"Let's see. The oven doesn't work in the guesthouse. My landlord is a tyrant. And I have no space to entertain."

What the fuck is she talking about?

"Well, if you'd like to throw a party in the next year, I suggest you let me do my job and you stick to wedding planning, yes?"

"Bite me, you broody bastard," she huffed as she stormed past me and joined my daughter at the table where she was coloring.

I rubbed my face and walked to the bathroom to tell the guys to stick to the plan.

Even though I highly doubted Violet wouldn't change her mind again tomorrow.

CHAPTER THREE

Violet

"How about hashtag 'I like big balls,'" I said a couple of weeks later as Blakely stood at the whiteboard jotting down potential hashtags for the next wedding we were planning.

"Absolutely not. That's offensive." Montana rolled her eyes and used her hand to cover her laughter.

Montana and I owned the Blushing Bride, the wedding planning business in town. After we graduated from college, she convinced me to move to this small town with her and start a business together. She grew up in Blushing, Alaska, and she'd been very persuasive about how much fun small-town living would be.

Blakely was our office manager, and the three of us worked really well together.

"Since when are big balls offensive? You don't mind Clifford's."

Clifford Wellhung was the gigantic moose in town who roamed the streets as if it was perfectly normal for a wild beast to cruise around downtown.

"Personally, I find Clifford's balls offensive, if I'm being honest. The way they just sort of dangle around like big ole melons." Blakely shrugged. "And I have to side with Monny on this one, Vi. I think referencing his balls in a wedding hashtag could be a questionable choice."

I laughed. "Well, his last name is Ballsy. It's shit luck, but you may as well have some fun with it."

Montana's jaw fell open, and she gaped at me. "His last name is Balmy, not Ballsy."

I winced. "Eek. Balmy balls would suck."

Blakely burst out in hysterical laughter, and Montana and I ended up joining in.

"Speaking of balmy balls, how is it going over at your place with your sexy landlord?" Blakely asked.

I rolled my eyes. "That grumpy bastard is working my last nerve. He's trying to tell me how to renovate my house. It's appalling."

"He's your contractor. That's his job." Montana chuckled. "Just like we tell people how to plan a wedding."

I thought it over. "Renovating a home is far more personal than a marriage. It's the place I'm going to live for years to come."

"Uh, I think a wedding is pretty personal, considering it's the person you're going to spend the rest of your life with." Blakely was looking at me like I had three heads, and Montana agreed, with that knowing look she liked to give me.

"Listen. I get inspired in the middle of the night sometimes. And he needs to deal with it." I moved to the whiteboard and took the marker from her. "How about hashtag 'it's getting Balmy in here.' You know, like it's getting hot in here, but obviously we go with Balmy."

"I don't know about that one." Montana tapped her lips as if she was deep in thought. I popped a few Skittles in my mouth while I waited for more ideas to get thrown out. "Hashtag 'here come the Balmys.' Hashtag 'Balmy, party of two.'"

I wrote them both down, but nothing was blowing us away. And at the Blushing Bride, we liked to be blown away.

"What about hashtag 'rollin' with the Balmys.' Like 'rollin' with the homies.'" I chuckled.

"I like that one," Blakely and Montana said at the same time.

I motioned to an invisible mic in my hand and dropped it on the floor dramatically.

"That's definitely the leader right now. I'll run them by Jules and see what she thinks," Montana said, referencing the future bride, who would most likely not agree to it, since she'd turned down every idea we'd given her thus far.

"All right, I've got a one o'clock meeting to go over the pricing for the tent and table rentals. I'll report back." I grabbed my hot tea and made my way to my office.

I set my phone on my desk and noticed a familiar face at the top of my Instagram app. My sister Velveeta had posted. Obviously, her name wasn't Velveeta, but I preferred it over her real name, which was Velveteen.

She'd always given me plastic cheese energy, while nothing about her gave me stuffed British rabbit vibes.

My stomach dipped as I picked up my phone and took in the family photo. My father and his second wife, Pissy Beaumont.

Fine.

Missy Beaumont.

But my nickname was much more fitting for her as well.

Surrounding them were their children, Velveteen, Paris, Huntington, and Brenton. They were celebrating their twenty-eighth wedding anniversary, and the caption read: "Sweet family memories celebrating twenty-eight years of love from Maui."

They clearly forgot to drop an invitation to daughter number one, per usual.

The bastards.

Twenty-eight years of marriage.

Even the number pissed me off, because I was twenty-eight years old as well. *Logically it appears the math is not mathing.*

However, my father decided to leave my mother when she was pregnant with me for Missy, the stepmother from hell. She'd never made me feel like part of the family, and she'd act like I was a distant cousin whenever I'd visit. My siblings and I were actually fairly close, aside from *Velveeta*, who was just a year younger than me because my father wasted no time remarrying and knocking up wife number two. Velveteen took on her mother's disdain for me, while my other siblings were a bit more rebellious, and they'd always welcomed the black sheep of the family with open arms. But in the end, I blamed my father for not standing up for me. For making me feel like I didn't belong and for giving me a lifetime of things to discuss in therapy.

My phone rang, and my sister Paris's face lit up the screen.

"Hey, Par, how are you?" I asked, knowing that she was calling because our jackass sister had posted.

"Hey," she groaned. "I'm sorry, Vi. I'm sure you saw the post from this morning."

"I just saw it. It was a Beaumont celebration, huh?" I said sarcastically.

"I didn't know if I should tell you. It was a super-last-minute trip, at least as far as including us kids, and Mom said they'd invited you and you were too busy to come. But then Dad had one too many Long Island iced teas, and he broke down to me one night at the beach bar and said that he was disappointed in himself for not insisting that you be invited." She sighed.

Oh, William Beaumont, you poor excuse for a man.

It pissed me off that I had daddy issues over a man who didn't deserve me and that I wasted my time analyzing the way he'd rejected me my entire life.

A man who was too weak to stand up for his own child.

I had zero respect for him at this point—yet, seeing them all together still felt like a punch to the gut sometimes.

"It's all right. It's not you that I have a problem with," I said. "Tell me about Maui."

Paris rambled on about the fact that my father and Missy had renewed their vows. It was the sixth time they'd renewed their vows since they'd married, which felt like a little overkill.

We get it. You're sticking to your vows this time around, Daddy Dearest.

"Well, you would have enjoyed seeing Ralph in all his glory," she said over her laughter.

Ralph was Velveteen's fiancé, and they were set to marry here in Blushing in less than three months. They'd be married at the Blushing Inn, the farmhouse that Montana and I had invested in with her fiancé, Myles, and renovated and was now our most popular wedding venue. They did not choose to marry in Blushing because I owned a wedding business here; they'd chosen this quaint small town because Harry Simon, the most famous boy bander on the planet, had chosen to marry Bailey Clark, a famous supermodel, here in Blushing a while back, which had put this town on the map. So even though I was enemy number one, I was also wedding planner extraordinaire and planning my sister's wedding. Ralph was what we called in the wedding business a "loose cannon." The man literally never disappointed at family gatherings, as he'd always drink one too many shots of Jägermeister and do something outrageous. My sister was uptight and pretentious, and they were the most mismatched couple I'd ever met. Who knew what Ralph would pull on his big day.

Needless to say, I was not looking forward to this wedding at all.

He'd streaked down the street three years ago at Thanksgiving.

He'd gotten wasted at Velveteen's holiday work event this year and knocked over the buffet table, and she'd considered breaking up with him.

I heard about most of the gory details from Paris, since Velveteen rarely opened up to me.

"Tell me." I leaned back in my chair and popped a few more Skittles in my mouth.

"Ralph had one too many tequila shots at the vow renewal, and he stepped on Mom's train and tore her dress completely from her body," she said, sounding horrified but also bursting out in laughter.

"Nooooo," I said, because Missy Beaumont was the most proper woman I'd ever met. She never left the house without a French manicure and a proper cardigan or with a hair out of place. I couldn't fathom her being stripped naked on the altar. "Like, completely off her body? Or she was holding it in place."

"Completely off her body. It all happened so fast. He staggered up there, tripped, Mom went to jump out of the way, and it just ripped away, like one of those magicians who makes the outfit disappear."

"My God. Missy must have been beside herself." I chuckled while trying to sound concerned. She was Paris's mother, after all.

"Well, luckily she was covered in shapewear from head to toe, so it wasn't like an ounce of skin was showing, but she had a meltdown, and we had to call the night short."

"Everyone appeared to be fully dressed in the family photo," I said, studying the post on Instagram again.

"That was taken before Tequila Gate." She laughed. "It was fine the next day. Ralph stuck to piña coladas the rest of the trip, per Velveteen's orders. Apparently, rum doesn't bring out his crazy."

"How the hell am I going to control him at this wedding?" I groaned.

"Yes. Your house better be done by the wedding, because I'm staying with you. Huntington and Brenton want to stay at your house too. Let the old people stay at the hotel."

"Velveteen is younger than me," I reminded her.

"But she's twenty-seven going on ninety. She's no fun. We want to stay with you. I bet Ralph would rather stay at your house too," she said over her laughter.

"That's a hard no. I still can't believe she's marrying this guy."

"I know. I think we're all shocked. But Mom loves that he comes from money, so she seems okay with it."

"At least she has her priorities straight." I chuckled before glancing at my email inbox to see a new message that had just popped up from Charlie Huxley. The subject line was in all caps.

URGENT!

"Maybe you should try giving her some sisterly advice. You know a lot about weddings, too, as you plan them for a living."

"I am the last person to give relationship advice. I avoid them like the plague. Plus, she never listens to me. She hates me," I said, because we both knew it was true.

"No. She's jealous of you. Always has been. And she might act like a spoiled brat around you, but she talks about you nicely behind your back."

A laugh escaped my lips. "Oh really? She's nicer behind my back, huh?"

"Yep. She also got a little loosey-goosey on the trip, and she made some comments that she wished she cared less about what people thought about her, like you do. She went on and on about how she wants to give less shits about the opinions of others, and she kept referencing you."

"The saying is 'less fucks.' And is that supposed to be a compliment?" I asked dryly.

"If Velveteen is admitting her flaws and mentioning being more like you—it's definitely a compliment." She chuckled.

I groaned. "That's up for debate. I've got to get to a meeting. I'll call you later."

"Love you, Vi."

A sharp pain hit my chest at her words. If not for my three youngest siblings, I wouldn't have any relationship with my father. But I loved them and they loved me, so it kept me in this vicious cycle with my father and his wife.

"Love you too." I ended the call and clicked on the email from Charlie.

> Ms. Beaumont,
> I received your change regarding the lighting in your primary bathroom. If you continue to make changes to the renovation plan, you can expect your timeline to change, as well as the price that

you were initially quoted, if I have to keep my guys on this jobsite longer than expected. Please be aware that this is the last change that we can agree to and if we want to finish the project in the three months that we agreed upon.
Charlie Huxley

What the hell was wrong with this man? I lived in his backyard. Why was he sending me a formal email?

My fingers fluttered above the keyboard as I thought over my response.

Mr. Huxley,
Thank you for the oddly formal email, especially seeing as we live on the same property, and you have my phone number as you texted me to tell me I parked in the wrong spot on the driveway just a few days ago.
As a contractor, I would assume that you want your clients to be happy. I found a fabulous vintage light fixture at the antique store downtown. So there is no hold up to the timeline, and I'm not asking you to return the other light. I was thinking of having the original light hung in the guest bath instead. Will thought it was a fabulous idea when I ran it by him.
Please be aware that I will continue to change my mind if I see fit, as I want my house to be perfect.
Ms. Beaumont

I hit send, then gathered my things to head to my meeting. I was slipping my coat on just as my laptop dinged with an incoming message.

Ms. Beaumont,
Chasing perfection isn't realistic. And for the record, Will isn't running this company, I am.

Mr. Huxley
P.S. If you got the text about the driveway, why did you park there again yesterday?

I chuckled. There was something about getting under his skin that I enjoyed.

Mr. Huxley,
I parked there because it's a big driveway, it's closest to the guesthouse, and I'm convinced that you're just being a dick for the sake of being a dick. And it's the perfect spot for my car, so I guess I was just chasing that unrealistic perfection.
Ms. Beaumont

I waited for a minute or three . . . But he didn't respond. I'd probably pissed him off. It wasn't my first time calling him a dick, nor would it be my last.

I walked out and said goodbye to Montana and Blakely as I walked the short distance to the party rental shop a few blocks away.

My phone dinged just as I arrived, and I glanced down at the email from Charlie.

Ms. Beaumont,
Once again, your obsession with my dick is alarming.
No. More. Changes.
Mr. Huxley
P.S. If you need to use the oven again, we'll be home by 5:30.

I tucked the phone back in my purse, and I couldn't hide the ridiculous smile from my face.

CHAPTER FOUR

Charlie

"You okay, Harps? Dinner's ready." I sat on the edge of my daughter's bed, where she'd gone as soon as we'd arrived home after I'd picked her up from aftercare at school. She had her back to me, and her brown wavy hair pooled on the mattress.

I felt like shit that she was one of the last kids to be picked up.

But I was buried at work, and she usually liked staying after school so she could play with her friends.

"I'm not hungry," she sniffed.

I reached for her shoulders and rolled her so she was lying on her back. It hurt me when I saw how puffy her eyes were. "Hey. What's going on?"

"Nothing, Daddy. I'm just not hungry."

These were the moments that I struggled with. I didn't know what the fuck I was doing parenting a little girl all on my own most of the time, and it was a constant battle in my head if I was fucking this up. All I knew was that I woke up every day and loved her enough for two parents.

I loved this kid enough for a mother and a father.

Hell, I loved her enough for two sets of grandparents as well.

Because I was a one-man show when it came to raising Harper.

I worked hard to provide for her and give her everything she needed.

But this kind of shit was out of my wheelhouse.

My little girl looking like someone stole her sunshine.

I didn't know how to handle that.

I had zero experience with little kids before my daughter was born. I grew up in and out of foster care, so I had very little experience with stability before my Harper came into the world.

I stroked her hair away from her face. "You might feel better if you eat something."

"I don't want to. I'm not hungry."

I sighed, trying to figure out if I should force her to eat or give her time.

There was a knock on the back door, which could only be one person.

The menace from across the yard.

The past few days had been filled with snarky emails, and she continued to come by the jobsite daily to check on the progress and question everything.

Every. Single. Thing.

"I'll be right back." I moved through the house toward the back door and yanked it open.

"What did you burn down now?" I leaned against the doorframe as I took in her face. Her eyes were a little puffy, unless I was reading into it. The biggest sign that something was off was that she didn't have a snarky comeback.

She wasn't spewing venom at me.

She just stood there looking a little—broken.

"Can I just put these in your oven and then come back in twenty minutes to pick them up? I'm too tired to go to the diner, and I don't have anything to microwave, and I need some comfort food." She held up the bag of pizza rolls.

I'd ordered a new oven for the guesthouse, and it was expected to arrive in a week to ten days. And now I felt like a big dick that she couldn't cook food for herself in the house where she was living.

"Yes, of course." I took the bag from her hand and moved toward the oven, still warm from the garlic bread I'd just pulled out for dinner. She followed me inside, and I handed her a cookie sheet. She poured several pizza rolls onto the pan before handing it back to me.

Her eyes were definitely puffy.

I wouldn't have guessed Violet Beaumont would ever let her guard down long enough to cry, but the signs were there.

She was quieter. Less combative.

Her eyes were puffy and red.

"Thank you. I'll be back in twenty minutes," she said as her gaze moved to the table with two plates of pasta sitting there, accompanied by a basket of garlic bread and some salad. "What's going on here? Looks like it's getting cold."

I put the pizza rolls in the oven and leaned against the kitchen counter before blowing out a frustrated breath. "I don't know. Harps says she doesn't want to eat. She's been in her room lying in bed since we got home, and I'm pretty sure she's been crying."

Violet narrowed her gaze at me. "You're pretty sure she's been crying? Does she not make any noise when she cries?"

"She was quiet on the drive home, and then I started dinner out here, and when I went to go get her, I found her in her bed. She kept sniffing, and her eyes were puffy."

Just like yours are.

"She's definitely been crying, genius." She rolled her eyes and crossed her arms over her chest, as if I'd been the one to make my daughter cry. "Did you ask her why she was upset?"

"I asked her if she was hungry, and she said no. I asked her if she was sick, and she said no." I trailed a hand down my face.

"Well, there's lots of other reasons for someone to cry other than being sick or hungry. Especially when you're six years old. You should always just ask the damn questions. Most people want to talk about it—they just don't think you care."

"Of course I care. She's never done this before, and I didn't know if I should push," I admitted, feeling like an insecure asshole because most of the time I didn't know what I was doing when it came to parenting.

"You always push, Charles."

"All right. Well, it looks like you've been crying too. What's going on with you?"

"It's none of your damn business, you big Neanderthal," she hissed.

"You told me to ask."

"And I have a right to tell you it's none of your business. Now watch my pizza rolls for me, and I'll go talk to Harper. I'm very good at figuring out why someone's upset." She moved past me like she owned the place.

The woman had a way of lighting up any room she entered.

Even when she was pissed off at me, which was most of the time.

Moving around on a mission, like a goddamn firefly.

"Thank you. It's the second door on the left." My house wasn't that big, so it wouldn't be hard to find her, but I needed to say something.

I poured myself a beer now because I was on edge. I was letting my ridiculously annoying yet sexy neighbor talk to my daughter when I should've been the one doing it.

But Harper had never closed herself off to me like this.

This was a first, and I was at a loss.

I took a swig of my beer, then moved down the hallway quietly, positioning myself outside the door so I could listen.

"It's okay to have a bad day every now and then," Violet said as I stood completely still. "I didn't have a great day today either. How about you tell me what happened, and maybe we can help each other?"

"You didn't have a good day today?" My daughter's voice cracked, as if she'd just stopped crying.

I had one fucking job in this world, and it was to give Harper a good life.

Yes, I ran a company, and I worked hard to provide for us.

But the one job that mattered, the only fucking thing that was my reason for waking up every single day and working hard, was the little girl on the other side of this wall.

And knowing that she was hurting did something to me. I felt it physically in the center of my chest, where a deep pain resided now.

Hell, I'd run away because I was too damn scared to ask her why she was crying. Harper had always been open with me. She'd never hesitated to tell me every feeling she had.

So why was she acting so strange about it now?

"I didn't. But here's the thing, sometimes you just need a good cry, you know? Like you just let it out, and you scream at the top of your lungs if you need to, and then you remember all the good things that happened in the same day."

I heard a sniff and assumed it was Harper before she spoke. "I got the most points in reading today. And I got one hundred percent on my math test."

Attagirl.

My chest puffed with pride.

"That's amazing. Sounds like lots of good things." Violet cleared her throat. "And then something happened that bothered you?"

"Yeah." My daughter's voice was just above a whisper.

"Do you want me to go get your dad so you can tell him about it too?"

"No," Harper said so quickly it felt like a punch to the gut. "I don't want to tell Daddy what happened."

Why the fuck not?

Had I done something to make her not trust me?

"Okay. That's fair. Do you want to tell me? I always feel better when I tell someone why I'm upset."

"Did you tell anyone why you were upset today?" Harper asked, and there was more sniffing.

"No. But what if we make a deal? You tell me what's bothering you, and I'll tell you what's bothering me?"

I wanted to peek in the room. Were they sitting on the bed together? Were they both sniffing, or was that just Harper?

"I like that," my little girl said. "I'll go first because it's scary going first sometimes, but I'm not scared to tell you."

"Thanks for being brave," Violet said. "What happened?"

"Denise Quigley was at aftercare today with me. That's for kids that stay late because their parents work."

"Yes. I always went to aftercare," Violet said. "So what happened there?"

"Denise said that my mama probably left me because my hair is too wavy and I'm short." I could hear the tremble in my daughter's voice, and I closed my eyes and tried to breathe slowly. "And she said I dress like a boy sometimes."

I wanted to storm into her bedroom. This was my daughter, and I should've been handling this.

But Violet's voice was strong and certain as she spoke. "Denise Quigley? Her mom works at the diner, right?"

"Yeah, she works at the Brown Bear Diner."

"Well, let me tell you, that girl is not nice. I saw her make her brother cry at breakfast once."

"You did?" my daughter asked, her curiosity impossible to miss.

"Yep. I watched the whole thing. He's much younger and he was trying to eat his pancakes, and her mom was talking on her cell phone, and I saw Denise pour her glass of juice over the poor little guy's pancakes."

"No," Harper said on a gasp.

"Oh yes," Violet said. "And I told her mama what she did when she finally got off the phone, and Denise called me a liar and told me to mind my own business. And her mother took Denise's side. So, I don't think I'd be listening to that girl. And for the record, you dress so great. I love your style. I mean, look at me, I'm in leggings and a hoodie. We've all got our own style."

"Denise wears glitter shirts, and she has pink tennis shoes," Harper said, and I made a mental note to take her shopping this weekend.

"Good for her. But anyone who has to make someone else feel bad is just insecure. Trust me, Denise is jealous of you."

"What's insector?"

"'Insecure,'" Violet said slowly on a chuckle. "She doesn't feel good about herself. So she probably lashes out at you because she wants to be like you."

"You think so?"

"I know so. I know her type," Violet said, her voice confident.

"But what if that really is why my mama left?" Harper said, her voice sounding wobbly again.

We'd never talked a whole lot about it. I'd just told her that I loved her so much, and that not everyone has two parents. Her mother came around once a year, and that was just how it had always been.

Obviously, it was time to have a chat about it.

"Well, I don't know any mamas who leave because their daughter has wavy hair. I've seen Denise's hair and it's very straight, and yours is long and dark and wavy, and everyone wants hair like yours." She took a breath, and I assumed she was thinking over her next words. "When did you last see your mama?"

"I saw Caroline last year on my birthday. She left me when I was just a little baby girl because she knew Daddy loved me enough for two parents."

I leaned my head back against the wall and breathed through my nose as I swallowed back the lump forming in my throat.

I do love her enough for two parents. I'd walk through fire for this little girl without hesitation. And that is the fucking truth.

"Well, that sort of blows Denise's theory to shreds, right? I mean, if you were a baby, she never saw your hair or how tall you were. Denise is a—" She paused, and I hoped like hell she wouldn't finish that sentence with any of the words that came to my mind. "Sad little girl, I think."

"You think she's sad?" Harper asked.

"I do. Because happy people don't like to hurt others."

"My mama does come back, but I don't call her 'Mama,' though. She only comes on my birthday because she wants to be friends. Her name is Caroline, and I don't remember her from last time, 'cause my birthday was so long ago. So, so long ago. But I don't think she thought I was short, or my hair was too wavy."

"Of course she didn't. Your hair is so pretty. I wish mine was that long and that color."

"Your hair is wavy, and you're so pretty, Violet."

They both chuckled, and my fucking chest squeezed. Because my daughter had just felt her first heartache, as far as I knew, and now she was laughing.

"I think *you're* so pretty," Violet said.

"Will you tell me why you were sad today too?" Harper asked, and I listened intently.

"I guess the same reason as you. I got my feelings hurt. Someone said something to me that made me feel extra sad."

"Who said it to you?" Harper pressed.

"Actually, it was my father."

Harper gasped dramatically, because I knew all her little sounds, and I could just picture her hands over her face as she looked at Violet. "Daddies are never supposed to make you sad. My daddy only makes me smile."

Damn straight, baby girl.

"Yeah. Well, mine isn't that kind of daddy. He's real selfish, but it's okay."

"Because he's insector?"

Violet's laughter poured down the hallway. "Yeah. He is very insecure. But I have a question for you."

"What's your question?" Harper asked.

"Well, you clearly have the best daddy. Why didn't you just tell him what Denise said to you? He would have told you what I told you, and you wouldn't have needed to be sad."

Exactly.

"We can't tell Daddy about this," my daughter said, and now her tone was very serious.

"Why?" Violet asked.

"Because I have the best daddy in the whole wide world," she said, a little giggle escaping. "I don't want him to think I'm sad that I don't have a mama. Because my daddy loves me enough for a mama and a daddy. He might not know why my mama really left, and I don't want Daddy to be sad."

A loud buzzing noise came from the kitchen, and I startled.

The fucking pizza rolls.

I hurried down the hall before they caught me eavesdropping and I turned off the buzzer.

And I listened as multiple footsteps padded down the hall toward the kitchen.

Violet had gotten my little girl to come out of her room.

I guess there was more to Violet Beaumont than I'd guessed.

I glanced over at her as she beamed down at my daughter, shining all that light her way like a goddamn firefly.

CHAPTER FIVE

Violet

It smelled like garlic and warm bread, and my stomach growled. My pizza rolls weren't sounding as appetizing as they did when I'd arrived here, desperate for an oven and some processed food.

We turned the corner into the kitchen, and Violet's whole mood had turned around.

Hell, even mine had turned around.

"Daddy, what you got cookin', good lookin'?" Harper giggled.

She was so cute it was hard for me not to unleash what I really thought about that mean girl, Denise. I knew the type. I'd seen the girl in action more than once. She picked on her little brother, all for attention that she never got, from what I could tell. Her mother ignored her, and I was certain she was jealous of Harper.

Harper Huxley was the rare jewel of children. She was an old soul, and we'd actually had a very nice conversation. She wasn't bratty. She was reasonable. She was sweet. And she was the cutest kid I'd ever seen.

So it was ludicrous to suggest that her physical appearance was the reason her mother had left.

Trust me, I'd experienced abandonment in a very similar way, and I knew it had very little to do with me. But it took me a long time to get here.

Charlie scooped up his daughter and hugged her, his eyes finding mine over her shoulder.

He didn't say anything, and he didn't need to.

I saw the gratitude there, and I nodded before making my way toward the oven to collect my pizza rolls off the pan and go back home to finish my pity party for one.

"I cooked your favorite, baby girl. You feeling better?" Charlie asked before setting her back down on her feet.

"I'm feeling all the way better. Can my best friend Violet stay for dinner?" she asked.

"Oh, I've got my pizza rolls here," I said, dropping them all onto the paper plate I'd brought with me.

"We've got plenty, and I think our dinner looks a lot better than your dinner." Charlie's lips twitched the slightest bit, and I'd come to learn that was what he did when he was trying to suppress a smile.

"Says a man who's clearly never had pizza rolls." I tucked my lips between my teeth as I considered the offer.

His dinner did look much better than mine.

And Violet was standing there with her little hands in a prayer position, smiling up at me.

Charlie surprised me when he popped a pizza roll in his mouth and chewed. "Ours is definitely better than yours. Just have some pasta and some salad, and then you can head home and think of new ways to torture me tomorrow."

"Fine," I said.

"Fine." He cleared his throat and made another plate.

"Fine! 'Fine' is my new favorite word." Harper took my hand and led me to the table. "You want a beer, Violet?"

"Hey," Charlie grumped. "Six-year-olds have no reason to ask that."

"I'm almost seven. And I know adults sometimes drink it."

I chuckled as Charlie set the plate down in front of me and then held up a beer bottle and raised a brow at me. I nodded, and he poured the bottle into a glass and handed it to me before taking his seat next to his daughter.

"So, is there anything anyone wants to talk about?" Charlie asked, clearly out of his comfort zone, because he stared down at his plate as the words left his mouth.

"Denise Quigley is insector, Daddy. So me and Violet think she's sad," Harper said as she twirled her fork in her noodles, preparing for the perfect bite.

Well, I personally think Denise Quigley is an asshole.

But I'd settle for "sad and insecure" because I doubted Charlie would want me to say what I really thought.

"Yeah? Why do you think she's sad?" he asked, and I wondered if he'd stood outside the bedroom door listening to us, because I sure as hell would have.

"We don't know, right, Violet?"

I could think of a few reasons, *She's a spoiled mean girl* being at the top of my list.

"Right. We don't know. But we know it has nothing to do with you," I said.

"Right. And isn't Daddy's sketti the best?"

"It's really good." *Possibly the best I've ever had, but we don't want to give the man a big head.*

"Better than pizza rolls?" Charlie asked, his voice lighter now, as he tipped his head back and took a pull from his glass. His hair was longer in the front and shorter in the back. His sapphire eyes were the color of the deepest sea, and his broad shoulders made it apparent that he wasn't a stranger to physical labor.

Yes. So much better. "Hmm . . . I'll have to think about it."

Charlie's eyes darkened as he looked at me, but he didn't say anything.

"Daddy, Violet's daddy is insector too." Harper popped a large forkful of pasta in her mouth just as I took a sip of beer, and I coughed a few times at how blunt she was.

"Tell me what 'insector' means?" Charlie asked his daughter, and the way he looked at her made me look at him in a different light. He was softer around Harper. He was everything a dad should be to his daughter. And now my curiosity was getting the best of me, wondering where Harper's mother was. She was clearly alive, because she saw her every year on her birthday, which was weird as hell.

Even my father had better stats than that, and he was an epic failure in the parenting department.

Who sees their kid once a year and only on their birthday?

Harper looked at me as Charlie told her to take a few bites of salad.

"Insector, or 'insecure,' is someone who isn't happy with themselves, so they make others feel bad because they're so miserable," I said, reaching for a piece of garlic bread.

Damn. The man could cook.

"Ahh . . . I know a lot of insectors." Charlie laughed. I rarely heard the man laugh, and when he did, it felt like a gift that you were lucky enough to witness it.

"Daddy, we need to feel sad for all the insectors." Harper was coming up with that all on her own. I wanted to tell her to put up boundaries with people who weren't kind to her, but it wasn't my place. And she quickly changed the subject. "Can Violet come to my Pinkalicious party? It's going to be so fun."

"It's here at the house in a couple weeks, and you'll probably still be living out in the guesthouse at the rate you keep changing your mind on every finish, so if you want to stop by, you're welcome to." Charlie smiled the slightest bit.

"That was the worst invite to a party ever. You insulted me while extending the invite."

Harper's eyes widened, and she wiped her mouth. "But Daddy's not insector, right, Violet?"

"I assure you. Daddy's a lot of things, baby girl, but he's not insector." Charlie's voice was gruff, and his gaze locked with mine.

Yeah. The man was a lot of things.

But insecure was not one of them.

I chuckled. I hadn't thought this night could turn around, and here I was having a good time at dinner with a man I normally despised and a kid I liked more than I ever thought possible.

Life was full of surprises.

"I'll for sure stop by," I said as I cleared my plate, and Charlie stopped me from rinsing it in the sink.

He said I'd done enough, and I knew there was a compliment in there somewhere.

"That's the best present ever, Violet. And you can even see Denise at the party."

"Sounds great. I hope she doesn't pour orange juice on my food." I looked at the little girl staring up at me as she burst into giggles.

I wondered if I'd meet her mother at the party.

But I wasn't about to ask. I just thanked them for dinner and made my way back across the yard.

And I didn't even feel the need to return to my pity party when I got home.

The Blushing Inn was our new venue for hosting weddings, and we were partial owners of the property. Montana's ridiculously wealthy fiancé, Myles St. James, had purchased the old farmhouse and allowed the Blushing Bride to invest in it, and Huxley Construction had done the renovations to make it exactly what we wanted. It was nice that we had control over the venue where we hosted the majority of our events now.

And today was wedding day for Jacoby and Geneva Whitacre, from Pennsylvania. Like many of our clients, they were not local, but they wanted to get married in the quaint town of Blushing, Alaska. My best friend and I worked well together. Like a fine-tuned machine. She liked dealing with the clients more than I did, and I preferred all the behind-the-scenes excitement. Blakely, our executive assistant, would oversee things and let us know when issues came up, so the bride and groom could enjoy their day and we could handle every challenge without a hiccup.

And when it came to weddings, we always had some sort of unexpected challenge.

I loved it. One could never be prepared, and just when I thought I'd seen it all—the shit would hit the fan.

Literally and figuratively.

Blakely's voice came through the radio earpiece, which was how the three of us communicated when it was game time.

"Uh, we've got a, er, issue in the main bathroom," Blakely said, and what followed sounded like she was dry heaving. "The FOG just dropped a bomb in there, and the toilet has overflowed. And let's just say that things are not contained to the toilet area."

The FOG was code for "father of the groom."

Serves him right, because who eats two chili dogs a few hours before their son's wedding?

Thankfully everyone was still getting ready for the big event, and guests hadn't arrived yet. I'd get this fixed immediately.

"Heading your way. Can we get Wayne over here pronto?" I asked.

"I already called. Wayne is down with the stomach flu," Blakely said.

"Shit. Pun intended," Montana groaned, and we all laughed, because that was the perfect description of the situation.

"How bad is it? Can we use a plunger?" I asked as I walked through the main entertaining space and down the hallway toward the guest bath.

"This is well beyond a plunger. It's like a murder scene in there," Blakely said, keeping her voice low. "And Jacoby's dad is lying on the floor near the bar area, and he doesn't look right."

"Monny, you handle Frank Whitacre, and I'll get the bathroom fixed."

"On it," Montana said. "Me and a large bottle of Imodium A-D are on our way."

When I turned the corner, Blakely was standing there with wide eyes, beside the closed door.

"It's that bad?" I asked.

"It's an epic shitstorm in there."

I blew out a breath at the smell coming from the bathroom. We didn't have a lot of time to remedy this situation. I grabbed both of Blakely's shoulders, and my gaze locked with hers. "Go get a few pine candles and infusers from the storage closet and place them on every surface surrounding this bathroom that you can find."

She nodded before hurrying away, and I opened the door.

Holy shitballs.

She was not exaggerating.

My God. The man had had the blowout of all blowouts. I reached in my belt bag and placed a face mask over my nose and mouth. Under the sink were all sorts of cleaning supplies, and I sprayed down every surface with disinfectant. And then I pulled out my phone and texted Charlie.

Me: We have a serious toilet situation at the Blushing Inn and we only have an hour to get it fixed before the guests arrive.

Charles: I suggest calling a plumber. I don't fix clogged toilets.

Me: Wayne has the stomach flu, and we have 125 guests arriving in an hour.

Charles: And I'm your first call? Interesting.

Me: I have no time for games. You strike me as someone who knows how to deal with a shit situation.

Charles: Good assessment. I'm dealing with a nuisance living in my backyard.

Me: Fifty-eight minutes and counting, Charles. Please. I'll owe you one.

Charles: I'll tell you what. I'll fix your shitter, if you help me with Harper's birthday. She wants some pink and white balloon thing with tons of balloons that hangs down the wall and I don't have a fucking clue what it is.

Me: It's a balloon swag you fool. I can make that in my sleep. If you handle operation shit show, I'll make Harper's balloon dreams a reality.

Charles: On my way.

"Charlie is on his way. The floors and walls are soaking in disinfectant. As soon as he gets the shit water to flush and I am not at risk of passing out from the foul smell, I'll go in with the mops and have it back to normal before the guests arrive," I said, placing one hand over my ear so I could hear better.

"Good work, Vi. Frank is groaning, and I sent him back upstairs to his room to rest until the Imodium A-D kicks in."

"I'm heading back with so many pine candles people will think they're shitting in the woods." Blakely chuckled, and I moved out to the hallway because I couldn't take the smell any longer. She was on a mission, lighting candles and placing them on every surface in the area.

I checked on the kitchen staff to make sure all was on track. Just then, Charlie came through the front door with a duffel bag over his shoulder like he was going into battle. I held out a face mask for him.

"You're going to need this," I said, arching my brow.

"This deal doesn't quite seem fair. I'm dealing with shit, and you're paying me back by blowing up a few balloons?" he grumped.

I held up my hands. "Do you see these? Yes, they have a beautiful French manicure, so it's easy to miss. But if you look closely, there are battle scars from the hundreds to thousands of balloons I've tied over the last few years. You have no idea how much goes into this. You have the opportunity to make your daughter's pink birthday dreams come true. Man up and get in there."

He shook his head and pulled the face mask over his mouth and nose. After he opened the door, he said something under his breath, but I got called to the bar and told a brooding Charlie that I'd be back.

"Hey, Vi," Benji said as I walked to where he stood behind the bar. He owned the Moose Brew, the local pub that everyone loved, and he handled the alcohol portion of all our events. Sometimes he tended bar himself, and other times he sent someone from his staff. Tonight we were lucky enough to have him.

"Hi. You all set up?"

"Yep, but we've got a little situation," he said.

"What's that?"

He leaned forward before clearing his throat. "The groom's brother has put back more shots of whiskey than I would have thought humanly possible. I've never had to cut someone off at a wedding before it actually started."

I glanced over to see Jamison Whitacre harassing one of the bridesmaids, and she didn't look happy about it.

"The freaking Whitacre family is a giant pain in my ass already. I'm about done with them. Okay, if he dares to come over to you the rest of the night, you pour a Coke in the glass and tell him it's whiskey. I'll get some coffee into his system, and if he can't pull himself together, we'll lock him in one of the guest rooms upstairs." I chuckled.

"I expect nothing less from you, Vi," Benji said with a smile.

I spoke to Jacoby, the groom, just to make sure he was aware that his brother was no longer going to be served alcohol. Blakely brought in a pot of coffee, and I sat Jamison on the couch in the men's parlor and told him that he had to drink two full cups of coffee, or he wouldn't be attending the wedding.

"You're not the boss of me," he slurred, and there was nothing worse than a sloppy drunk who was supposed to be the best man at a wedding.

"Oh, you're very wrong about that, my friend. Today is about your brother and his beautiful bride. And I won't hesitate to lock you in a room if you don't straighten up now. Drink this coffee. You've got a best man speech to give tonight, and I'm sure you don't want to make any more of a fool of yourself than you already have."

His eyes widened, and he didn't argue.

My job was to keep our clients happy, and Jacoby's brother was not my client.

And I think he got the message loud and clear, because he didn't say another word for the next thirty minutes.

It was just another day at the office for me.

CHAPTER SIX

Charlie

I washed my hands in the sink and packed up my supplies. I'd dropped Harper off at her best friend Lily's house earlier, and I was looking forward to a few hours to relax alone, because it didn't happen often.

But here I was dealing with the aftermath of a dude who'd binged on chili dogs.

And why does the entire house smell like a Christmas tree now?

I was drying off my hands just as Violet came around the corner.

Blond waves fell around her shoulders, and I tried not to stare at the way her white sweater outlined her perfect tits like pieces of art. Or the way her jeans hugged her cute little ass.

Or the way she continued to light up every room she entered.

Even the shitter.

Damn. I needed to get laid.

It had been a while.

Dating wasn't easy, considering I was balancing a busy work schedule with raising my little girl. But I had a few women I occasionally got together with.

They knew I didn't have much to offer outside a good time every now and then, and they were fine with it.

"All fixed," I said, pulling the strap of my duffel bag over my shoulder.

Violet glanced around the bathroom and gaped at me. "You didn't need to clean up the mess. I was going to come in and do that."

"It's fine. Better I end up covered in shit than you. You've got a wedding to pull off tonight."

"Why are you being so nice to me? Are you up to something?" Her voice was laced with humor. "You got a hot date tonight, Charles?"

"Nope. I just can't wait to see you tie hundreds of pink balloons and pay me back. I'll see you later."

She was still watching me as I walked backward toward the door, and she smiled as the words left her mouth. "I'm going to head out to my house tomorrow morning and check on the progress."

"No more changes, Firefly." The name slipped from my lips without a thought. She looked at me, but I kept talking like it was nothing. "We're trying to stay on track so you can get back in your house."

"Sick of me already?" she said with a smirk.

No, actually. I didn't mind her staying in the guesthouse in the backyard, even though I liked to pretend I did. Nor had I minded her using my oven. She'd been patient about the fact that the new oven had arrived damaged, and I'd had to ship it back and reorder another one all over again.

So I'd told her to just use my kitchen as often as she wanted.

"Don't change the subject. I'm serious about not making any more changes. I feel like you're up to something."

"Then you know me well, Mr. Huxley." She chuckled as Montana came running around the corner, looking a little frantic.

Violet informed her that the bathroom was fixed, and she thanked me before telling her best friend that the groom's brother had just puked all over the groom's tuxedo.

"That's my cue. I'll see you ladies later." I made my way out to my truck.

My phone rang, and it was Jeanne McAffrey, Lily's mom. "Hey, Jeanne, how are the girls doing?"

"They're great. Um, Lily asked if Harper could spend the night. I know she's never slept away from you, but she seems like she wants to give it a try. I could always call you if there's an issue."

I rubbed my face. The McAffreys were good people. I'd known Jeanne since elementary school, and her future husband, Tim, had moved to Blushing when we were in high school.

But my daughter had never spent a night away from me. I didn't have much family, so she didn't have grandparents. She'd been close to my cousin when she'd stayed in the guesthouse, but she hadn't spent the night with her.

I was all she had, and I never wanted her to feel abandoned or not cared for, so it had always been her and me against the world in a way.

I wanted to shield her from every hard lesson life would throw at her.

And so far, I'd been able to do that, to an extent.

"She wants to spend the night?"

"She said she does. But why don't you speak to her so you can feel it out?" Jeanne said.

"All right."

Harper's voice came through my Bluetooth in the truck: "Hi, Daddy."

"Hey, baby girl. Are you having fun?"

"Yep. So much fun. Lily wants me to sleep over, and she got those bunk beds for Christmas."

I chuckled. "That's cool. Do you want to sleep over?"

"I do want to sleep over. But will you be sad if you're by yourself?"

I'll never figure out how an asshole like me got lucky enough to have this sweet angel as my daughter.

"You never need to worry about me, Harps. I'm just fine. I want you to have fun."

"Mrs. McAffrey said if I change my mind, I can call you and go home anytime."

"Anytime, baby girl. I'll have my phone on me, and I can be there in five minutes if you get homesick," I said. "Do you want me to drop off a bag with your pajamas and your toothbrush?"

"Lily has a pair of jammies that I can wear, and Mrs. McAffrey said that they have extra toothbrushes. We're going to have a slumber party, Daddy."

I pulled into my driveway after the short trip from downtown and turned off the engine. "Have the best time, and if I don't hear from you, I'll be there first thing in the morning."

"Love you more than all the stars in the sky, Daddy."

"Love you more than monkeys love bananas," I said, which I knew would earn me a fit of giggles.

Jeanne came back on the phone, and she was laughing now too. "You're a good dad, Charlie Huxley."

"Thank you. And thanks for having her. If you need anything, just give me a call."

"Hey, there is something I wanted to run by you."

"Sure. What is it?"

I heard Tim say something in the background, and she told him to stay out of it, but they were both laughing. "I think you know my hairdresser, Julia Warren?"

I groaned, knowing where this was going. "I know Julia. Our town is the size of a postage stamp. She's been living here for a while now."

"Just hear me out. She thinks you're . . . What did I tell you she said, Tim?"

Tim grabbed the phone from his wife as I was making my way inside my house. "Hey, Charlie."

"Why do I feel like I'm going to regret this call?"

"I don't know?" He chuckled. "But I believe Julia called you a 'hot daddy.'"

"Give me that phone!" Jeanne shouted, and soon she was talking to me again. "She thinks you're good looking."

"Thanks. Good to know." I cleared my throat, because I didn't like being set up. That type of thing came with different expectations. "Listen, Jeanne, it's nice of you to think of me. But I'm not looking to get into anything serious."

"Neither is she. It's dinner and drinks. We were thinking we could double-date. You and Julia and me and Tim. That'll make it more casual. Just four friends out having a good time."

I roughed a hand through my hair. "It's tough to get a babysitter, so how about we play it by ear."

"I'm sure Abigail Howard would happily babysit if it meant you could go out and have some fun," she said, as if she had it all figured out. Abigail was my neighbor, and she adored Harper, and she was always offering to babysit for me.

Tim shouted into the phone that he had nothing to do with this.

I groaned. "I'll think about it."

"We could just do dinner and a beer at the Moose Brew. It doesn't have to be a big deal. When was the last time you had some fun?"

"You don't need to worry about me. I'm doing just fine." I chuckled.

I usually grabbed a drink with my friend Myles at the Moose Brew once or twice a month, and I played poker every couple of weeks with Benji and a few other guys.

"Fine. Do it for me. I want to get out. Tim and I haven't gone to the Moose Brew in a while, and I can't get him to go anywhere, but if we were going with you and Julia, he'd be much easier to convince." I heard Tim teasing her in the background that she was being a little dramatic. "You can just go as friends and see if there are any sparks. No pressure at all. How does next weekend sound?"

"Fine," I grumped, not happy that she was forcing my hand. I'd run into Julia several times, and she always came on real strong. I just didn't feel an attraction there, so I made it a point to avoid her whenever I saw her out. And now I'd be trapped at a table with her. "I'll meet for dinner and a drink, but I like to be home to put Harps to bed."

"You do remember those crazy nights we used to have in high school, right?" Jeanne said. "You're still young, and according to Julia, you're still hot."

"Good night, Jeanne," I said, and I held the phone away from my ear when her loud laughter boomed through the phone. "Call me if Harper gets homesick."

"Thanks, Charlie. I'll text you the details this week. Julia is going to be thrilled. We didn't think you'd agree to go."

"I feel like you kind of forced me into this, if I'm being honest."

More laughter.

We said our goodbyes, and I fixed myself some dinner.

It was quiet in the house, which wasn't the norm.

My phone vibrated with a text.

Myles: Hey, any chance Abigail could hang with Harper tonight?
Me: Nope. Harper's having her first sleepover. What's up?
Myles: Want to meet at the Moose Brew for a drink? Montana has the wedding so she'll be late.
Me: To think you were a bachelor not that long ago. Now you're lonely when your lady is gone for a few hours?
Myles:
Myles: Am I to believe that you aren't twiddling your fucking thumbs sitting on your couch alone?

I had to laugh. He knew me well.

Me: I'll meet you there in fifteen minutes.

The snow had finally melted, and it was a nice night for a walk, not that downtown was too far from my house. I slipped on my coat and made my way outside. This was my favorite time of year, with winter on the way out and spring not quite here yet. It was still cool in the evenings, but not so bone chilling that you couldn't be outside.

When I opened the door to the bar, Myles was already there, talking to Dakota, one of the bartenders who worked for Benji, and Dean Walker was standing beside them.

I groaned internally.

The dude owned the only used car lot in town, and he thought he was a big fucking deal. I'd grown up with him, and he was always the guy who liked to point out the fact that I was a foster kid.

I hadn't forgotten it, all these years later.

I noticed that some people liked to kick others when they were down in an attempt to feel better about themselves.

As Harper and Violet would say, the dude was very insector.

I pulled up the barstool next to Myles and gave them a nod. "Hey."

"I see Huxley is his usual chatty self," Dean said with a laugh as he tipped his head back and finished what was left in his glass.

Dakota set a beer down in front of me, knowing exactly what I ordered when I did swing by, before he stepped away to wait on a few customers who'd just walked in. I knew Benji was still working the wedding for Violet and Montana tonight.

"Just didn't want to interrupt the conversation," I said, holding my bottle up to the asshole still standing beside Myles, who'd just informed me that he had to take a phone call real quick, and he stepped away.

I shot him a look, letting him know that he'd better hurry his ass back.

I had zero patience for Dean Walker.

"I was just asking Myles about Violet, seeing as she's best friends with Montana," he said, and for whatever reason, my shoulders stiffened at him inquiring about her. "I'm taking her out tomorrow, and I wanted to see what I could find out about her. I've been working on getting a date with that woman for months, and she finally agreed to go out with me."

"Is that so?" I said, the words coming out much harsher than I expected.

Why the fuck would she agree to go out with this asshole?

"Wait a minute. You're renovating her house, aren't you?" he asked. "She's renting your guesthouse while she's waiting to move back in?"

I raised a brow. "You haven't been out with her once, yet you seem to know a lot. And do you always try to see what you can find out about someone before you take them out?"

He laughed loudly like we were buddies and I was just giving him shit. But that was not the case, as I was basically insinuating that he sounded like a stalker.

"When you've been trying to get a woman to go out with you for months, you do what you can to present yourself a certain way when she finally gives in, you know? I don't want to have put in all this effort for nothing."

This fucking guy.

He had a reputation, and he was known for banging every tourist who came through town. Why hadn't Montana given her best friend a heads-up about what a piece of shit this guy was? She'd known him as long as I had.

"'All this effort'? From what I've heard, you've been keeping plenty busy with the tourists coming through town. But now you're into Violet, huh?" I took a long pull from my beer.

"You keeping tabs on the competition, Huxley?" He laughed, and I wrapped my hand so tight around my bottle I worried the glass would shatter as he continued talking. "Obviously we're two of the most eligible bachelors in Blushing. I get it. And you know my motto—'Hit it and quit it.'"

I didn't know his motto. I didn't keep up with who the eligible bachelors in town were. And I didn't give two shits about this fucker.

But I didn't want him anywhere near Violet.

So, I'd have to play the game.

"Well, I don't think you're going to have any luck with that motto when it comes to Violet." I shrugged, glancing over at Myles, still talking on his phone in the far corner of the bar. He looked pissed off, which didn't mean much because it was also his normal state.

"Oh, what do you know? Myles didn't tell me shit. But he's a moody fucker, right?" More annoying laughter.

"I mean, if you're crazy about her, like you claim to be, I think you should go for it. She's staying in my guesthouse, and she's a great girl. She's got plans, though, so be aware."

"Dirty plans?" He smirked.

"Nah, that's not her thing. I helped her move into the guesthouse, and she has a whole bulletin board of her plans to be married by the end of the year. She wants five kids, and she's already got their names picked out. I mean, you've got to respect a woman who knows what she wants." I shrugged, reaching for my beer again and then taking a sip as he gaped at me. "But your 'hit it and quit it' might not be aligned with her motto that I noticed she uses as her screen saver."

Shit. I'd never been great at thinking on the fly, but by the shocked look on his face, I was doing a damn good job.

"What the fuck? I thought she was wild. I was hoping for a good time. What's her motto?"

This fucker had it coming.

But now I had to think of something quickly.

I cleared my throat. "I shouldn't be sharing her secrets, so keep this between us."

"Always. Bros before hos, am I right?"

No, you fucker. You're not right.

I plastered a fake smile on my face. "It was something like, 'Saving myself for Mr. Right.'"

"No shit. She's a fucking virgin? How did I misread her so badly?"

"Maybe you're just a clueless fuck," I said dryly like I was kidding around. He roared in laughter, and I pretended to join in.

"Well, she won't be the first woman I deflower." He moved his brows up and down, and I cringed at his words. "Challenge accepted."

Well, that didn't go the way I hoped it would.

CHAPTER SEVEN

Violet

The last hour had been the longest sixty minutes of my life. I wanted a new car, one with snow tires, and the only place in town to get it was at this dipshit's car lot.

He'd been hitting on me for months, and I dreaded the idea of spending any time with him. I'd considered going to Anchorage to avoid this interaction, but I'd noticed the cute white Bronco that was parked on his lot last week, so I decided to just bite the bullet. Dean Walker was not the first asshole I'd ever dealt with.

I could handle him for a brief time, right?

"You sure you don't want to discuss the finances over lunch?" he asked, flashing his Cartier watch around his wrist several times to make sure I saw it.

"Yes, I'm sure. I'd like to buy a car, Dean. Are you able to handle the paperwork for me? Otherwise, I'm happy to go to Anchorage and purchase it there."

He whistled. "Honey, they don't call me the Car King for nothing."

I'd never heard anyone call him the Car King, nor did I care what they called him. He had a Bronco that I wanted, and I hoped we could do this painlessly, but he'd already proved that wasn't going to be possible.

He'd talked about himself ever since I'd arrived. When I said that I liked the tan interior in the Bronco, he suggested that I should take a look inside his sports car and see the red leather interior.

I'd declined the offer and inquired about the snow tires on the Bronco.

He'd then offered to take me to his house to see his garage full of snow tires.

I'd declined the offer.

Again.

The man was working my ever-loving nerves.

"So let's go over what you're going to give me for the trade-in and negotiate the price of the Bronco, yeah?" I asked.

He chuckled and nodded. "I like a woman who knows what she wants."

"Great." *I also know what I don't want, asshole.*

We spent the next thirty minutes going over the price and the financing, and it was painful, but we agreed on everything, and he had one of his employees draft up the contract. He reached down in his desk drawer and pulled out a bottle of wine and two glasses.

Is this guy for real?

With a wink, he took a wine opener from the top drawer and opened the bottle.

"What exactly are you doing?"

"I'm celebrating with you. You're a woman who knows what she wants, right? And I'm a man who knows what I want. Don't be afraid, Violet. You can trust me."

I intertwined my fingers and rested my elbows on the desk across from him as he poured two glasses of wine and set one in front of me.

"What exactly would I be afraid of?" I asked. "And I won't be joining you for that drink because I've got a half day of work left."

"All work and no play makes Violet a dull girl."

My. Blood. Is. Boiling.

"I assure you, no one has ever called me dull. But I'm curious, Dean. Do you harass all of your customers who purchase cars?"

"Nah, just the pretty ones." Loud laughter bellowed from his mouth, and it took everything I had not to dive over the desk and throat punch him.

"I see. So, you're not hiding the fact that you're a chauvinistic pig then?"

"Hey, you don't need to do all that. I know your secret. You've got all this pent-up frustration because you've never allowed yourself to feel good."

Okay. I was definitely going over this desk and kicking his ass if he took this any further.

"Are we talking about cars, Dean? I'm a straight shooter, so how about you just tell me what the hell you're talking about, and then we can get the keys to the Bronco and I can get out of here."

"Darlin', you give such mixed signals with that mouth of yours," he said, and I had to close my eyes and count to ten because this guy was actually doubling down on this.

"How many sexual harassment lawsuits have you dealt with over the years?" I crossed my arms over my chest and met his gaze.

He took a long sip of his wine before swirling it around and staring at it. It took everything in me not to inform him that he was doing it backward, as you normally swirled the wine before you sampled it, but the man was too clueless to waste my breath on.

"Sweetheart, this is Blushing, not the city. We don't sue one another. We like to have a good time."

"I see. And I'm too dull to have a good time?" I asked.

"You have too many rules. And that's probably why you've been avoiding me all this time. I scare you."

"I wouldn't say I'm scared of you. But I would say your mere existence is frightening to all females." I leaned back in my chair.

He let out a full-bodied laugh. "I like this game we're playing, pussycat."

"And I'd like to get the keys to my new car before I scratch your eyes out."

"Listen, I know I have a reputation." He held his hands up and smiled, and it was easy to see that the man thought he was charming as hell. He was not capable of reading the room, because he was too egotistical to see how offensive he was. "But I'd be willing to bend the rules for you. Now I don't know about the five kids, but I'd walk down the aisle with you today if it means that much to you."

What in the flying fuck is this man talking about?

"That's it, Dean. I don't think our signals are crossing here." I stood up, because no one needed a Bronco this badly. I'd walk through the snow before I sat here one more minute. "I'm going to call this done."

"I know you're a virgin, Violet. I know you're saving yourself for marriage. I know about the five kids, and it's not something I've ever wanted, but I'd consider it for you." He was on his feet now with a creepy smile on his face.

I turned around to look at him. "What in the absolute hell are you talking about? I came here for a car. What is this?"

"Don't be mad at Charlie. He was helping his boy out. He told me about the screen saver. About all of it. And I could consider the rules, if you'd just give me a little something. A sign that you want this too." He walked closer to me.

Charlie freaking Huxley.

He was behind this.

"Dean. If you take one more step, I will kick you so hard in the balls that you'll be singing soprano for the rest of your days." I held up a hand, making it clear that I did not want him to take one step closer to me.

"Tell me what you want, pussycat." He smiled, like he was conceding to a challenge I was no part of.

"I wanted a freaking Bronco. I want you to never call me 'pussycat' again. I don't want to date you. I don't want to get married. I don't have any desire to have five children, and I don't have a clue what you're talking about. I came here for a car. And I no longer want a car. So I'd say your sales skills are as bad as your dating skills."

"You don't need to be ashamed of wanting what you want, Violet. I'm okay with it," he insisted.

I need to get out of here.

The door flew open, and his assistant walked in with the paperwork. I took the contract from her hands and tore it in half and tossed it on the desk.

"Deal's off. You're lucky I'm leaving without causing you physical pain, Dean." I marched out of his office.

"What if I throw in an extra year warranty on the Bronco?" he shouted from the other side of the door, and I held my hand up and flashed him my middle finger.

I didn't need snow tires now anyway. I'd made it through the worst of winter, and I had plenty of time to find a car before next winter.

I'd walked here because it was close to my office, but I was going to make a pit stop before I went back to work.

I knew Charlie was working at the hotel today, and I beelined for the entryway. They'd made a lot of progress on the place.

Will smiled when he saw me coming; he usually spent his mornings here and his afternoons at my place. His face straightened when he saw the look on mine. "Where's your boss?" I hissed.

He thrust his thumb over his shoulder, and his eyes were wide. "He's in the kitchen, getting the appliances set up."

I nodded, and my eyes went to the bags from the Brown Bear Diner sitting on the card table. Charlie's name was written across one of the six bags. "Great. Is this his lunch?"

"Yes, ma'am." Will looked a little terrified of me, and I only hoped I'd put the same fear in his arrogant, jackass boss.

"I'll take it to him." I yanked the sub sandwich wrapped in tan parchment paper out of the bag and stormed toward the kitchen.

A few guys were just coming toward me from there, obviously heading toward the front room, where they ate lunch when they were working here. But Charlie wasn't in the group, and I hoped I'd catch the bastard off guard.

They all said hello, and I gave them a curt nod, because I was on a mission.

I stormed through the swinging door to the kitchen, and there he was, arms crossed over his chest, broad, muscled shoulders stretching against his white henley as he stared at the commercial refrigerator like he was about to ask it on a date. His gaze moved to me when I stepped inside, and I pulled my arm back like I was going to pitch a ball in the World Series and hurled the foot-long sandwich of deli meat wrapped in homemade bread at his head. The bastard raised his hand on reflex and caught it.

I searched the area for something else to throw at him.

"Hey, hey," he shouted, moving around the island across from me. "What the hell is going on?"

I saw a newspaper still rolled up with two elastic bands around it, so I chucked that at him, hitting him in the chest this time.

"You bastard!"

"I didn't get back to you about the tile you want to change on the kitchen backsplash, because I need to see if it's even in stock." He set the sandwich down beside the newspaper now resting on the stainless steel island and stared at me.

"This isn't about the freaking tile, you asshat!" I shouted.

"*Asshat*'s a new one. You haven't called me that yet." He smirked, and I wanted to wipe that smile right off his handsome face. "What did I do now, Firefly?"

Damn him with the cute nickname. Although it probably had some sort of offensive meaning, for all I knew.

His hair was a disheveled mess. Ocean-blue eyes locked with mine. He was enjoying this.

I stormed around the island, stopping in front of him. "Well, buckle up, buddy, because I have a slew of names for you."

"How about you tell me what you're so pissed off about first."

"You don't know?" I moved closer.

"I don't know."

"Charlie."

"Violet," he said, mimicking me.

"Does me being a virgin, saving myself for marriage, and holding out for five kids ring a bell?"

I saw it on his face the minute the words left my mouth. He winced. "Oh, that. I can explain."

I shoved at his chest. "You can explain? I highly doubt that."

"He was telling me that you'd agreed to go on a date with him tonight, and—he didn't have your best intentions in mind." He shrugged, wrapping his hands around my wrists to hold them still.

"Ah . . . the womanizer didn't have my best intentions in mind? What a shock."

"You know he's an asshole?" he asked.

"Uh, yeah, genius. Everyone knows he's an asshole. We were never going on a date. I was buying a car from him this morning. But that did not happen after he proposed marriage and offered to take my virginity and allow me to birth his demon spawn."

A wide grin spread across his face, and he chuckled. "All right. Well, he misled me a bit on that, and I was trying to help you out."

"You were trying to help me out by telling the biggest perv in town that I'm a virgin waiting to be deflowered?" I yanked my arms away and stomped on his foot, because it was the only thing I could think of.

He yelped, and I turned on my heels to walk away, but he wrapped both of his big arms around my waist and held me still. My back to his front. "Will you just relax and let me explain?"

I wrestled to get out of his hold, but the man was strong, yet he managed to be gentle at the same time. I didn't feel threatened or nervous, and I stopped fighting him.

"Fine," I huffed. "Let me go, and I'll listen to what you have to say."

His arms relaxed, and I moved out of his grasp and turned to face him.

"I hate that guy," he said. "I didn't like the way he was talking about you. I thought if I told him those things, he'd leave you alone."

"But you thought I was willingly going on a date with him?"

"Yes, that's how he made it sound."

"Yet you were trying to ruin my date?"

"Wait a minute. One minute you're mad that I said those things to the biggest asshole in town, and now you're mad that I was trying to ruin your date?" He threw his hands in the air.

"Well, if you thought I wanted to go out with him, and you told him what you told him—that was a dick move. Either way, you're the asshole."

"I'm the asshole?"

I glared at him. "You're definitely the asshole."

"You can twist this however you want, Firefly, I was trying to help you out."

"Well, that's a funny way of helping someone out."

"Did you get the car?"

"I did not. After he talked about my virginity and tried to woo me with a glass of wine, I got the hell out of there." I shook my head with disgust and then glanced over at his sandwich and reached for it. "I haven't had lunch yet, so I'll be taking this with me. I would suggest you watch your back, Charles."

"What is that supposed to mean?" he grumped.

"I'm just saying . . . karma is a patient gangster. And this mother of five will be waiting for the right moment to strike."

He groaned as I stormed out the door.

But I had a big smile on my face when I reached the guys who were all sitting around the large card table eating.

Will looked up at me, his lips turning up on one side. "Everyone alive in there?"

I glanced at the empty chair that I assumed was for Charlie, and I made my way over and sat down. "He's alive for now. But I can't promise that will last long."

They laughed as Charlie walked out of the kitchen, his gaze moving to each of us.

"I'll be back. I'm going to grab a sandwich," he growled as he walked past the table. "You're all a bunch of traitors."

The group erupted in laughter as I took a bite of the sandwich.

I wasn't sure how I'd pay him back, but I was determined to think of something.

CHAPTER EIGHT

Charlie

"I think we should all take a shot," Julia said to Benji when he stopped by our table to grab our order. The woman's enthusiasm was giving me a headache, and we'd only been here for fifteen minutes.

She'd texted me half a dozen times today because Jeanne had taken it upon herself to give Julia my phone number, even though this was supposed to be a casual get-together with friends.

She'd asked what I was going to wear tonight, which was weird as fuck to ask a dude.

She'd asked if my babysitter could spend the night, which was not happening, and I'd made that clear.

She'd asked if I thought we should try to bail on Jeanne and Tim, so we could be alone.

Also, a hard no.

The last few texts were ridiculous. She'd inquired about food allergies, if I had any sexual kinks, and if I was open to threesomes.

To say that I didn't want to be here would be a massive understatement.

"I'm totally down for shots," Jeanne said, and Tim gave me an apologetic look, as he didn't seem thrilled about being here either. Benji had a wicked grin on his face because he was enjoying the fact that I was miserable.

"I'm going to stick to a beer," I said, and Tim asked for the same.

"Great. Well, you two can do your thing, but me and Julia are going to have a good time," Jeanne said with a big smile on her face.

"Yes. Our men can take care of us tonight," Julia said, leaning against me in the booth.

What the hell was going on? We barely knew one another. I hadn't agreed to anything more than four friends having dinner.

Thankfully, Benji soon returned, and the two women downed the shots in a matter of seconds. We placed our dinner orders, and Julia requested another round of shots for her and Jeanne, as well as some Long Island iced teas.

Tim looked a little panicked, since Jeanne wasn't a big drinker.

Benji and I traded a look, and I knew I'd be getting a text from him later tonight about the madness that was this moment.

I took a long pull from my beer as Jeanne told us all about her PTA meeting today and the fundraiser they had planned next month.

"I was hoping you'd help me again with building the set for the spring performance this year," Jeanne asked as Benji set down two new shots of tequila for the ladies as well as their Long Island iced teas.

"Let's drink to Charlie building a sexy prop for the kids!" Julia reached for her shot glass and clinked it with Jeanne's, and they both tipped their heads back.

"Not quite sure a sexy prop for a kid performance is the goal." Tim reached for his beer bottle and took a sip.

"Well, I just think being a single dad is sexy. And I think you're sexy," Julia said to me. "And do you know what else I think is sexy?"

I didn't respond. I just stared at her, because this wasn't a conversation that I felt like having. Julia was sucking down her Long Island iced tea like she was preparing for an episode of *Girls Gone Wild*, and Jeanne was leaning against Tim as if she was already two sheets to the wind.

"Well, I'll tell you," Julia said, keeping her voice low. Benji was back and setting our dinner plates in front of us. "A limp dick is never a bad thing, Charlie. There are work-arounds."

What the actual fuck?

"Thanks for the fun fact," I said, turning my attention to the burger in front of me.

Benji chuckled as he walked off, and my phone vibrated shortly after with a text from him that was simply an eggplant emoji. I guess she was speaking louder than I thought she was.

I responded with a head-exploding emoji.

"Try to take a few bites of your chicken sandwich, baby," Tim said, pulling the plate closer to his wife.

"Okay. My man is taking care of me, I guess." Jeanne's eyes were already showing signs of intoxication, and her words were slurring. But she reached for her cocktail and sucked half the glass down through her straw.

I had a feeling this date would be ending much sooner than anticipated, and I was fine with that, but I felt bad that Jeanne was going to be sick as hell tomorrow.

Julia held her glass up and whistled to get Benji's attention. She held her glass up and two fingers, and he nodded.

"I don't think Jeanne needs any more to drink," Tim said, and I could hear the irritation in his voice.

"She never goes out. Let her have some fun," Julia said, turning her attention back to me. "Speaking of never going out. Why don't I see you out much?"

"Because I work and have a child to raise. I go out plenty, but I'm not downing shots anymore. I'll have a beer or two with the guys, and that suits me just fine," I said before reaching for my burger and taking another bite.

"But I bet you like your woman tipsy and relaxed, huh?"

"Actually, not really." I shrugged. "It's tough to have a conversation with someone who's tipping back the shots, you know?"

Julia was young, and it showed tonight.

Her hand found my thigh beneath the table, and she leaned close to me. "Conversation is overrated, Charlie."

"I don't feel so well," Jeanne said from the other side of the booth, just as Benji set down two more drinks before telling us he'd get us some refills on our waters. Tim helped his wife out of the booth, and they walked toward the bathroom.

"Good. I thought they'd never leave," Julia said, sucking down more than half the liquid in her tall glass with one sip.

"Well, at the rate you're pumping booze into her, I think they'll probably be heading home soon. And I'm happy to get you home, but I plan on heading out when they do, so if you'd like me to walk you home, I'll be leaving early."

"Charlie, you don't have to worry. It's not an issue for me. I think you're sexy as hell. We can work around the other things, you know? I'm a creative girl." She smiled, and then her tongue slowly slid across her bottom lip as if she was trying to draw me in. But at this point, I was already one foot out the door and eager to get the hell out of here. I wasn't going to let her drive home or walk home alone when she was this intoxicated, so I'd walk her there before heading to my place. I wasn't a complete asshole.

"Julia, I don't have a fucking clue what you're talking about. But I'm actually okay with that, because I'd rather not know. How about we just finish our burgers, and I walk you home and we call this done."

"Charlie," she said before her hand moved between my legs, and she gripped my cock over the denim of my pants. "I'm talking about your little problem."

I wrapped my hand around her wrist and tugged it away. "What the fuck are you doing? Read the room. This is not happening. And that is not the way to make it happen, I can promise you that."

She wasn't even remotely deterred by me tugging her hand away. "I know about the medication, Charlie, and clearly it's working from what I just felt there."

I sighed and closed my eyes for a second, hoping I could will her to stop talking.

No such luck.

"I can help you with your situation. You won't even need the medication," she said, her words slurring.

Okay. This wasn't going to go away, so I just sat there waiting to hear whatever the hell she was going to say, and I made no attempt to stop her this time.

"You won't be my first limp dick that I've dealt with. I can get you there. I could climb right under this booth right now and get you there, Charlie. I've got one magical mouth."

I coughed, choking on the long pull of beer I'd just taken.

I hadn't been laid in a while. This woman had just grabbed my junk right under the table and was basically talking about having me fuck her mouth right here.

And yet, I wanted to get out of here.

I was clearly not attracted to her at all.

"Do not climb under this table," I said when she started to move. "Julia, I'm not sure where you're getting your information, but I don't take medication. My dick is just fine. But I am not looking for a relationship, and I think we're best off as friends. I appreciate the offer, though."

"She said you'd say that. I know it's embarrassing," Julia said. "But you aren't going to push me away. Hell, I don't even care about your doll collection. I think it's cute."

"Who were you talking to? Jeanne?" I asked with a glance over toward the bathroom. Still no sign of Jeanne or Tim, which meant things must not have been going well.

"Okay, you can't say I told you, because I promised her that I wouldn't say a word. But Monique does Violet's hair, and her booth is next to mine. Violet was in the salon today, and I know she lives in your guesthouse and you two are friends. And she wasn't betraying your trust—I promise she wasn't. She was just trying to help a girl out." She smiled up at me.

Sure she was.

"What exactly did she say?"

"She told me that the guys all give you a hard time about your situation." She kept her voice low once again, as this was apparently a sensitive subject. "She said they have all sorts of names for you—Limp Biscuit, Limplestiltskin, Sir Limps a Lot—and we both agreed it's cruel. And that's when she told me about the doll collection you keep in your bedroom. Listen, saving all your great-grandmother's old-fashioned dolls on shelves in your bedroom is not anything to feel bad about. And I don't even care that you brush their hair every single Sunday to keep them looking nice. I'm a hairdresser, Charlie. I admire your commitment." She reached for Jeanne's untouched cocktail, and my eyes widened because this woman could hold her liquor.

Un-fucking-believable.

Tim walked toward the booth, and he did not look pleased.

"Hey, guys, we need to get going. Jeanne is pretty sick. I'm sorry to bail early, but I need to take her home." He reached for his wallet, and I waved him off.

"I've got it. Just get her home. We're going to leave as well."

Julia made a little whiny sound and then pushed her bottom lip out to me, and I stood and made my way over to Benji.

"Can you close this tab out, please?" I said, handing him my card.

"Of course," he said, swiping it through the machine. "Your date appears to hold her liquor very well. Poor Jeanne is going to be miserable tomorrow."

"Yeah. I'm going to take Julia's drunk ass home so I can go give Violet a piece of my mind."

Benji handed me my card back and smirked at me. "You two love to give one another shit, don't you?"

"She clearly does." I signed the piece of paper and told him I'd talk to him later.

Getting Julia out the door was a whole other issue. The two-block walk felt like a full marathon.

"Are you seriously not going to come inside? Even after I said I'm fine with your Limp Biscuit dick and your baby doll obsession?" Her words were slurring now as I walked her up to the front door.

"I'm not coming inside, but I appreciate the support." I chuckled, because the whole thing was ridiculous.

"Fine. It's your loss," she hissed as she put her key in the door.

"I'm sure it is." I held up a hand, and she slammed the door in my face, which was a perfect ending to a horrific evening.

I made my way home and cut through the side yard, because I had a bone to pick with my neighbor first. The light was coming through the window, so I knew she was still up. I knocked on the door, then shoved my hands in my pockets, suddenly second-guessing myself.

What if she had a dude here?

She might not be alone.

What the fuck was I even doing here?

I was turning to get out of there when the door flew open.

"Charles. How was your date?" she asked as a mischievous grin took over her face.

"Don't you mean Limp Biscuit?"

"Sir Limps a Lot is my personal favorite, although I think Get Limpy with It is another good option," she said, and my eyes moved from her pretty face down her body. She wore a thin tank top, and my gaze zoned in on the two hard peaks poking through the fabric. She caught me staring and shrugged. "It's cold outside."

"Apparently. And thanks for making that the most uncomfortable night of my life," I said, trying to hide the smile that I couldn't fight any longer, because the evening had been laughable at the very least.

"Maybe you can cozy up to your baby dolls and brush their hair and snuggle them in bed tonight to comfort yourself from your horrible date?" She smirked.

"You know how insane that sounds, right? Me and my limp dick curled up with a bunch of creepy dolls?"

"Hey, your great-grandmother's dolls could be keepsakes. And Julia didn't have any issues with it. I think she actually liked the idea of you being a little—*unusual*. It can be intimidating when someone appears too perfect."

I stepped closer, and I noticed the way she sucked in a breath. "Too perfect, huh? Is that what you think of me, Firefly?"

"Me? No. I find you to be very imperfect." She cleared her throat, and her voice was a little husky now. "Moody, bossy, and what you did with Dean was a dick move."

"What is your obsession with my dick?" I asked, my voice so gruff it was barely recognizable.

"I could care less about your limp package," she said as her hands fisted my shirt and she tugged me closer, completely contradicting the words leaving her mouth.

"I think you do care." I leaned down, my lips so close they grazed hers, my hand moving to the side of her neck as my thumb traced her jawline.

Have I ever wanted anyone more?

It made no sense. This woman drove me mad.

She tangled her hands in my hair, and her green eyes locked with mine. "Obviously you want to kiss me."

"I think you want to kiss me just as bad as I want to kiss you, Firefly," I said, our lips still brushing against one another's.

"I mean, it's normal to be curious," she said, her words breathy. "We could agree to one kiss, and we never speak of it again."

That was all I needed. My mouth crashed into hers. Her lips parted in invitation, and my tongue slipped inside. Her hands were pulling at my hair, tugging me closer, and I gripped her ass and lifted her feet off the ground. I stepped inside to get out of the cold and kicked the door closed behind me. I pressed her back against the door, and I moaned when she ground up against my cock.

I had one hand supporting her ass and the other on the side of her neck, tipping her head to the side so I could take the kiss deeper.

Her fingers tangled in my hair, tugging me closer as she moved faster.

Our lips attaching to one another.

It was frantic and needy.

Her hands moved to my shoulders, her mouth pulling back from mine as she gasped and dug her nails into my shoulders as she continued grinding up against me with a fury.

Faster.

Harder.

My dick was so hard I was certain he'd tear through the denim.

And she used every inch to get herself off.

I thrust into her and watched as she went right over the edge.

It took everything in me to remain still as she rode out every last bit of pleasure.

I was desperate to follow her into oblivion. But I did not need to appear like a teenage boy who couldn't control himself.

Even if that was exactly how I felt.

I just stared at her, watching the way her eyes fell closed.

The way her cheeks flushed.

Her lips were red and swollen where we'd kissed like two feral animals.

And even if I didn't let myself finish, watching her fall apart while grinding up against my cock was the next best thing.

Apparently, Limp Biscuit still had it.

CHAPTER NINE

Violet

Hells to the yes!

Damn. Charlie Huxley had just lived up to every fantasy I'd had about him, and our clothes had remained on.

I blew out a breath and smiled as I slowly slid down his body. "Well, I think we're going to have to change your name to Hard as a Rock Huxley."

He roared in laughter, and when Charlie Huxley did that, it always felt like you were witnessing something special.

Something that he hid from the rest of the world.

But maybe I was just being nostalgic after having the world's best orgasm.

I have a new theory that dry humping is an underestimated form of foreplay.

"It beats Sir Limps a Lot."

"I feel a little bad that I ruined your date, and now I just humped you like a rabid horndog, and you are still, er, in a state of discomfort." I glanced down at his tented pants.

"I wasn't going to come in my pants like a prepubescent teenager and allow you to taunt me for the rest of my life," he said, feigning irritation, but he looked like he was quite proud of himself.

"You're a wise man, Charles." I bit down on my bottom lip because I was still completely turned on, but I didn't want to appear desperate. "I guess it's better to suffer than to let me gloat."

Should I offer to help him out?

No. This was a one-kiss deal. I just got greedy and tossed in a little happy ending for myself.

"Damn straight. And don't you worry," he said, smirking the slightest bit as he reached for the door handle. "I'll go take care of myself in the shower, thinking about you grinding that sweet pussy of yours all over my cock, all desperate and needy."

Oh. No. He. Didn't.

I squeezed my thighs together and did my best to act unaffected. "Impressive dirty talk for a man who doesn't like to speak all that much."

He tossed me a wink and walked right out the door. I watched as he crossed the yard and stepped inside, and then I closed the door and leaned my back against it.

Was I sweating?

And why was I panting?

Damn you, Charlie Huxley.

"So, after giving all those hashtags to Jules and Carter, I hate to tell you, but they settled on hashtag 'we said yes,'" Montana said.

I closed my eyes and feigned sleep, even adding a few fake snores for dramatic effect. "Damn. I hate when they go with the boring option," I groaned. "Why not spice it up? Live on the edge. You only get married once, right? I mean, that's the goal, but I can't say that failed marriages are bad for business. That just means we get to plan the next one."

I tossed a Skittle in the air and caught it in my mouth before doing it a few more times with the handful of candy I had in my palm.

Montana paused, hands on her hips, as she studied me. "What is going on with you today? You're all hopped up."

"I agree. I mean, you're normally sort of hopped up, but today you seem, I don't know, like you ate an energy bar—or six," Blakely deadpanned. "Did Velveteen change her hashtag?"

"Of course not. She's sticking with hashtag 'we said I Doobie.'" I rolled my eyes, because it wasn't my favorite, but God forbid my sister take my advice. She was the one who'd be stuck with the name Velveeta Doobie, so who was I to judge.

Actually, I am a wedding planner, that's who.

It's what I did for a living.

"Nope. It's not about that," Montana pressed. "She's hiding something. I can tell. She's got that look on her face."

I leaned back in my chair, propping my stilettos on the conference room table like a boss lady. "I had a hot make-out session with Charles last night."

Montana's mouth fell open, and Blakely pushed back in her chair abruptly. The wheels slid a little too fast before it slammed into the wall behind her.

"You made out with Charlie Huxley?" Blakely shouted.

"Way to be discreet," I hissed. "And this is why I hesitated to tell you."

"I think you hesitated to tell us because you don't want to admit that you like him, when you are so determined to hate the man." Montana was laughing hysterically now.

"I do hate the man," I said dryly. "But that doesn't mean I hate kissing him."

"I'm guessing it was good then?" Montana asked as she took the seat beside me and leaned in, like this was a dirty little secret we were sharing.

I guess it was in a way.

I made out with the enemy, after all.

"Of course. It figures, right? The man I despise is hot as hell, and let me tell you, he's packing the goods."

Blakely clapped her hands together. "How do you know? And did he find out about what you'd told Julia?"

"He sure did. He came barreling over to the guesthouse to give me a piece of his mind, and instead, I climbed the man like a tree."

"Oh, this was more than just a kiss?" Montana said, then turned her attention to Blakely, who groaned, moved to her feet, and stormed out the door.

"Where is she going?" I asked.

"You'll see," my bestie said with a playful grin on her face.

Blakely soon returned and handed Montana ten bucks. "I did not see it going down this quickly."

"'Going down'? No one went down. Though I'm sure the man would do magical things with that mouth of his," I said with a laugh. "Why are you paying her?"

"We had a bet that you and Charlie would hook up before the end of the month." Montana shrugged, tucking the money in her pocket.

"Well, it was a one and done. He already annoyed me this morning when I went over to cook some eggs before work."

"You sure spend a lot of time over there." Blakely pursed her lips like she'd just put me in my place.

"I have no oven." I tossed my hands in the air.

"Please," Montana said. "You live on Skittles and pizza rolls. You hardly need an oven. Now you're cooking two meals a day at the Huxleys', like you're Martha freaking Stewart."

"I think you want to bone big bad Charlie," Blakely said over a fit of laughter.

I shook my head with disbelief. "We can't stand one another. It was a buildup of sexual frustration that we worked out in one epic make-out session."

"You know attraction doesn't just usually fizzle that easily," Blakely said. "I mean, if the make-out session had been a disappointment, or an epic fail—sure, I'd buy the 'one and done' idea. But I don't think that's the case here."

"Agreed. You could always just have one of those flings where you just get it out of your system," my best friend said, as if she'd invented the idea.

"No way. We aren't going there. The man is still renovating my home, and I'm living in his backyard. What if he got attached? I can't risk it." I chuckled.

"It's Charlie. He doesn't seem like the clingy type," Montana said. "I think you're afraid that *you* might get attached. Would that really be the worst thing in the world?"

I rolled my eyes before popping a few Skittles in my mouth and then glancing down at my phone when it vibrated. I read the text and held my phone up for them to read it.

Sexy Tourist Brayden: Hey there, beautiful. Are we still on for dinner tonight?

"Oh, yes. The lawyer from Boston. I forgot about him," Blakely said, clapping her hands together. "You said he was very charming."

"He was." I grinned at her before typing a response.

"Well, he is persistent. I'll give him that," Montana said.

Me: Yes. I'll meet you at Sonny's Ranch House at 6pm?
Sexy Tourist Brayden: Are you sure I can't pick you up?
Me: I'm sure. I'll see you there.

I preferred to meet a guy at a public place, because I never wanted to be trapped in someone's car. I liked to have an exit strategy.

Always.

I'd met him at the diner last week when I was having lunch with Montana, and the man kept smiling at me before he finally walked over and introduced himself. He was charming enough, and he'd asked where I worked, and he later sent flowers to the Blushing Bride. He asked me to dinner on the card and left his cell number. I'd texted a thank-you message, and we'd chatted a few times over the last few days. I'd agreed to dinner tonight, and we'd go from there.

"Exactly. I hadn't expected him to keep messaging, but apparently, he's in town for a couple weeks, and dinner with a good-looking man doesn't sound like a terrible idea."

"You're taking your own car, right?" Montana asked.

"Yes, Mom. I'll be taking myself to and from dinner." I laughed. "Unless I feel the need to extend our evening."

"I want text updates about your whereabouts." She reached for her phone when it buzzed, and I promised I'd keep her updated before I made my way to my office.

I had a meeting with my stepmother and my sister in an hour and a bunch of paperwork to finish.

Once I'd sat down at my desk and turned on my computer, Charlie's name was at the top of my email, and I clicked to open his message.

> Ms. Beaumont,
> I received your lengthy email with the list of things you'd like to add to the job, and I think we can fit them all in and still stay on track with your timeline. We are hanging the chandelier (the one you most recently chose after three changes) in the dining room this afternoon and the kitchen cabinets will be installed today and tomorrow.
> Also, thank you for the eggs this morning. Harper refuses to eat eggs, yet she ate all of the eggs you made for us this morning, so whatever you put in them was pure magic. I appreciate it. But if you tell anyone I said that, I'll deny it.
> Mr. Huxley

I chuckled. I'd started going over every morning to make breakfast, and this morning they were running late for school, so I just made extra eggs. It wasn't a big deal if I scrambled two eggs or six eggs.

Mr. Huxley,
Thank you for the update. I'll be stopping by later today to check on the progress. That third choice on the chandelier was a real winner. Can't wait to see it. I'm also very excited about the new cabinets.
As far as the eggs go, I hate to give my trade secrets away, but I used salt and pepper. It's an old family recipe that I planned to take to the grave, but seeing as you're so interested, I thought I should share.
Ms. Beaumont

The emails were ridiculous because we also texted throughout the day. Usually about the renovation at my house, or something with the guesthouse. Or sometimes it was just to give one another shit.

I got back to work, typing up a few contracts and updating a few things on QuickBooks before getting ready for my Zoom meeting, when my phone vibrated with a text.

Charles: You were right. It looks great. <photo of the dining room chandelier>
Me: Damn. It's perfect. Thank you for arguing with me and insisting I was wrong.
Charles: My pleasure. It's what I do best.
Me: I'll head over as soon as I get out of my meeting.
Charles: No changes, Firefly. We're cruising now. Everything is ordered and we're on track.

I chuckled before turning my laptop to face me, and I clicked on the Zoom link. I spent the next forty minutes being insulted by Pissy Missy, who asked me multiple times if I was sure I could handle an event like this.

She also wanted reassurance that Montana would be there as well.

Velveteen was actually more pleasant than usual. I kept my cool, showed them the drawing for the outdoor space with the tents and chandeliers, and finalized the colors of the linens and floral arrangements.

Missy continued to grill me, and I did my best to bite my tongue before ending the call.

I made my way to my house and was thrilled with the progress. The chandelier looked great, as expected from the photo that Charlie had sent. The cabinets were partly installed, and I loved the sage-green color that I'd chosen even more in person.

But there was no sign of Charlie, and it surprised me that I was disappointed that he wasn't here.

Was I a glutton for punishment?

Did I get a sick joy out of being aggravated?

I mean, look at your family. Maybe you are predisposed to this type of behavior.

"It looks great, Will. Thank you so much," I said, making my way toward the door.

"Yeah. You've got a great eye. Even Charlie said so." He chuckled. "He likes to give you a hard time, but between me and you, after we installed the chandelier and he looked at the cabinets, he told me that you could be an interior designer."

I couldn't help the smile that spread across my face. "Wow. A compliment from Charlie Huxley, huh?"

He shrugged. "There's no denying you've got talent. Look at this place. It's really something."

"Thank you. I'll see you tomorrow."

I was proud of the fact that I'd purchased my first home. And as much as the flood had been a frustrating experience, I was enjoying renovating the place and making it my own.

And I didn't even mind living in Charlie Huxley's guesthouse.

In fact, I was enjoying being there.

I sat on a barstool in the tiny bathroom getting ready for my date, and for whatever reason, I couldn't stop thinking about that damn kiss with Charlie.

I'd definitely need to kiss Brayden tonight so I'd have something new to think about.

I slipped into my dark jeans and a cream sweater that hung off one shoulder, showing a little bit of skin. I wore my heeled black boots and drove the short distance to Sonny's Ranch House. Brayden was waiting for me outside when I pulled into the lot. He was tall, his blond hair was cut short, and he wore a black trench coat. He helped me as I stepped out of the car before placing his hand on the small of my back and leading me inside.

We found a quiet table in the back and ordered steak and lobster, and the conversation flowed. He was nice and smart and even a little funny.

But I wasn't feeling it.

Not even a little bit.

I kept checking my phone to see if Charlie had texted, as I usually went over to make something for dinner.

But he hadn't messaged.

I tried hard to focus on Brayden as he told me about a recent case he'd taken on against a large corporation.

It was interesting. But my mind was elsewhere.

"So tell me about the wedding business. You've built quite a company, from what I can tell."

I nodded and finished chewing the most delicious lobster. "Yes, we're packed for the next year, and business is good."

My gaze moved as if it were being pulled by a force.

Steve the owner moved past our table, with Charlie Huxley beside him.

The man I was trying hard not to think about just walked right past me.

CHAPTER TEN

Charlie

It had been a day, and now here I was at Sonny's Ranch House at eight o'clock at night. Harper had a project I needed to help her with after school, and a bottle of glitter had exploded in my face. I'd gotten her fed and bathed before Steve Johnson called, sounding frantic because his refrigerator was acting up, and seeing as I'd built the home that he and his wife Cora lived in, he knew he could call for an emergency. I was fairly decent at fixing things, and I said I could get it going temporarily until he could get it replaced. I'd called my neighbor Abigail, and she'd come over to the house to sit with Harper until I got back. She and Cora were close friends, so she was happy to help.

But I hadn't expected to see Violet sitting at a table with some dude on a date.

I hadn't expected it to bother me.

It shouldn't matter.

It *didn't* matter.

But for whatever reason, I was agitated now.

I glanced over, and my gaze locked with hers before I quickly looked away and followed Steve into the kitchen.

I spent the next hour working on the commercial refrigerator, and I was fairly certain it was just a wiring issue. I hoped my tweaks had done the trick, because it was up and working now.

"I can't thank you enough, Charlie. Are you sure I can't pay you for your time?" Steve asked.

"Nah. It's not a problem. I'm just going to use your restroom and wash my hands before I take off."

"All right. Well, the kitchen packed up some steaks and side dishes for you and Harper, and we sent one for Abigail as well, so I'll have that bagged up and waiting for you when you come out." He clapped me on the shoulder before I made my way down the hallway to the restroom.

And there she was walking my way. The hallway had very dim lighting, but I could still make out her pretty green gaze as it locked with mine.

"Charles, what brings you here tonight?" she purred.

"Steve was having issues with the refrigerator, so I came down to see if I could help out."

"And did you get it fixed?" she asked. The smell of lavender and vanilla wafted around me, and I cleared my throat to keep from reacting. She was standing too close, and the hallway was narrow.

"I think so." I studied her. She was so goddamned beautiful, it got under my skin. Her blond waves tumbled over her shoulders, and those kissable lips taunted me as she smirked.

I couldn't get that fucking kiss out of my head.

I assumed it hadn't affected her the same way, as she hadn't said anything about it since, and she was here on a date with some rich-looking dude who was probably more her type.

Hell, she despised me most of the time.

Her hand came up and grazed along my cheek, and I startled at her touch. "Is this glitter?"

"Yeah. Harps had a project, and I went to battle with a bottle of glitter, and it sort of exploded all over me."

She smiled, moved closer, and reached up to my hair before running her fingers along the front and chuckling. "You've got a bunch in your hair."

"Sounds about right. I'll jump in the shower when I get home. You better get back to your date. You don't want to keep him waiting." I stepped back, turning my back to her before making my way to the men's bathroom.

"Where's Harper?" she asked, and I got the feeling she didn't want to get back to her date.

"She's at the house with Abigail," I said as I shifted to look at her. "She stopped by the guesthouse earlier to see if you wanted pizza. We had to work on her project, and there wasn't time to cook. So we saved you some in the refrigerator, if you want it later."

Her teeth sank into her bottom lip. "I do love pizza."

I nodded before pushing into the restroom. I needed some distance there. Ever since that kiss, I'd been consumed by thoughts of Violet Beaumont, and that was not a good idea.

Hell, the fact that she was on a date with another dude being the most obvious reason. Not to mention the fact that we couldn't go five minutes without fighting.

I washed my hands and looked in the mirror, laughing as I took in the lingering glitter.

I made my way out of there, thanked Steve for the to-go food, and groaned when I realized Violet and her date were just a few feet ahead of me.

For fuck's sake. I was covered in glitter, I needed to get home to my daughter, and now I had to watch the woman I couldn't stop fantasizing about get escorted out by another man.

The dude was holding the door open for her just as I came up behind them.

Once we were outside, Violet turned around and saw me. "Oh, hey, Charlie. This is Brayden. I was just telling him about you and Harper."

"Nice to meet you, buddy," Brayden said, extending a hand, and I gave him a quick shake.

"Yeah, you too."

"Nice of you to offer Violet a place to stay while you renovate her home. Is that common practice?" He smirked, but I didn't miss the edge in his tone.

"Is what common practice?" My voice came out harsher than I meant it to, but I didn't like the guy. Not because he'd done anything in particular, but because he was on a date with Violet, and it pissed me off. It wasn't rational, but I never claimed to be a rational guy.

"Offering your clients housing while you work on their homes? Or do you save that just for the beautiful women you work for."

Well, now I really don't like the dude, because that was a dick thing to say.

"It's a small-town thing. And Violet is best friends with my buddy's girlfriend, and they asked me for a favor. But I agree, she's a beautiful woman, and you're lucky she agreed to go out with you," I said, surprising myself as the words left my mouth. But if he wanted to be a dick, two could play that game. Violet's gaze locked with mine, and she cleared her throat.

"Okay. I really do need to get going. I've got to call my client back, because you can't leave a bride in crisis. Brayden, thank you for dinner." She extended a hand to him, which he did not look happy about, but he kept it together.

"Yeah, of course. I'll give you a call soon." He went for the hug, and I started walking toward my truck, unable to wipe the smile from my face.

A fucking handshake.

She shut that shit down, and I wasn't going to lie, I was happy about it.

I climbed in my truck, watching in the rearview mirror as he stood outside her car and she slipped inside and waved. I started the engine and drove right behind her to my house.

She pulled in the driveway ahead of me, and I put the truck in park.

We got out at the same time, and she sighed. "Sorry. That was a little awkward."

"For him maybe," I said with a laugh. "The handshake was cold, Firefly."

"We're friends. It wasn't cold. I just wasn't feeling it. He probably wasn't feeling it either."

I moved closer to her. "Oh, he was definitely feeling it."

"How do you know?"

"Because I'm a dude, and we know these things." I shrugged.

"Well, that was a nice touch, you playing the jealous neighbor and acting like he was lucky to be out with me. You must have picked up on the fact that I wanted to make it a quick goodbye," she said, her gaze searching mine.

I glanced over at the house, knowing Harper was most likely waiting up for me to say good night to her. I reached forward and tucked a strand of hair behind Violet's ear, because I just needed to touch her. "I didn't pick up on anything, and I wasn't playing the jealous neighbor. I was just being honest."

And I turned toward my house, then paused at the door to find her staring at me from her door with a big smile on her face. "You're smoother than I would have guessed, Charles."

"Get inside and lock up, Firefly."

She laughed as she stepped inside, and I waited for her to shut the door before I walked into the house. Abigail was sitting on the couch, knitting a sweater for Harper that she'd been working on for weeks.

"Sorry I'm late."

"Oh please, you weren't even gone that long. And Harper is sound asleep. She left you a little card on the counter." My neighbor moved to her feet. The elderly woman was a lifesaver to me. I was lucky to have her right next door. "And you didn't need to rush Violet inside—you could have continued chatting."

I gaped at the woman. "Were you spying on me?"

"Of course I was. I'm old. I don't get a lot of excitement in my life these days, but I saw some sparks out there." She whistled.

"We just happened to get home at the same time. She was actually on a date with someone else."

"Well, from where I was watching, she wished she was on a date with you." She patted me on the cheek before dropping her yarn into her tote bag.

"You're letting your imagination get the best of you," I said before grabbing the bag that Steve had sent for her and handing it to her. I opened the door and left it open as I walked her the short distance to the edge of her backyard, where I could watch her step inside.

"Maybe you should be a little imaginative too, Charlie. You're young. You don't need to be so serious." She chuckled before waving and stepping inside the house.

I wasn't always serious. But yeah, I had a pretty routine lifestyle. I was raising a child all on my own, which required a certain responsibility.

I glanced at the guesthouse, saw that the lights were still on, stepped in my house, and grabbed a beer. I put the to-go food away in the refrigerator and moved down the hall to check on Harper. She was sound asleep, and I kissed her forehead, pulled her comforter up to her chin, and moved back out to the living room. I opened the note from my daughter, where she asked if I could make her pink pancakes sometime and then wrote that she loved me more than all the pink pancakes in the world.

I glanced down at my phone, wanting to text Violet, and I found the perfect excuse.

Me: Hey. Where does one find pink pancakes?
Firefly: Are you talking dirty to me?

I laughed, just as another text came through.

Firefly: You can make pancakes any color you want with food coloring. Does Harper want pink pancakes?
Me: Yes. Is food coloring safe for me to put in her pancakes?

Firefly: Oh Charles, you clueless man . . . there is food coloring in lots of food that we eat.
Me: Shit. I didn't know that. Thanks for educating me. How do I know how much to put in the pancakes?
Firefly: How about I handle it for you. Just let me know when, and I'll make them. Because if you do too much, they will be red. And that's a whole different vibe.
Me: Ah . . . thank you. Did you have fun tonight?

I leaned back on the couch, then took a long pull from my bottle before setting it on the coffee table. I wasn't much of a talker usually, but there was something different about Violet.

I always wanted more.

Even when she was pissed at me, I wanted more of it.

More of her.

Firefly: The food was good. He was fine. I just wasn't feeling it.
Me: He seemed like a good guy. Why do you think you weren't feeling it?

Why the fuck did I just ask that?

Firefly: I don't know. It's all about a connection. Why do you think you weren't feeling it with Julia? I mean, she was willing to look past the limp penis and the doll collection. 😆
Me: She doesn't do it for me. And I think you can vouch for me . . . my dick is anything but limp.

He agreed by springing to life the minute she mentioned him.

Firefly: Ahhhh . . . the kiss that we shall not speak of.
Me: Looks like we're speaking about it now.
Firefly: It was a good kiss, Charles.

Me: It was a fucking amazing kiss.

Firefly: I thought so too. But I feel bad that you didn't get to walk away feeling as good as I did.

Fuck me. Apparently, Abigail was wrong, because my imagination was working just fine at the moment.

Me: Watching you fall apart, riding up against me all hot and needy . . . I couldn't walk away any happier, Firefly.

Firefly: Did you take care of business later?

Me: About a dozen times since it happened.

Firefly: It happened yesterday. That's a lot of relief happening over there.

I finished off my beer and set the bottle on the coffee table. I couldn't believe I was doing this, but I sure as hell didn't want to stop.

Me: I guess you must do it for me then, huh?

Firefly: I thought you couldn't stand me.

Me: It's not like that, Violet.

Firefly: Tell me what it's like.

Me: You challenge me. You're strong and determined, and even if it frustrates me from a working standpoint, it doesn't mean I don't admire that about you. And clearly it doesn't mean that I'm not attracted to you.

Firefly: So you're attracted to me, huh?

Me: Not going to deny that. But it doesn't mean acting on it is a good idea.

Firefly: Well, we finally agree on something.

Me: Good night, Firefly.

CHAPTER ELEVEN

Violet

"Violet makes the best eggs," Harper said as I set down the plate in front of her. It had become our routine the last few weeks. "But now that you got her a new oven, she won't come make me eggs."

"I do know how to make eggs, Harps," Charlie grumped, like I had caused his daughter to turn against him and his cooking.

The new oven had arrived yesterday, and Charlie was going to install it today.

"Hey, don't shoot the messenger. My eggs are clearly better than yours." I smiled, and he rolled his eyes.

Harper was laughing, and what I'd quickly learned is that Harper Huxley was not the norm for a six-year-old. I didn't typically like kids, but this little girl could be my Mini Me. She was the wittiest six-year-old I'd ever met. She gave me all the first-grade classroom gossip at the end of the day, because I cooked dinner over here most evenings. So I was spending a lot of time with these two, and I didn't mind it at all, which was also weird. My biggest issue . . . the fact that I was ridiculously attracted to the world's most aggravating man. We texted all day, mostly about my house renovation, a lot of it unnecessary but a reason to talk, but occasionally it would turn flirty. We hadn't crossed the line again, but that kiss was still haunting me.

"She's six. She's hardly a reliable critic." He stood and reached for our plates.

"Daddy, your eggs aren't bad, they just aren't as good as Vi's. But I still love you. And all your other food is my favorite."

"Well, that's a good thing, seeing as you're kind of stuck with me, baby girl. Now go brush your teeth, and I'll get you to school."

"You know I love you more than all the stars in the sky, Daddy." Harper moved to her feet.

"Yeah, yeah, yeah. Love you more than all the fish in the sea, Harps. Get going," he said.

These two. They were something else.

And seeing Charlie with his daughter did something to me.

Something I couldn't explain.

I glanced over to see his back to me as he rinsed off the dishes. His broad shoulders strained against the black long-sleeve henley he was wearing. My gaze moved down his long, lean legs covered by dark denim, leading to a pair of brown work boots.

Why does he have to be so sexy?

I moved to my feet abruptly. "Okay, I've got to go. I forgot I have a meeting. Tell Harps I'll see her tonight to go over the party plans."

He turned around, grabbing a towel to dry his hands as he studied me. "It's nice of you to do this. It'll make her happy to be included."

I'd basically taken over Harper's birthday party, as she and I had been discussing it for a while now.

"Not a problem. We need to go over the balloon design for the swag anyway." I cleared my throat, as it was getting more difficult to be around this man. "And you have the key to the guesthouse to install the new oven today, right?"

He had a slight smile on his lips, as if he found the question comical. "I do, Firefly. I'll take care of it."

The words rolled off his tongue like butter.

Melted butter.

Melted hot butter.

I'll take care of it.

My God, what was happening to me?

I walked backward and tripped over the leg of the chair before righting myself and rushing out the door.

Air.

I needed air.

I took a few deep breaths once I was outside and decided to walk to work, seeing as the sun was shining and the weather was warming up. I needed to clear my head.

My phone vibrated with a text from Brayden. The man was relentless. It was clear the way the date had ended weeks ago that there weren't any sparks between us, yet he was a persistent guy.

Brayden: I'm leaving town tomorrow and thought I could buy you dinner tonight and maybe enough drinks to convince you to come home with me? 😁

The comment rubbed me wrong, but it wouldn't have mattered if he was a complete gentleman, because my mind was on one man, and one man only.

Getting hung up on Charlie Huxley was not the norm for me. He was admittedly not looking for a relationship, and he aggravated me more often than he didn't—not to mention the fact that I'd have to be around him often due to our mutual friends.

This is why we both knew it was just a bad idea to even go there.

I promised Harper I'd draw the balloon swag design for her and we'd work on the final details for her big day, and I was actually looking forward to it. She had so many ideas, and I wanted to make this seven-year-old's birthday wishes come true.

Me: Sorry I can't make it tonight, but I appreciate the invite. Safe travels home.

I came to a stop when I spotted Clifford Wellhung walking down Main Street. He had his back to me, his unusually large balls dangling between his legs as he swayed from side to side. He stopped in front of the Blushing Bride and stared in the large front window. This was a daily routine for him.

And who was I to rush an alpha moose with big balls?

"Hey, Violet," Brit Hansen said as she walked up to stand beside me. She owned the mobile spray-tan business in town, which was a huge thorn in the side for Montana and me. She'd spray-painted more brides neon orange than she hadn't.

"Hi, Brit, how are you?"

"Good. Just heading to the Brown Bear Diner for some breakfast, but I sure as hell don't want to get in Clifford's way." She chuckled.

We both waited until the giant moose decided to move on.

"Let him get a few feet farther before you start walking," I said.

"You know, I was actually going to call you today. I know you're living out in Charlie Huxley's guesthouse, and I wondered if you had any intel on the man?"

I looked at her. "'Intel'?"

"You know, does he bring women home? I heard from Julia Warren that he liked to play hard to get. And let's just say, I don't mind chasing that man if it means I could catch him." She laughed, and my hands bunched at my sides.

Why does this infuriate me?

Why did I have the sudden urge to scratch her eyes out?

"I don't know, Brit. I'd try treating him with some respect, and not like a piece of meat," I hissed.

"What?" she shrieked. "You can't stand the man. Everyone knows that."

"Correct. He's aggravating as hell, but he's also a really decent man. A good father. A good contractor. A good friend. Maybe if you just try talking to him instead of talking about him, he'll actually engage." I stormed off and reached for the door handle, hearing her mutter apologies behind me, but I just walked inside.

"What is happening here?" Blakely asked as I made my way to the candy jar, took off the lid, and grabbed a handful of Skittles.

"Oh boy. We're diving into the Skittles before eight a.m. That's never a good sign," Montana said, motioning for us to follow her into the staff lounge. It's where we ate lunch. Where we brainstormed on the whiteboard. And where we usually had full-blown therapy sessions.

I dropped to sit in my usual seat at the table. Montana settled beside me, and Blakely was directly across from me.

"What's with the attitude today?" Blakely asked.

"Brit Hansen and Julia Warren are talking about Charlie like he's a piece of meat. It's appalling." I threw my hands in the air. "No. It's disgusting, that's what it is. Absolutely disgusting!"

Montana smirked. "Well, one woman turns people an unnatural mango color for a living, and the other asked Myles if she could test her pink hair color out on Porky."

Now it was Blakely's turn to laugh. "She wants to color your porcupine's hair?"

My bestie and her fiancé had had a full mini house built outside for Porky, the local porcupine who was a bit of a nuisance in their backyard. But that spiky little rodent was living his best life.

"She does. Obviously, we told her that we would never expose our little boy to toxins like that. And he doesn't even have real hair. It's ludicrous," Montana huffed.

"I mean, it's not any more ludicrous than the fact that you just called a porcupine 'our little boy.'"

"Okay, enough about Porky. We can go over his long-term hair goals later." Montana laughed. "Why are you so pissed off about two women you aren't even friends with talking about a man you despise?"

"Because she likes Charlie," Blakely said, looking between us.

"Duh." Montana rolled her eyes. "I'm trying to get her to admit it."

"I do not like Charlie. Not the way you think I do. That's not my thing. But that damn kiss is messing with my head. And I don't want to go out with anyone else because it's like this itch that needs to be scratched," I said, as if I was figuring it out as the words left my mouth.

"Oh, you know what my college roommate called this?" Blakely said, glancing around to make sure no one else could hear her, even though we were the only three people here.

"Sexual frustration?" Montana asked.

"Nope." Blakely leaned forward, like she was about to tell us the most sinister thing she'd ever shared. I leaned in, too, because no one liked sinister news as much as I did. "Banging it out of your system. I think that's what you and Charlie need to do. One time. Get it done, and then move forward. You can go back to being irritated with one another, but the elephant in the room will be gone."

"Is the elephant in the room Charlie's giant schlong?" I asked.

"Didn't you just get offended by Julia and Brit treating Charlie like a piece of meat?" Montana smirked.

"Correct. But I just admitted that Charles is a good man. It's not offensive to assume the man has a giant penis. I've dry humped him, for God's sake. I know it's there. I'm just sharing the facts. It's just science at this point. I mean, just look at the man's hands and feet," I said over my laughter.

"I don't pay much attention to the size of Charlie's hands and feet." Montana leaned back in her chair and studied me. "But I don't think this is a bad idea. Neither of you is looking for anything serious, but you're both clearly attracted to one another."

"So they can just bang it out," Blakely said, her cheeks turning bright pink as she continued. "Hashtag 'bang it out with big boy Huxley.'"

"You don't think this is a bad idea?" I asked Montana, surprised that she was on board with it.

"I actually think it's a great idea. For both of you. And you're moving out soon and back into your house, so things will go back to normal. And who knows, you might hate it."

I thought it over. "You're right. And for all I know, Charles could be a big dud in the sack."

"Well, he wasn't a dud when you humped him like a dog in heat a few weeks ago." Blakely reached for her coffee, and I chuckled.

"Correct. But in truth, he was just sort of standing there like a tree. I did all the humping." I shrugged.

"You said he was an amazing kisser," Montana reminded me.

"That's true, but you can be a fabulous kisser and a lazy lover. And how the hell am I going to get him on board? He thinks us taking this any further is a terrible idea."

"What if you approach it like a business deal," Blakely said. "You know, you just lay out the facts. Remind him that you're both attracted to one another. You're both a little, er, frustrated. And you could have a 'bang it out' moment and call it done. Never speak of it again."

"Hmm . . ." I tapped my finger against my lips. "It would have to be during the day, when Harper is at school. I mean, we can't be acting like feral animals with her in the house."

"No way. I wouldn't even expose Porky to that kind of passion," Montana said with a laugh.

"The last thing I want is to jump Charlie's bones with your freaky rodent watching. But I need a plan if I want this to happen. I'll have to tease him a little and feel him out before I just ask if he's game. Making him jealous would probably do the trick, because he looked wounded that night he saw me out with Brayden. So if he got jealous, it might cause him to be the one to suggest the 'bang it out' idea." I pulled out my phone as my fingers hovered over the keyboard.

> Me: Let Harper know I will be over tonight to go over the party details.
> Charles: Yes. We already discussed this.

The girls hovered over my shoulder, reading the texts along with me.

Me: Well, you're a little older than me, so I wasn't sure if you remembered. I've got a busy night.
Charles: We're available. Come over anytime.

"Damn this man. He didn't take the bait," I grumped.

"Well, it wasn't super clear," Blakely said just as the phone vibrated again, and we all turned our attention back to my phone screen.

Charles: You got a hot date tonight?

I rubbed my hands together mischievously before typing my response.

Me: Would it bother you if I did?
Charles: Nope. And your oven is fixed if you want to have someone over for dinner.
Me: Great. I'll have to invite him over to the house then seeing as it doesn't bother you at all.
Charles: I don't have a problem, but it seems like you do. I think you're having a hard time shaking that kiss.
Me: Don't flatter yourself. You're the one who can't stop taking cold showers.
Charles: I'm fine. But if you're struggling, I'd be happy to help.
Me: Hardly. I'm the one who has a date.

"Damn you, Charles. You're not going to make this easy on me," I hissed.

"Who are you going to invite to the house?" Blakely gaped at me.

"No one. It's all part of the plan. Make him jealous. Get him to come up with the idea about Operation Bang It Out," I said.

"I'm so here for this, but I don't think this is the way to go about it." Montana shrugged. "I think you could just suggest it. Pretending you have a date seems like a bad idea."

"Just trust me. Charles is a complicated man. I need to make him jealous and then let him come up with the idea to seduce me." I kicked my feet up on the table, crossing my stilettos at the ankles as I popped a few Skittles in my mouth.

It's game time.

CHAPTER TWELVE

Charlie

I pulled the cornbread from the oven and set it on the stovetop just as my daughter squealed thirty decibels louder than any human should be able to.

"Vi's here!"

I stirred the tortilla soup and turned around as the little hellion came through the back door. My eyes bulged out of my head as I took her in, and I did what I could to act unbothered.

She was wearing a pair of fitted jeans and a red fitted shirt that slid off one of her shoulders. She wore sky-high black boots, and her hair was pulled back in a ponytail at the nape of her neck.

My mouth watered at the sight of her exposed golden skin.

"Hey, Harps," Violet said, her green gaze moving to mine, and I swear I stopped breathing for a minute.

She was too damn beautiful for her own good.

"You look so pretty. Are you ready to draw the balloons and eat some tortilla soup?" Harper asked as she jumped up and down.

"I think Violet has a date, so she's not eating with us," I said. I thought she'd been bullshitting me about the date when she texted earlier. She liked getting under my skin, or at least that's what I'd assumed was happening at the time.

But now I was second-guessing myself.

Would she dress up and pretend to be going on a date, just to irritate me?

Either way, it was working.

"Well, I could eat a little bowl of soup while we sketch out the design." Violet smirked before taking the seat at the table that had somehow become hers over the last few weeks.

"Aren't you cooking for . . ." I said, waiting for her to fill in the last part of the sentence.

"Of course. I'm cooking for my date," she said, eyes locking with mine.

"Who is it?" I pressed, and she held my gaze.

"His name is . . . Dav-eed. Daveed." She dragged out the last syllable unusually long.

"Daveeeeed?" Harper mimicked her, and it took everything in me not to call bullshit and laugh.

"Yes." Violet cleared her throat. "Daveed Beck . . . art. Daveed Beckart. That's his name."

I set a bowl of soup down in front of each of them; the tortilla chips and shredded cheese were already on the table. I crossed my arms over my chest. "His name is Daveed Beckart? That's quite a name."

This was a stretch even for her.

"Yes. He's here on a visa. He's an international supermodel and a professional athlete." She had a ridiculous smile on her face.

"What sport does he play?" Harper asked as I grabbed my bowl of soup and sat down.

"He plays several. Professionally, of course." She shrugged before crunching a bunch of tortilla chips into her soup.

"Wow. A supermodel and a professional athlete of multiple sports. I guess that explains why you're so dressed up," I said, trying to keep my voice steady because it was hard not to laugh. "This is a pretty big date."

"Yep. He'll be over later, so I just stopped by to go over this design with you, Harps. Then I'll go make a romantic dinner for my Canadian soccer/basketball player."

"He plays professional soccer *and* professional basketball. That's quite a catch. And he's here in Blushing, Alaska, huh?" I asked, using my napkin to cover my mouth and hide my smile.

"Yep. Just here on some fancy athlete modeling trip." She took a bite of her cornbread and smiled.

She moved her attention to my daughter and flipped open her notebook.

"I love it. Look at all the balloons!" Harper squealed over a mouthful of soup.

"Harps, manners," I said.

"Daddy, pink balloons."

I had to laugh, because my little girl owned me, and she knew it.

"So, I thought we could go with three shades of pink and then some pops of gold." Violet sketched out some sort of crown as Harper watched intently. "I ordered a few large gold crowns that she wears in *Pinkalicious*. And then we can do the number seven as well and just have a massive balloon arch to take photos in front of."

"This is going to be the best party ever. I don't know if Caroline should come because there will be lots of kids here and the big balloon swaggy. Do you think she's going to come, Daddy?"

My shoulders tensed. I hadn't heard jack shit from Caroline, but she usually just showed up around Harper's birthday. She used to check in every couple of months, but that hadn't happened in the last few years.

I scratched the back of my neck. "I haven't spoken to her, Harps."

Violet's eyes bounced between us as if she was trying to figure out why I wasn't saying more. "Well, she'd be a real fool to miss this party because I happen to have a warehouse full of pink goodness, and I'm pulling out all the stops for you, Harps."

"You're pulling out all the spots!"

"'Stops,'" Violet said, giggling. "Meaning every kid in Blushing is going to want to have a party just like Harper Huxley."

Harper fist-pumped the sky. "Even Denise Quigley is going to wish for a party like my Pinkalicious party."

"Yes, ma'am," Violet said, leaning back in her chair and smiling.

"I think the balloon swag and the food and cake are plenty. You don't need to go overboard," I said, reaching for my beer and taking a pull.

"I'm a wedding planner, Charles. I always go overboard. And we've upgraded the balloon swag to an arch. Swags are lame. This is the big leagues." She leaned forward, resting her elbows on the table as her gaze locked with mine. "I like to go all the way."

Fuck me.

I was a horny bastard, and she knew what she was doing to me.

"Do you mean you like to go all out?" I corrected her, and she had a wicked grin on her face but she didn't respond.

"I'm so excited. And you're going to stay the whole time at the party, right, Vi?"

"I wouldn't miss it for the world," Violet said. "I just need to know if you want me to add any unicorns or glitter to the theme, because you mentioned those last week."

"Anything pink and sparkly, right, Daddy?" My little girl smiled up at me, and it took my fucking breath away.

"Anything pink and sparkly, baby girl." I pushed to my feet just as Violet stood and started clearing the dishes.

"Thank you, Vi. I can't wait for everyone at school to see the Pinkalicious goodness! Are you going to bring your special friend Daveed with you to my party?"

I chuckled as I stood at the sink before glancing over my shoulder at Violet. "Yeah, maybe he can sign soccer balls and basketballs during the party?"

"Unfortunately, Daveed Beckart has to get back for some big games over the weekend. He's leaving right after our date." She wiped down the table, and it took me a minute to realize how comfortable the three of us had gotten with our routine.

"Well, that timing worked out nicely," I said.

"It sure did. I better get going. He'll be here anytime now." Violet leaned down and hugged Harper as I dried my hands with the dish towel.

"Good night, Vi. I'll see you tomorrow morning. I'm going to go look at my Pinkalicious books and see what else we can do." Harper ran down the hall.

"Thanks for doing this for her party." I held her gaze, because it meant a lot that she was stepping up for Harper.

"Of course. Harper's my favorite. We're going to knock it out of the park with the decor." She walked backward toward the door.

"So, you're going to go meet Daveed, huh?" I chuckled.

"Yep. Unless you don't want me to go for some reason? Last chance to tell me if it bothers you."

"Not going to happen, Firefly. I have far more restraint than you think I do." I moved closer to her. "But you could just tell me you want to stay."

"Please. I'm not even tempted." She swiped her tongue along her bottom lip slowly. "Just concede. You know you want to."

"Shit. I must have spilled some soup on my shirt," I said, the lie slipping so easily from my lips. I reached over my head and tugged my hoodie off. My jeans were hanging low on my hips, and I tossed the sweatshirt on the table. "I'll have to get some stain remover on that as soon as you leave."

Her eyes widened as she took in my chest and my abdomen, raking me over like it was her day job. I didn't miss the way her gaze scanned the tattoo across my chest.

Harper.

My little girl was my heart, my soul, and my reason.

This was my reminder.

"You play dirty, Charlie Huxley." Violet's voice was gruff.

"Maybe I like it dirty," I said, leaning down and grazing my lips against the lobe of her ear. "Tell me you want me."

"You say it first," she whispered.

"Not going to happen." I smirked. This game we were playing wasn't smart. We both knew this couldn't go anywhere. But that didn't seem to stop either of us from having fun.

"Then I guess you and your blue balls can enjoy a cold shower, while I go enjoy some big balls on my hot soccer/basketball star." She pulled back, a wicked grin on her face.

Loud laughter rumbled from deep in my chest. I couldn't deny that I was laughing more since Violet moved into my guesthouse than I had in years. "You sure about that?"

"I'm sure, Charles," she purred before stepping back. "Daveed is probably waiting for me now."

"Have a good night, Firefly."

She turned and walked toward the door before pausing and glancing over at me. "Do you think Harper's mom is going to show up to her party?" she whispered, and the question caught me off guard because it was laced with concern.

I shrugged. "Not sure. We haven't spoken. She usually just shows up on her birthday."

Violet's gaze narrowed as her hands landed on her hips. "She gets to just show up for a party and that's it?"

"It's complicated." I cleared my throat, the topic making me uncomfortable.

"It's selfish." She shook her head. "She deserves better. Hell, you deserve better."

And then she turned and walked out the door.

"Time for my bath." Harper came around the corner, and she gaped at me. "Daddy, why are you naked on the top? Where's your shirt?"

I chuckled. "I spilled some soup on my sweatshirt. I'm going to throw it in the wash."

She followed me to the laundry room, and I tossed it in the washer, even though there was no stain on it.

"And I'm not naked, baby girl. I've got my pants on." I reached for her hand and led her down the hallway before stopping in her bathroom and turning the water on in the tub.

Once the water was deep enough, I turned off the faucet, and she stepped into the bathtub. I dropped to sit on the toilet as she told me all about her day. But I couldn't get Violet's question about Caroline out of my head, even though I tried to shake it off.

"I can't believe Violet's going to make me the prettiest party I ever had." She chuckled. Her cheeks were pink, and she had some bubbles on the tip of her nose.

"That's nice of her, huh?" I pushed to move closer to the tub before tipping her head back and using the spray hose to wash her hair. We had our routine, and she didn't fight me on it. I handed her a washcloth to hold over her face to keep the suds away.

"Yes. I wish she didn't have to move back to her house," Harper said. "I like having her here."

"We do just fine on our own, Harps." I leaned forward, my elbows resting on my knees. I hated the thought that I was failing her in some way. She only had me. A grumpy asshole who didn't have a clue what he was doing half the time. "And you'll still see her. She only lives a few blocks away."

"But she won't come make eggs in the morning. And she won't come over for dinner." She frowned.

"Maybe we can invite her over sometime," I groaned. "Now let's talk about your party. Are you excited?"

"I'm so excited. I can't wait to put on my new pink dress you got me. Do you think you can paint my nails before the party?"

"I'm sure I can figure it out," I said, pushing to my feet and grabbing a towel for her, because she was ready to get out. I didn't have a fucking clue how to paint tiny fingernails.

Harper stepped out of the tub, and I wrapped her up in the towel before lifting her and setting her to sit on the sink and drying her long hair with another towel. I brushed through the tangles in her hair until it was all free of any knots.

"Do you think Caroline will come to my party this year?" she asked, meeting my gaze in the mirror.

"Do you want Caroline to come to your party?"

"I'd like everyone to come to my party. But I don't really remember Caroline anymore. But I do remember she had pretty fingernails."

My ex was always pampering herself. We had nothing in common, even back before Harper came into the world. She was rich and spoiled and selfish.

But she was also the mother of my baby girl, and because of that, she'd always get a pass.

Even if this arrangement of ours wasn't making a whole lot of sense anymore.

I'd do whatever I could to keep the peace.

As long as I had Harper, nothing else really mattered.

CHAPTER THIRTEEN

Violet

I'd just said goodbye to Montana and made sure she hurried down the driveway keeping her hoodie over her head, just in case Charlie was watching.

My best friend had made fun of me for sneaking her into my place to make it look like I had a man over.

I knew he was onto me, but I wasn't going to give it up just yet.

I poured myself a glass of wine and slipped into the bathtub. The hot water was heavenly, and I reached for my phone when it vibrated.

Charles: I see your lover just left.

Me: Stalker.

Charles: Hey, you had me at two-time professional athlete and supermodel. I thought I might be able to get his autograph. Maybe even a selfie.

My head tipped back in laughter. Charlie would never in a million years take a selfie, nor did he strike me as someone who would fanboy over a professional athlete.

Especially one we both knew didn't exist.

I reached for my wineglass and took a sip before setting it back on the ledge.

Me: He's a pretty private guy. He was in a hurry to get out of here without getting harassed by nosy neighbors.
Charles: Really? He didn't seem that worried about it when I pulled his hood off. Montana screamed so loud I'm surprised you didn't hear her.

Note to self: My best friend was not invited to any future undercover operations.

Me: I didn't hear anything.
Charles: That's all you have to say about it, huh?
Me: What would you like me to say, Charles? I was trying to get you to concede.
Charles: Because you want me?
Me: Because you're an arrogant jackass, and I'd like you to say you want me first.
Charles: I think we both know we're playing with fire. We already irritate the hell out of one another, and we haven't crossed any lines other than you climbing me like a tree a few weeks back.
Me: You love to point that out. You're the one who had to take multiple cold showers just to get the thought out of your head.
Charles: Not denying it, Firefly. But doing it again would be a bad idea.

I chewed on my thumbnail. I was the one who thought it was a bad idea, but I was offended that he thought it was a bad idea.

Me: Hey. You should be so lucky to spend a night with me.
Charles:
Me:

We hadn't even done the deed, and we were already fighting by way of emoji.

Charles: You are the one who said it was a bad idea in the first place.
Me: So you're throwing my words in my face?
Charles: Violet.
Me: Charles.
Charles: We fight more than we don't. Neither of us are looking for anything. Acting on an attraction is a bad idea.
Me: Have you not heard of the Bang It Out theory?
Charles: Is this something one learns in school, Firefly?
Me: It's something one learns from street smarts, Charles. Keep up, buddy, and you might get lucky.
Charles: I'm on the edge of my seat.
Me: Smartass.
Charles: Explain.
Me: We have one designated night to get the sexual tension out of our system. That kiss really got in my head, and I need to move forward, but I'm stuck.
Charles: Because you're obsessed with my dick?
Me: 🖕
Charles: So we have sex, and it's a one and done?
Me: I'm certain you've done that before.
Charles: You'd be correct. It's the only way I've done it over the last few years. But it's never been with someone living in my backyard.
Me: Lucky for you, I'm moving out in a few weeks.
Charles: You think it's that simple?
Me: Oh, Charles. Life can be as simple as you make it. I don't like you. That's simple.
Charles: You sure about that? You did get all dressed up and pretend to have a date, because you wanted me to get jealous.

Me: Because I wanted you to admit that you want me.

Charles: I want you. That's the easy part.

Me: What's the hard part.

Me: Oops. Pun intended.

Charles: It can't be weird after. Harper likes you. We have mutual friends.

Me: I like Harper. I like our friends. You're the one I have a problem with most of the time. So that won't change. But we'll be riding the high of the Bang It Out theory and we'll be done. For the record, I don't get attached.

Charles: You've never been with me, so you don't know for certain that it will be that easy to walk away.

Me: Please. I have years of daddy issues I'm overcoming. One grumpy contractor with a nice body is not going to undo years of damage.

Charles: You're fucking funny, Firefly.

Me: Remember that when you're falling in love with me. I'm not looking for a boyfriend.

Charles: What are you looking for?

Me: A good time, Charles. A one and done. We bang it out and we walk away. Capisce?

Charles: Capisce? Am I now to believe you're an Italian mobster?

Me: Believe what you want. I've got this figured out. What do you say?

Charles: Fine. I'm in.

Me: Very romantic.

Charles: I don't do romance, Firefly.

Me: Neither do I. We're on the same page.

Charles: So we're doing this?

Me: Yes. Tomorrow when Harper is at school. We'll meet at your place on my lunch break, and we'll do the deed.

Charles: I've never made an appointment for sex.

Me: I'm a wedding planner. We love appointments. Bring your A-game, Charles.
Charles: I always bring my A-game. I'll be there.
Me: Prepare to be blown away.
Charles: Your foreplay game is weak sauce.
Me: Bite me, Charles.
Charles: Count on it.

"This is crazy, even for you," Montana said as I packed up my briefcase and grabbed the smoothie Blakely had brought me for lunch.

I'd be skipping our normally scheduled lunch break for a little afternoon delight with Charles.

"Why? We're on the same page. There's no confusion. We meet. We do the deed. Hopefully we both enjoy it. And then I never have to fantasize about the man again, because he'll be out of my system."

"She makes a good argument," Blakely said, taking a bite of her sandwich. "Plus, it's very modern-day 'I am woman, hear me roar.' It's about not being afraid to just ask for what you want and then be done with it."

"Exactly," I said, nodding my head, grateful that at least one of them was on board with the plan. I pumped my fist. "Tonight we ride, my friends."

"Well, it's lunchtime, so that doesn't really work," Montana said with a laugh.

"I've got to go. I need to beat him to the house so I'll have the upper hand," I said, pulling my purse over my shoulder.

"What are you going to do? Put on some lingerie and lie in his bed?" Montana asked.

I shrugged. "It's a game-day decision. I need to go scope out the area. I've never been in his room. For all I know, his decor could freak me out. You know I scare easy. What if he has photos of himself blown up and hanging on the walls?"

"She's got a gift for expecting to be let down." Blakely narrowed her gaze at me before looking at my best friend.

"It's called self-sabotaging. She's one of the best I've ever seen," Montana said as she winked at me.

I rolled my eyes before taking a sip of my smoothie. "I'll keep you posted. Hopefully I'm back in a few hours, and I've banged Charles Huxley out of my system. No looking back."

They were both laughing as I strolled out of the office. Clifford Wellhung was lying across the street at the park, and I saluted him.

I felt like I was ready to take on the world.

It had been a while since I'd had sex. I'd been in a rut. A self-inflicted dry spell, so to speak, and today I was going to let Charlie Huxley blow my mind for one day, and then I'd be back in the game.

My phone vibrated when I pulled in the driveway at his home.

Charles: Are we still doing this? I'm finishing up at the hotel in ten minutes.

Me: I'll be waiting.

I chuckled as I walked into his home and dropped my purse on the counter. I needed to set the mood. I found the lighter in his kitchen drawer and lit a candle on the counter, then brought one to his bedroom and lit it there as well.

He had an Alexa, which made playing music very easy.

I chose a very romantic station on XM radio and then second-guessed myself, because this wasn't supposed to be romantic.

This was a one and done, not a date.

Shit.

I found a channel that definitely wasn't romantic but was still going to get us in the mood.

A little raunchy R&B for the win.

I moved to his closet and pulled out a white button-up. I slipped my dress and heels off and pulled the oversize shirt over my head. I left several buttons open, exposing the red lace of my bra, and climbed onto his bed, positioning myself in the center.

One leg bent.

I propped myself up on my elbow.

I tugged my hair over one shoulder.

Okay, this would work. But first I needed to pee. I ran to the bathroom, snooped around, and couldn't find any condoms.

My God. What if Charles didn't keep condoms at the house?

I didn't carry them.

I dug through his bathroom drawers and came up empty.

Was I sweating now?

I texted the girls in a panic.

Me: He's not here yet, but I can't find condoms.

Montana: Where did you look?

Me: Bathroom.

Blakely: Should you check the garage?

Montana: She needs condoms not a snow shovel.

Me: Focus. I can't Bang It Out with a man I despise and not have a condom. The jig is up. This isn't going to happen. What was I thinking?

Blakely: Ahhh . . . is this an example of the self-sabotaging?

Montana: Yes, ma'am.

Montana: Try the nightstand.

Me: Oh. Why didn't I think of that?

Me: Charlie's room is very tidy. He's ridiculously clean.

Blakely: And that's a bad thing?

Me: I'm just saying. The man is uptight. Checking the drawers now.

I set my phone down and pulled open the top drawer.

There was a pair of nail clippers.

ChapStick.

Vaseline.

Hmm . . . what have you been up to, Charlie Huxley?

There were a few books about construction and architecture, and I fumbled around beneath the books and gaped at what my hand found.

I dropped to sit on the bed, holding the freaky contraption in my hand.

What the actual hell was this?

It was some sort of scary-looking baby doll shoved inside a condom.

I picked up my phone and typed as quickly as my fingers would allow.

Me: This is bad.

Montana: Are the condoms a size mini?

Me: Focus, Monny. Charles has a doll shoved inside a condom in his nightstand drawer. Operation Bang It Out is DONEZO. He's a serial killer.

Blakely: Screenshot please.

I took a fast picture, dropped the weird doll back in the drawer, and quickly got dressed, leaving his dress shirt on the bed. I needed to get out of here, pronto.

Montana: This is alarming.

Blakely: Maybe he was wrapping her in a cocoon like a butterfly?

I did not have time to respond. I sprinted through the house, blew out the candles, told Alexa to zip it, and ran toward the back door.

"You're leaving?" Charlie's voice called out just as he entered through the front door.

"Sorry!" I shouted. "Wedding emergency. I'll have to take a rain check."

I raced toward my car, then zipped down the driveway like I was running from the law.

Because there would be no rain check.

Call it self-sabotage.

Call it whatever you want.

But that condom doll had me running for the hills.

CHAPTER FOURTEEN

Charlie

I should have known this woman was up to something. It was always some sort of game with her. She'd been the one to push for this, and then she'd fled without even giving me a second glance.

This was why I didn't mess around with women I knew.

Violet was anything but simple.

Yes, I was attracted to her.

But the woman was giving me whiplash.

One minute she's trying to seduce me, and the next she can't stand the sight of me.

I walked down the hall to my bedroom, where I found my dress shirt lying on the edge of the bed.

Had she changed her clothes?

My bedroom smelled like pine, and I glanced at the candle sitting on the dresser, noting the wax was still melted.

She'd come to my house, worn my clothing, lit candles, and what?

Rolled around in my bed?

This was some weird shit, even for Violet.

I sighed. I'd expected her to cancel this morning. Hell, even up until about an hour ago, I'd assumed she was fucking with me.

But then when she'd texted that she'd meet me here, I guess I got on board with the plan.

It was a disaster in the making, and we both knew it.

This was for the best.

My phone buzzed, and I saw an incoming call from Caroline.

I was already irritated, and I couldn't think of anyone I'd rather not talk to at the moment.

"Hey," I hissed.

"I haven't talked to you in a year, and that's how you greet me?" she asked, her voice sugary sweet.

This woman could put on a show with the best of them.

"What's up, Caroline?" I ran a hand down the back of my neck as I dropped to sit on the edge of my bed.

"Well, I just got back from the South of France. Wyatt proposed while we were there," she said.

Wyatt was her longtime boyfriend, and I was actually shocked they hadn't tied the knot yet. She claimed he knew about Harper, but he just didn't want anything to do with her.

So, as far as I was concerned, Wyatt could go fuck himself.

We didn't want anything to do with him either.

"Good for you."

"We were gone for a couple weeks, and I think we can both use some space." She chuckled, like we were fucking girlfriends discussing the things that irritated us about our boyfriends. She'd called the wrong dude if this was why she was reaching out.

I glanced at the nightstand, noting the top drawer wasn't closed all the way. I pulled it open and knew immediately that the little deviant woman who'd been taunting me with her hot little body had been up to something. It looked like she'd rifled through my drawer looking for something.

My God, had she attempted to rob me?

And that's when my eye caught on the red cap.

Clementine Claus Huxley.

The motherfucking Elf on a Shelf from hell.

I'd survived another Christmas of make-believe and magic for my little girl, even if it had nearly been the death of me.

This motherfucker had hung from our ceiling fans, set up camp on the toilet seat, even skied down a long piece of toilet paper that I'd attached to the ceiling. Hell, I'd done home renovations that were less complicated than deciding where this elf would be stationed when Harper woke up every morning. I'd been on websites that some of the moms from school had recommended to me, because Harper loved to find Clementine the minute she woke up, from the first day of December until the last.

So maybe I had a backup Elf on a Shelf, because I'd gotten her stuck in a goddamn balloon on Christmas Eve. She was supposed to look like she was in some sort of snow globe, but it looked more like a newborn alien resurrection.

So I'd used my backup elf and shoved this failed attempt in my nightstand.

Because my daughter wasn't a snoop, unlike Violet Beaumont.

"Hello? Earth to Charlie."

"Yeah, I'm here." I tucked Clementine in my coat pocket and walked back to the kitchen. "What do you need, Caroline?"

"So, is there a birthday party this year?" she asked.

"She's a kid. There's a birthday party every year," I said dryly.

"I'm going to fly into Blushing for a few hours, but I don't want to spend it with a bunch of loud kids, you know? I'd rather just hang out with you and Harper."

She said it like we should be so thankful to have her grace us with her presence.

I wasn't thankful in the slightest.

I tolerated her because she was Harper's mother.

I was annoyed that the woman who'd given birth to my daughter thought it was fine to fly into town for a few hours one day a year, and she thought Harper owed this day to her.

I was annoyed that the woman living in my backyard, haunting every filthy fantasy I'd had for weeks, had asked to spend a few hours with me, and then she'd been run off by Clementine the fucking elf.

I pinched the bridge of my nose. "The party is tomorrow afternoon, here at the house. If you're coming Saturday, that's what we're doing."

"You can't move it to Sunday?" she whined.

The fucking nerve of this woman.

"No, Caroline. It's a party that's been planned for weeks. It's Harper's day. Come or don't come, but don't fucking ask a six-year-old to move her party to accommodate you."

"What is with this attitude, Charlie?" she snipped. "I thought we agreed I could come once a year."

"Yeah. You just sort of said that's what you were doing. But Harper is getting older, and things are changing. She doesn't know you. And her birthday should not be about wondering if you're coming or not."

"Well, I'm coming."

"Fine. Party's at noon. I've got to go," I said, grabbing my keys and ending the call.

I drove the short distance to the Blushing Bride and put my truck in park before jogging inside. Blakely was sitting at the front desk, and her eyes widened when I walked in.

"Hey, Charlie. Nice to see you," she said.

"Yeah. You too. I just need a quick minute with Violet." I moved toward her office, because I wasn't waiting one more minute to call her out.

"She, um . . ." I heard Blakely fumble over her words, but I ignored her and kept walking.

I rounded the corner, finding the door to Violet's office open. She was staring at her monitor as she reached for a handful of Skittles. Her head snapped up when I moved toward her desk, and before she could speak, I tossed the damn elf on her desk. "Do you normally snoop in people's nightstand drawers before you . . . what did you call it . . . 'bang it out'?"

"Charles," she said before her eyes moved to the monstrosity that had just landed on her desk.

I crossed my arms over my chest and waited.

"I mean, I find it interesting that you're more disturbed by the idea of me looking in your nightstand drawer than the fact that you shoved a doll into a condom, and you keep it beside your bed."

"What are you talking about?"

"The doll. The condom. You don't find it alarming?" she snipped.

I ran a hand down my face. An hour ago, we were planning to have sex, but instead I was dealing with this complete insanity. "I don't know what kind of condom you think that is, but it's actually a balloon. And that's not a doll, that's Clementine."

"This is supposed to make me feel better?" She rolled her eyes.

"If you hadn't snooped in the first place, this wouldn't be an issue."

"Don't turn this on me. I was looking for a condom, and I stumbled upon this *Silence of the Lambs* type of serial killer stuff."

"You know, Violet, if you'd just picked up the damn phone and asked where the condoms were, I would have been happy to tell you that I didn't have any at the house. I don't bring women to my home. This was going to be a first. That's why I was late, because I stopped by the drugstore to grab a box on my way home, while you were ransacking my house like you work for the goddamn CIA."

She stood up, grabbed the elf shoved in the latex, and shook it in front of my face. "It still wouldn't have explained this!"

I stood, leaning over the desk as I yanked it from her hand. "Don't shake Clementine like that. Harper's attached."

"I'm sure Harper doesn't know you shove her dolls in balloons, nor do I think she'd be happy about it."

"For fuck's sake. It's an Elf on a Shelf. I tried to make a snow globe out of a balloon on Christmas Eve. A mom in her class told me I could shove it in the balloon and then blow it up and I could put snow in there, and some other fancy shit. But I got the damn thing stuck in the balloon and couldn't get it out. So I hid it in my nightstand, and I had to have Will run to town and get me another elf to use on Christmas morning. I just forgot I shoved it in my drawer. Why the fuck did you think I'd stuck it in a condom?"

She sat back down in her chair as she processed my words, and I reached for the scissors on her desk and cut the end of the balloon, freeing Clementine from the latex. I held it in front of her. "This is our Elf on a Shelf. Her name is Clementine Claus Huxley. Harper has had her since she was three years old, and she's obsessed with her. This thing has caused me more stress than the Wilsons' nightmare renovation last year. I've sewed clothing for her, I've built props that could rival a Hollywood movie set, and apparently now she's the reason I'm currently standing here instead of having sex with you."

"Oh," she whispered. "She's cute."

"'She's cute'? Are you fucking kidding me?"

"I mean, you have to understand why I would be concerned?" She threw her hands in the air.

"And this is why this is not a good idea. Look how quickly you jumped to the wrong conclusion. You didn't even give me a chance to explain, you just decided I was, what—a doll serial killer?"

"Well, it sounds crazy when you say it like that." She sighed. "I should have asked you, but I guess I freaked out."

My phone vibrated, and I glanced down to see a text from Will that there was an issue at the hotel. "That's an understatement. I've got to get back to work."

"Wait. We've still got time." She moved to her feet just as I stood.

"Listen. I'm calling this done. Five minutes ago, you thought I was a serial killer, and this has disaster written all over it." I moved toward the door after shoving Clementine in my back pocket.

"Charlie," she said, and I paused in the doorway and turned around. She just stared at me, her gaze searching mine. "I'm sorry for snooping."

"Don't beat yourself up, Firefly. Everything happens for a reason."

"I've always hated that saying. I mean, it's not true at all. Fires and natural disasters and murders, none of those happen for a reason. But maybe I wanted to find a reason to run out of there—I do have a habit of doing that. I tend to self-sabotage."

It was the first time I'd ever seen a vulnerable side of Violet Beaumont, and it caught me off guard. "Hey, nothing wrong with self-preservation. I'll see you later."

But I wouldn't see her tonight. She had a working oven. She wouldn't need to come by the house to prepare her meals anymore.

"I, um, I wanted to run something by you." She hurried to her feet and held up her phone. "I know I'm setting up the party in the morning, but I saw this cute idea on Pinterest to do the morning of a kid's birthday, and I wanted to see if I could come by early and do it for Harper?"

The photo was of a bedroom covered in balloons with a note taped to the door with birthday wishes from the birthday fairy.

I wanted to tell her I had it covered. But I didn't do this kind of shit. I'd been pretty decent with Clementine the elf, but that was as far as my creativity went.

"You don't need to do that. But I'm not going to tell you that you can't. She'd fucking love it." I shrugged.

"That's all I needed to hear," she said. "I'll be over tomorrow morning before the sun comes up. She needs to be asleep, and I'll just come in the back door and work my magic, and slip right out."

"Really? You don't plan on bringing a forensics expert to swab our DNA?" I smirked.

"You aren't going to let me live this one down, are you?"

"I don't plan on it." I knocked on the doorframe and walked out.

Me and my large set of blue balls had to get back to work.

CHAPTER FIFTEEN

Violet

I'd totally messed things up with Charlie. I'd wanted to have a one-night stand with the man, and instead I'd managed to accuse him of heinous doll crimes and offend him so badly that he had no desire to sleep with me anymore. And now, of course, it was all I could think about.

But today wasn't about me or my horny lady parts.

I'd gotten up early and blown up more pink and white balloons than I could count. The good news was that I'd be able to reuse these balloons in my balloon arch later at the party.

I wanted today to be magical for Harper.

Maybe in a way I was reliving my own failed birthday parties through her.

My father had never shown up to celebrate my birthday.

Not once.

My mother spent most of my childhood bitter and angry that her husband had left us.

So, I usually got a cupcake, and we'd go to the diner and have dinner after school.

There were no Pinkalicious balloon arches or birthday fairies.

I sent a quick text to Charlie.

Me: Just wanted to remind you that I'm coming through the back door with the balloons, so don't attack me for trespassing please.
Charlie: I always get up early on Harper's birthday. Plus, I want to make sure you don't set me up for a crime I didn't commit.
Me: I see we're over the drama from yesterday. 🙄

I grabbed the three large garbage bags full of balloons and was dragging them across the yard when I heard his deep chuckle from the doorway.

"Are you going to stand there laughing or help me with these bags?" I grumped.

"I was worried you'd think I was going to murder you, seeing as less than twenty-four hours ago, you thought I was a serial killer." He moved toward me and tugged two of the bags from my hands, leaving me with just the one.

"You're hilarious."

"They say most serial killers are."

"Shh . . . we don't want to wake her up," I hissed once we stepped inside.

"She's a deep sleeper. Tell me what we need to do," he whispered.

I glanced around, and the way he'd decorated the kitchen took my breath away. A garland of colorful flags hanging above the kitchen island read Happy 7th Birthday, Harps. Several doughnuts were stacked on a cake plate, and a pile of presents on the island had been wrapped in pink gift wrap with white ribbons.

Charlie Huxley is a rock star dad.

Sure, I'd briefly thought he was murdering dolls in his free time, but I never doubted that he was a good dad.

But damn, this was next level.

I pushed away the lump in my throat and looked up at him. "This looks nice."

"Thank you."

"Okay, we just need to quietly place these all over the floor in her room, and we'll put a few on the foot of her bed. So when she wakes up, she'll know the birthday fairy was here," I said, keeping my voice low.

"She's been talking endlessly about this birthday fairy. I take it that came from you?"

I nodded. "Yes. This kid in my class used to talk about the birthday fairy when I was in third grade, and I literally waited every year for her to come."

"Did she come?" he said, gaping at me.

"No. My mom wasn't big on the fairy thing, apparently. But at least I can use my childhood trauma for good now." I shrugged.

He smirked and shook his head. "Every time I think you're pure evil, you go and surprise me."

"That's the nicest thing you've ever said to me," I said, my voice laced with sarcasm. "Come on, let's go."

Charlie led the way down the hallway with the two bags in hand. He pushed the door open, and Harper was sound asleep in her bed. She looked so peaceful and happy. Her bed had several stuffed animals in it, and the unicorn night-light allowed just enough of a glow for us to see the balloons and quietly spread them around the bedroom. I placed four balloons on the bed, and then we quietly tiptoed back out of the room and down the hall.

Once we got to the kitchen, he took the empty bags from me and balled them all up and tossed them in the trash.

"I'll see you later," I said, assuming he was done talking to me.

"You want a doughnut? I've got plenty."

Maybe he doesn't hate me anymore.

"Sure. That sounds great. I can never fall back asleep once I'm up." I moved to sit on the barstool at his kitchen island.

"Coffee?" he asked as he poured himself a mug, and I nodded.

He set it down in front of me, clearly remembering that I took my coffee black, and he put the box of doughnuts in front of me as well, as he had several that he hadn't taken out yet.

I chose the white cake doughnut with sprinkles on it.

"Man, I could sleep any time of day," he said, his voice low and deep. "Even if just for fifteen minutes, I'd take it."

I took a bite of my doughnut and studied him. "Have you always been that way?"

"Yeah, pretty much. I've never slept deep, so I think little catnaps work for me."

"Why didn't you sleep deep as a kid? I thought all kids sleep deep," I asked.

He took a sip of his coffee. "I was in and out of foster care, so I never slept well. I moved around a lot and saw some shady shit, so I was always on edge."

I got a vision of a young Charlie, with dark hair and ocean-blue eyes, watching everyone cautiously.

My heart ached at the thought.

"How old were you when you went into foster care?"

"Around Harper's age, and I was there until I graduated from high school." He leaned forward and used the pad of his thumb to swipe something off the corner of my lip. "You had a sprinkle there."

"Thank you," I whispered. "Was it lonely in foster care?"

"I don't know. I didn't know any different, and I've never minded being on my own." He shrugged. "Don't feel sorry for me, Firefly. I don't do the pity thing."

"I don't feel sorry for you, Charlie."

"What do you feel then? You're looking at me like someone just ran over your puppy." He chuckled, but it wasn't genuine.

It was a painful memory for him, whether he wanted to admit it or not.

"I feel like there's so much more to you than I realized. I feel like you're an amazing father. I feel like you've been really kind to me by letting me live in your guesthouse and renovating my home, while I've tortured you." I got up and stood in front of him. "I feel like I was scared to cross the line yesterday, so I found a ridiculous excuse to call it off. I'm sorry for doing that."

He reached for my hand and laced his fingers through mine. "It's all right. I understand that more than you know."

"I feel like I want to kiss you, Charlie."

"So, kiss me then."

I leaned down, tangling my hands in his hair before my lips found his.

It wasn't frantic this time.

My lips parted and his tongue slipped inside. His hands moved to my ass and pulled me onto his lap, where he sat on the barstool.

Our tongues tangled, exploring one another's mouths as I groaned.

His hardness grew between my legs, and I moaned into his mouth.

I pulled back and looked at him. His heated gaze studying me.

"Okay, we should probably stop, huh? Harper's going to be up soon," I whispered.

"Yeah. Let's sit with this for now." He nipped at my bottom lip before helping me to my feet.

I glanced down to see the obvious tent in his gray joggers, and I chuckled. "I sure seem to leave you frustrated often."

"I think torturing me is your superpower." He winked, and my stomach fluttered.

What the hell is that about?

I didn't do stomach flutters or get all flustered over a good-looking man.

But Charlie Huxley was doing something to me.

"We've all got our strengths." I chuckled. "I better go get dressed so I can come back and decorate for the party in a little bit. Thanks for the doughnut and the coffee." I chewed on my bottom lip. "And the hot make-out session."

"Not a bad way to start the day, Firefly. Thanks for making Harper's birthday so special. She's going to love it."

"I'll see you in a little while." I made my way out the back door and through the yard. Once I was inside, I leaned my back against the door and slid down to the floor.

What is happening?

I dialed Montana's number, and she picked up on the first ring.

"Hey, it's Saturday. Why are you up so early?" she asked. My bestie was an early riser, where I preferred to sleep in.

"I went to do the fairy surprise for Harper," I said.

"Oh yes. I forgot you were doing the balloons in her room this morning. So why do you sound so defeated? Did you wake her up when you were setting things up?"

"No. But I kissed Charlie again."

She chuckled. "Vi, it's okay to say you like Charlie."

"I don't like Charlie. I just like kissing him."

"If you just liked kissing him, you wouldn't have run out of his house yesterday because you found that stupid elf in the balloon. You panicked. You're nervous because you actually like him. This is not a 'bang it out of your system' type of thing. You. Like. Charlie," she said, pausing on each of the last three words, which infuriated me.

"You aren't helping," I groaned. "Plus, I can't like Charlie. He doesn't like me."

"Charlie likes you," she said, giggling. "He came down to your office yesterday and tossed that weird elf in your face because you hurt his feelings. Because he likes you. Why is that so hard for you to believe?"

"He's not my type. And he's not looking for anything either. He doesn't do relationships. So liking him is a bad idea. Banging him was one thing, but I can't like him. It'll be a disaster."

"You told him you weren't looking for anything. Maybe you both just said it to protect yourselves, you know? Just go with it, and don't overthink it. See where it goes. Stop with the games, and just tell the man how you feel."

"I did not call for rational advice, Monny. I called for you to tell me to pull my head out of my ass and walk away now. I'm just confusing lust with feelings. I'm attracted to him. I can't like a man who irritates me all the time." I got up and headed to the bedroom to get dressed.

"That's not true. Myles irritates me all the time," she said before loud laughter bellowed from her. "But I love that man like crazy. I think it's good that you're feeling things. You've had this guard up around you for so long, and I'm happy to see it come down for someone."

"What if he rejects me?" I whispered.

Because at the end of the day, that was what I was afraid of.

I'd had a lifetime of rejection from my own father.

I wouldn't allow anyone to make me feel like I wasn't good enough ever again.

"Violet," she said, her voice wobbling as she said my name, "you can't spend your whole life protecting yourself from heartache. Look at what happened with Myles. I put myself out there, and it hurt like hell when he left. But he came back to me, and everything worked out. Had I not put myself out there, we wouldn't be together now. Sometimes you'll get hurt, but you've got to take risks to get what you want. It's part of life."

"I don't think I can go there," I said, my voice low as I swiped at the single tear streaming down my face. "The thought of him not feeling the same way about me would be too much. And we're friends. I love Harper, and I want to keep her in my life. I don't have it in me to hate Charlie Huxley, and if he rejected me I would have no choice."

"Because you have actual feelings for the man. The fact that we're even talking about this is huge for you. You've always been one foot out the door in every relationship you've been in. Just enjoy this right now and see where it goes. Don't decide anything yet, okay?"

"Well, I don't have time to decide anything anyway. I've got a Pinkalicious party to set up, and I think Harper's mom might be coming to the party, so for all I know, they still have feelings for one another." I pulled on a pair of jeans and a pink blouse before moving to the bathroom.

"I don't even know his ex, and no one in town has ever mentioned her. It's weird that she just comes to town once a year, right?" she asked.

"It's very bizarre. I want to see how the dynamic is. So I'm shaking it off, and your job is to forget this conversation ever happened. I'm already over it." I put a few curls in my hair before pulling it into a low ponytail.

"Good luck with that," she chuckled. "Unfortunately, feelings are not something you can just decide to get over. But I know you're in party mode now, and I can't wait to see you work your magic. We'll see you at the party in a few hours. Call me if you need me. Love you."

"Love you," I said before ending the call.

I put on some lip gloss and mascara and stared into the mirror. "You don't like Charlie Huxley. Shake it the hell off."

And that's exactly what I intended to do.

CHAPTER SIXTEEN

Charlie

I'd never experienced anything like the whirlwind that was Violet Beaumont in party mode. Harper was still floating on air after waking up to a roomful of balloons and dancing around the house that the birthday fairy had come to visit her.

I personally was still floating on air that the birthday fairy and I had shared a hot kiss in the kitchen this morning.

I didn't know what to make of it.

She was so hot and cold with me, and I couldn't read her.

Violet had insisted that I take Harper to the Brown Bear Diner for pancakes so she could get the inside set up for the party, as she wanted to surprise my daughter with the decor.

I normally bought some paper plates and cups and a cake, but this year, I'd agreed to let her do all the shopping for the party and take over the whole thing.

When we pulled up to the house, I sent her a text, per her instructions.

She was a bossy little thing.

Harper unbuckled and climbed into the front seat once we were parked in the driveway.

Me: We're home. Can we come inside now?

"What did she say, Daddy?" Harper asked.

"I'm waiting for a response. Seems kind of silly that we can't go in our own home, doesn't it?" I grumped, even though I thought it was sweet that Violet wanted to set this up for Harper.

"I don't think it's silly. Violet likes to make everything special. I can't wait to see what she did."

My phone dinged with a text.

Firefly: Come on in!

"All right. We can head inside," I said, and my daughter was immediately out of the truck and running toward the house. That's when I noticed the front porch now had a bunch of balloons, and she'd moved the banner I'd put up this morning in the kitchen out front and strung it across the railing on the front porch.

"She even did stuff out here, Daddy!" Harper shouted just as Violet opened the front door.

"Welcome to Harper Huxley's Pinkalicious party," Violet said as my daughter lunged herself into her arms.

Harper had grown attached to Violet, and as much as that made me nervous, I understood it. They were drawn to one another, and it wasn't my place to stop my daughter from having those connections.

I didn't want her to be closed off the way I was.

"Thank you, Vi!"

"Come on, let's go take a look." Violet set Harper down on her feet and took her hand, leading her inside.

My jaw hung open at how much she'd gotten done in just the time that we'd been gone. The foyer had a grand pink-and-white balloon arch, with gold crown balloons and a giant number seven balloon. In the kitchen, the island was covered in pink-netted fabric, with flowers and platters labeled where the food would go.

Pinkalicious Pinkerton turkey subs.

Pinkerton potato chips.

Pinkalicious fruit kabobs.

What the hell was a fruit kabob?

Pink and white lanterns hung from the ceiling, some striped and some with polka dots. There were streamers and more balloons every which way we turned. A photo booth with a huge backdrop said Harper's Pinkalicious Party.

"Violet!" Harper's voice cracked, and I startled when I saw tears streaming down her face. "This is the prettiest party I've ever seen. Thank you."

"Oh, Harps." Violet bent down to get eye level before wrapping her arms around my baby girl. "You deserve the most beautiful party. You're seven years old, after all. And you and your daddy have been so nice to let me stay in the guesthouse. It's the least I could do."

For fuck's sake.

I was at a loss for words now.

"Daddy, what do you think?"

"It's perfect." I cleared my throat. "Thank you."

Violet stood up, and I noticed that she blinked several times as she looked down at my daughter. "I'm glad you guys like it. I know your daddy got you the pretty pink dress, but I have a little something for you too."

Violet walked to the kitchen table and brought over a rectangular box wrapped in pink-and-white-striped paper with a big pink bow. She handed Harper the package. Harper's eyes were wide as she tore it open, and then she gasped when she lifted the lid. Inside the box was a pair of pink high-tops covered in pink stones with pink ribbon laces.

"Are these real diamonds?" Harper asked as she ran her fingers over the shoes.

"They're rhinestones. I put them on the shoes because I wanted you to have the sparkliest shoes to wear to your party." Violet bent down and hugged her.

"These are the most prettiest and most sparkliest shoes I ever saw." Violet bent down and slipped the shoes on, and I helped get them laced up.

"I'm so glad you like them," Violet said.

"They're my favorite."

"You should go get dressed, because the food will be here in twenty minutes, and then guests start arriving in less than an hour. We can take some photos of you in the photo booth before everyone gets here."

"Okay, I'll be right back!" Harper giggled all the way down the hall as she ran to her bedroom.

"Violet," I said, my voice gruff.

She turned to face me. "Yes?"

"That was—" I blew out a breath. "That was really kind of you. Thank you."

"Of course. I wanted this to be special for her."

"Well, you've succeeded. I saw the charge on my card for the food and the cake, but you didn't charge me for half of this stuff."

"I've been living rent-free in your home. You're also renovating my home for me. I would have paid for the food as well, if you hadn't been so pushy about making me use your card." She chuckled. "I wanted to thank you for everything you've done for me."

I nodded, fighting the urge to pull her into my arms.

Damn this woman for getting under my skin in every possible way.

"Thank you. I appreciate it," I said, moving a step closer as her tongue swiped out along her bottom lip.

I placed a hand on the side of her neck, my thumb stroking along her jaw.

And the motherfucking doorbell rang.

Violet chuckled as Harper ran down the hall in a pink dress with a big gold crown on her head and her pink sparkly shoes.

"I wonder if it's my Pinkalicious cake!" she shouted, moving toward the door.

I beat her there and pulled the door open. Caroline stood on the other side.

There was an awkward silence as my daughter processed who it was.

It wasn't her cake.

It wasn't her sandwiches.

It was her mother, who showed up once a year to spend a few hours with her.

"Happy birthday, Harper. Do you remember me?" Caroline's blond hair sat on her shoulders, and she had a smile plastered on her face. Our daughter had her mother's green eyes, but everything else from her hair color to her golden skin color to her expressions seemed to come from me.

"Hi, Caroline." Harper's tone was colder than usual, which had alarm bells going off in my head.

Maybe these visits weren't healthy for her anymore.

"Well, are y'all going to make me stand out here all day? I came for the party." Caroline chuckled as if it was perfectly normal to show up to her daughter's party when they hadn't spoken in a year.

I stepped back. "Sure. Come on in. I wasn't sure if you were coming, because you said you didn't want to do the big party thing."

"Well, you refused to move it, so you didn't give me much of a choice. And this is the only day I could come. I've got a wedding to plan, and we're building a new home," she said as she fluttered her hands around. "Look at my ring, Harper. I'm getting married."

Harper glanced down at the gargantuan diamond and shrugged. "Okay."

"Wow. This place is very pink. You don't usually decorate quite this much. Who did the decorating?"

"My Violet decorated for the whole party," Harper said as we moved toward the kitchen.

"Who is Violet?" Caroline asked, not making any effort to hide her irritation.

It was hard to wrap my head around the fact that this woman flew in once a year and had the audacity to be annoyed that we had our own shit going on.

"This is Violet," Harper said, running over to wrap her arms around Violet's legs as she stood at the counter filling a large white tub with waters and sodas.

"Are you a party planner?" Caroline asked, and her tone had an edge to it.

I forgot how rude she could be.

"I'm a wedding planner, but I also do parties for special little girls," Violet said as she adjusted the ponytail on Harper's head. "You must be Caroline?"

"Yes. I'm Harper's mother." Caroline crossed her arms over her chest.

What the hell was she doing? She was going to give Violet attitude for decorating Harper's party, when she didn't even want to come to it?

"Well, you're only my mama one day a year," Harper said, and Caroline gaped at her.

I was surprised she'd said it as well, but it was the truth.

"I just come to visit one day a year. I'm always your mother," Caroline snipped before setting her purse on the counter and handing a gift bag to Harper. "I'd like you to open this now, before the guests arrive. I probably won't stay for gifts."

Shocker.

What the fuck are we even doing having her show up like this once a year?

Harper looked inside the turquoise bag and pulled out a matching box. She opened the lid and stared down at the necklace. "Is it a necklace?"

"It's a necklace from Tiffany's. They're very expensive, so you need to take extra-special care of it."

I rolled my eyes. She was seven years old. She didn't want a fancy necklace. She liked to play outside in the dirt. She liked to swim and run and have fun. She was a kid. But we'd put it in her drawer with all the other expensive gifts from Caroline.

"Okay. Thank you."

"You aren't going to put it on?" Caroline asked, and Harper turned to look at me.

"Listen, it's a party. She's going to be playing outside. This isn't the time to put it on," I said.

Violet arched a brow as my gaze met hers, and I could read the look easily.

This entire interaction was insane, and she was right.

I'd thought this was an acceptable idea when I'd agreed to the ridiculous arrangement all those years ago. Allowing my daughter to see that her biological mother still thought of her, still wanted to be in her life, even if just briefly, once a year. We'd spend a few hours with Caroline, and she'd leave, and I figured I was doing the right thing by my daughter. I was not a man who'd had any sort of example of how to be a parent. I'd basically raised myself. So I was just trying to do the right thing.

But nothing felt right today.

Not Caroline's attitude, or the way that Harper appeared to be keeping her distance from her as if her mother made her feel uncomfortable.

"Oh, I didn't realize it was that kind of party. You should save it for a special occasion or when you go to a fancy dinner," Caroline said, bending down to meet Harper's eyes.

"I don't go to fancy dinners, Caroline. I eat dinners at home or at the diner," Harper said, and there was an awkward silence.

"How about I take the necklace and go put it in your room?" Violet reached for the box, clearly trying to make this situation less uncomfortable.

"Aren't you the party planner? Why would you know where her room is?" Caroline huffed.

"She lives in the backyard, and she's my best friend!" Harper shouted, catching us all off guard.

"What is with this attitude? I came a long way to be here, and I don't appreciate it," Caroline hissed, and Harper burst into tears and ran down the hall.

"What the fuck are you doing?" I growled at Caroline as Violet moved down the hall after my daughter.

"I'm coming to celebrate my daughter's birthday, like I do every year." She stared at me as if she was completely stunned that she'd been the cause of Harper's outburst.

"I told you that things are changing, and this isn't working anymore. I should have put my foot down, but I didn't realize it was this bad." I shook my head. "This is Harper's special day, and you showing up is not a good idea."

"So, I'm not welcome to attend my own daughter's birthday party?" She shrugged, her eyes watering because she was a narcissist, and of course she was going to make this about her. "She is my daughter, Charlie."

"No. She's my daughter, Caroline. You don't even know her. You didn't want to be a mom, and we didn't know how to navigate all of this seven years ago. But this isn't working." I ran a hand down my face.

"Because you have a girlfriend now, and she doesn't want me here?" She poked me hard in the chest with her long fingernail. "You don't get to push me out when it's no longer convenient for you."

"Are you fucking kidding me? No longer convenient for me? You don't call, you don't check in on her, you don't fucking know anything about her. You don't know that she's the best reader in her class. You don't know that she's artistic, that she's got a wicked sense of humor, and that her favorite food is pancakes. I've been here every single day since the day she was born. You gave me a choice, and I chose my daughter. You had the same choice, and you chose your life. And I don't judge you for it, but you don't get to stroll in here and ruin her birthday party because you want to call yourself a mom one day a year. Do your parents even know you're here? Does your fiancé know you're here?"

She swiped at the single tear running down her cheek. "No. No one knows I'm here. I'm trying to do the right thing."

"No, you're not. You're playing a part, and it's not working anymore. If you looked me in the eyes right now, and you told me that you wanted to be a mother, that you wanted to spend real time with her. That you were willing to sit up at night with her when she's sick. That you wanted to go to her school and meet her teacher and meet her friends? Hell, I wouldn't deny you that. But you want to live your life and still call yourself her mother? It's not right, and you know it, Caroline."

"I'm not going to let some low-rent construction worker who knocked me up one summer call the shots," she said, her voice laced with venom. "I have more money than you'd know what to do with. I could take you to court and destroy you. I could have her full time if I wanted to."

A sharp pain hit my chest at her words, but I knew she was full of shit. Her parents hadn't wanted her to keep our daughter. Her future husband didn't even know she was here. She was trying to intimidate me, which was probably what she did all those years ago, when I'd agreed to this ridiculous arrangement.

"Good luck with that. Shoot your shot, Caroline. There isn't a judge in the world who would grant you custody, considering you've been completely absent from your child's life for seven years. You haven't paid one penny in child support. You've been doing your own thing, while I've been showing up every fucking day. So if you want to come in here and threaten to take my daughter, you best be prepared, because this low-rent construction worker has a lot more money saved up than you can imagine. And I only have one thing to lose, and I promise you, you won't take her from me. You don't have enough fight in you to take on the wrath I would bring to protect my little girl."

"I'm over this conversation. I came here to celebrate a birthday, not to debate who's the better parent." She grabbed her purse from the counter.

"There is no debate. You've never been a parent," I said, my hands fisted at my side as I followed behind her when she stormed toward the door.

She whipped around to face me just after pulling open the door. "We had an agreement, Charlie. You said it was fine if I didn't want to be involved."

"It is. But you can't show up and expect things from Harper when you aren't in her life."

"I could make your life very uncomfortable if I wanted to," she said, glaring at me.

"For what, huh, Caroline? What is it that you're so pissed off about? You had a baby that you weren't ready for, and I happily raised her. I've loved her every day since the minute she came into this world. I didn't fault you for your choices, so don't roll into my home and threaten me or my child just because you don't like the way things are going for you now."

She glanced over her shoulder as a car pulled into the driveway. She'd hired a driver, obviously, because God forbid she drive herself or do anything on her own.

"Goodbye, Charlie. Let Harper know she can keep the necklace, even though she wasn't very grateful for the gift."

Those were her final words.

Very fitting in the grand scheme of things.

She stormed off and flashed me the bird, and then her car door closed and they pulled out of the driveway.

Two cars pulled in before I even had time to close the door. I took the platter of sandwiches and the bakery cake and set everything on the kitchen counter before making my way down the hallway to Harper's bedroom.

I stopped in the doorway and found Violet sitting on the floor with a crying Harper tucked beside her as she held her close.

"Hey, we can't have you crying on your birthday, Harps," I said. "This is your special day. We aren't going to allow anyone to ruin that for you, okay?"

"I don't like Caroline, Daddy."

"Yeah, well, she's gone, and I don't think she's coming back."

I just hoped like hell that was true.

CHAPTER SEVENTEEN

Violet

I'd held Harper for the last twenty minutes while Charlie and his ex from hell had remained out in the kitchen. And now Charlie had strolled into the room like some sort of superhero, and I was mesmerized at the way he was talking to his daughter.

"Come on now, baby girl. It's your special day. It looks like Pinkalicious puked out in the kitchen—we can't let all those decorations go to waste." He was bent down low to the ground as he stroked her hair.

She giggled for the first time since she'd run down the hallway.

"Pinkalicious doesn't puke, Daddy."

"No? Well, there's a lot of pink out there, and your friends should be arriving any minute," he said, his voice calm and deep.

"I didn't want to wear the fancy necklace." Harper sat forward and sniffed a few times as her father pulled her from my arms and wrapped her up as he pushed to a full stand.

"You don't have to wear the necklace. I shouldn't have allowed her to come here. I didn't handle that right, but I will handle things differently moving forward, all right?" he said as he rocked her back and forth and she clung to him.

"Because it's you and me against the world, right, Daddy?" she said before glancing over at me. "And Violet can stay here with us as long as she wants. She's our family too."

I felt my chest contract, and I stood up.

"Aw . . . I'll give you two a few minutes to clean up. I'll meet you out there." I'd started to move when Charlie's hand wrapped around my wrist, and he pulled me close.

"She's right. You can stay as long as you want. Thanks for taking care of my girl for me." He tucked me into his chest, and the three of us just stood there hugging.

It felt wonderful and overwhelming all at the same time.

I was getting too attached.

I'd never felt like I fit anywhere, and in a way, that was safer than hoping I'd fit somewhere.

It was both exciting and terrifying. I liked how I felt when I was with them, but I also didn't want to be another person who let Harper down if this was all just a temporary situation.

The doorbell rang. Charlie let his arm drop as I stepped back, and he put Harper down on her feet.

"I'll get the door, and you can help Harper get cleaned up," he said, winking at me before he mouthed the words *Thank you*.

And when Charlie Huxley appreciated you, it felt like you were on top of the world.

I nodded and took Harper into the bathroom, where I fixed her ponytail and cleaned up her face.

"You look like you're ready for the best party ever," I said, kissing her on the cheek as she stared in the mirror.

"Violet," she said, reaching for my hand. "I love you."

A large lump formed in my throat, and I nodded. "I love you too, Harper Huxley."

"Let's go party." She clapped in excitement and then skipped out of the room, tugging me along with her like I belonged right beside her.

A few of her classmates had arrived, and I hurried to get the food out and the cake set up on the dessert table. We had the doors to the backyard open, and the kids were running in and out.

Harper's best friend Lily had already asked me if I'd plan her birthday party.

"Thanks a lot, Charlie," Tim said with a laugh. "Now we have to hire party planners for our kids."

"Hey, they only have so many birthdays. I'm not against it," Jeanne said, bumping me with her shoulder. "But I didn't know you did birthday parties. I thought you only did weddings."

"She does," Montana said as she and Myles walked over. "But she made an exception for Harper. Although I will say, I wouldn't have guessed kids' parties were your thing, but this is pretty spectacular."

"Well, Harper is pretty spectacular," I said, and I looked up to see Charlie watching me. He had a beer in his hand, and his gaze never left mine.

"Excuse me, lady," a loud, whiny voice said as she tugged my hand unusually hard.

"Um, yes?" I gaped at her, unsure why she was being so aggressive.

"I'm Denise Quigley," she said, and then I remembered her from the diner.

"Ah, yes. Denise Quigley. What can I do for you?"

"You can do my party in a few weeks." She smiled up at me, and her mom hurried over.

"Sweetie, we already booked your party at the country club," her mom said, reaching for her hand.

"I don't want my party at the country club. I want a Pinkalicious party!" she shouted.

And this is why I normally don't care for children.

Harper would never behave like this, and I glanced over to see her and Lily at the photo booth with a couple of other kids, holding up the props as their parents took photos.

"A country club party sounds amazing," I said.

Charlie interrupted and called everyone to come get sandwiches, and thankfully Denise Quigley and her mother moved on to more exciting things.

Harper came over and pulled me around the corner. "Denise Quigley said this is the best party ever."

"The best party for the best girl," I said.

Lily came hurrying around the corner and called for Harper to come eat, and we walked hand in hand back into the kitchen.

All the kids ate, as did the adults. Harper loved her Pinkalicious cake with its big gold crown on the top.

Montana helped me clean up most of the decorations when the party finally started winding down. Lily and Harper were going through her gifts after all the other kids had left. Charlie, Myles, and Benji were having cocktails with Lily's parents. Montana told Myles she was ready to head home, and I was exhausted myself. I hugged Harper goodbye, and I said goodbye to everyone who was still lingering.

I avoided Charlie, and I didn't know why.

Things had gotten heavy today, and my gut told me I should put some distance there. I made my way to the guesthouse and went to the bathroom immediately, turning on the water to run a bath.

It had been a long day.

I undressed and slipped into the tub, groaning at how nice it felt to soak.

I closed my eyes and smiled, thinking about all the times I'd looked over at Harper and found her laughing and smiling.

After all that had gone down with her mom, I was happy that she was able to rebound.

My phone rang, and I saw my mother's name flash across the screen. I hesitated, as it was well past dinnertime, and I knew that meant she'd be deep into a bottle of whiskey, which was never a great time to speak to her.

But I answered.

"Hey, Mom," I said, holding the phone in one hand while the other rested in the tub water.

"Hey, yourself. I haven't talked to you in a week. What's going on?"

"I've just been swamped with work. I'm still renovating my house, so I've got a lot going on over there too," I said.

"Must be nice to own your own home."

Actually, yes, it is. I've worked damn hard for it.

"I'm looking forward to getting settled. You'll have to come see it."

"If you buy me a ticket, I'll come," she said.

"I told you to let me know when you have a few days off, and I'll book the ticket."

"Okay, I'll let you know. I was calling because I didn't get my check yet for this month, and money's tight," she said, her words slurring a little bit as she spoke.

"I don't send checks anymore, Mom, remember? I transferred the money directly into your account three days ago. Just like I do every month."

"Oh. I didn't look at the account. I kept checking the mailbox," she said.

She didn't thank me. She didn't tell me that she appreciated that I contributed $500 a month toward her living expenses. She just expected it. Like I owed her.

"It's in the account."

"Well, you can thank your father for that, because if I had a partner, I wouldn't have to rely on you."

I closed my eyes and counted down from ten. Nine. Eight. Seven.

"You know what, Mom," I said, sitting forward in the tub because I was over this same conversation, "Dad left both of us before I was born. You need to stop blaming him for everything and take control of your life. That's what I'm doing."

She was quiet for a few beats, so I knew she was going to weaponize her next words.

"You've always been ungrateful. You know, your father and I were very happy before I had you." Her words were dragging, and I knew she was drunk.

I knew she didn't mean it.

But it still hurt.

So, I did what I always did—I pulled my hard outer shell over my heart to shield it.

"Well, I wasn't born yet, so I'm sorry that me being in the womb was such a struggle for your relationship."

I was tired of her guilting me about something that I had no control over. Blaming me for her life not going the way that she wanted it to. Normally I could just bite my tongue where my mother was concerned. I'd had years of conditioning. But today, today felt different.

Seeing the way that Caroline treated Harper wasn't sitting well with me. And maybe things were just hitting too close to home now. I was proud of Harper for having an outburst and sharing her discomfort with the situation, and maybe it was time I started doing the same with my own mother.

"What's with the attitude, Violet?"

"I'm tired, Mom. You're welcome for the money. You're welcome for tolerating your abusive behavior my entire life. How about you call me when you have something nice to say, all right?"

"I wouldn't hold your breath," she hissed, and I knew it was the booze talking.

I shouldn't have answered the phone.

"I won't." I ended the call and stepped out of the tub, drying myself off with a towel before slipping on my robe.

I will not cry.

I will not cry.

I will not cry.

I was a pro at pushing away my feelings.

The knock on the door startled me, and I tightened the belt on my robe and peeked through the little window beside the door.

Charlie.

I cracked the door open. "Hey, what's up?"

"Can I come in?"

"Yeah, of course. I just got out of the tub, hence the robe." I stepped back, opening the door farther.

"Even better." He chuckled before studying me after I'd closed the door. "Are you all right?"

"Yeah. I'm fine."

"You don't look fine." He followed me into the small living space, dropping to sit on the couch.

"Where's Harper?" I asked as I took the seat beside him.

"She ended up going home with Lily for a sleepover."

"Oh," I said, surprised, because I knew she'd only slept away from home one other time.

"I actually asked them if they would be okay to have her tonight." He cleared his throat, appearing nervous, which was not the norm for this man.

"You did? Why? I would have had her spend the night here if you needed a night off."

He smiled just slightly. "I didn't need a night off, Firefly. I wanted to come talk to you, actually."

"What did you want to talk to me about?"

"Well, first, I wanted to thank you for everything you did today. For my daughter. For me." He shrugged. "It meant a lot. I don't like relying on people, and you just seem to keep showing up for us. I wanted you to know that I'd noticed, and that I appreciated it."

"Charles," I said, making no attempt to hide my smile. "That might be the most words you've ever said to me in one sitting."

He smiled. "I have more to say."

"Okay."

"I like you, Violet Beaumont. Even when you're aggravating me and changing your design plans for the hundredth time. Even when you're challenging me, or accusing me of being a serial doll killer. I. Like. You."

I don't know why his words triggered something in me.

I should have just been happy that he'd admitted that he felt the same way I felt.

But instead, I did the one thing I never in a million years thought I'd do.

I tried to speak, and my voice cracked.

And before I could stop myself—the tears started falling.

And I broke down in front of Charlie Huxley.

CHAPTER EIGHTEEN

Charlie

Seeing Violet vulnerable did something to me.

I didn't even think about it, I just leaned forward and pulled her onto my lap and wrapped my arms around her.

She was always so stoic and strong, and in a way it felt like a gift that she was comfortable enough with me to let me see this side of her.

I just held her there and let her cry it out.

Once her sobs had slowed, I took the opportunity to speak. "A wise woman once told me that you should always ask someone why they're crying."

She chuckled and sat up, looking at me with those pretty green eyes. "I don't know why I'm crying."

"Yes, you do. And maybe if you tell me, it'll make you feel better. It worked for Harper that day you got her to tell you what was going on." I stroked the hair from her face.

"It's embarrassing, Charles. I'm a grown woman crying because I have a shitty family." She shrugged, as if it was a relief to say it aloud.

"Nothing to be embarrassed about. I have a shitty family too. We have no control of that. Tell me what happened."

"I mean, how far back do you want to go?" She chuckled again before sniffing a few times and looking away.

Man, I fucking understood it more than she knew.

This shame that came with feeling like you weren't good enough as a kid, something that followed you right into adulthood.

I reached for her chin and tipped it in my direction, meeting her gaze. "As far back as you want to go, Firefly."

"So, my father is a piece of shit. He left my mom before I was born, and he has a whole new family, and I'm an outsider there. A third wheel. My mother resents me for my father leaving us, and she's a severe alcoholic, and my call with her tonight just reminded me that I don't fit anywhere, you know?" Her bottom lip shook, and I wrapped my hand around the back of her head and waited for her gaze to meet mine. "And I'm so tired of trying to find my place, you know?"

"Those don't sound like people that you want to fit in with, right?" I asked, choosing my words carefully. "You just haven't found your people, Violet. Anyone who makes you feel like you don't belong, or like a third wheel. Fuck them. You were clearly born to be a goddamn unicycle, and anyone who knows you knows that."

She studied me for the longest time, her smirk turning into the brightest smile. "A unicycle, huh?"

"Yeah, it sounds like your parents don't see you. But I see you. The minute I met you, I knew you could ride solo. A firefly who lights up the sky all on her own."

"Says the man who likes to ride solo himself. With his little girl in the sidecar." She chuckled.

"Yeah, maybe that's why we're drawn to one another. We have more in common than we thought," I said, using the pad of my thumb to stroke her jaw.

"Well, we both have messed-up childhoods. We're stubborn and set in our ways," she said, listing things off. "We both think Harper is the coolest kid around. We have the same taste in friends."

"We're both great kissers," I said.

"Even if I sort of blew the 'bang it out' plan, huh?"

"You know, I don't think that was really supposed to be our thing. I think you found a reason to call it off, and as much as I was disappointed, a part of me was relieved." I regretted my choice of wording when I saw the way her face fell.

"Yeah, probably good that we don't cross that line."

"That's not what I meant, Violet." I waited for her eyes to find mine. "I don't want to bang anything out with you. I mean, yeah, I'd like to bury myself so deep in you that I can't see straight. But I don't think once will be enough for me. I also don't want to pretend it didn't happen after. If—and that's only if you decide you want to go there—but if we did cross the line, I'd want to take my time. I'd want to do it over and over until you didn't want anyone but me."

Her eyes widened, breath quickening.

"I thought you didn't do repeat customers?" she said, her voice low and hesitant.

As if she was afraid to ask the question.

"I don't. I mean, I haven't since Harper came into the world. It's just been me and her. But I also don't question things that feel right. And yes, you aggravate the hell out of me most days," I said on a laugh. "But I go to bed thinking about you. I wake up happy that you're in my kitchen cooking breakfast. So, this is different. I don't know what it means. Maybe it's something we do a couple times and it ends. Maybe you'll be sick of me after the first time. But from where I'm coming from, I'd like to see where it goes, if you're open to that. One day at a time, Firefly. Maybe we get two days, maybe we get ten. Hell, maybe we last longer than we can count before we want to murder each other."

She blinked a few times like she was processing my words.

Maybe this was too much for her.

"And there's no pressure to do anything. I just wanted you to know that I was open to more than a 'bang it out' type of thing." I cleared my throat, suddenly feeling like an asshole for saying anything. Maybe she wanted this to be done.

"Stop, Charles." She put her finger to my lips. "I like you so much it makes me nervous. I prefer to be annoyed with you. It's safer that way."

I nodded. I understood it.

"I think you could like me and still be annoyed by me," I said as I nipped at the tip of her finger.

She laughed and said, "I mean, this relationship is doomed. We tried to have a one-night stand, and I thought you were a serial killer. Then you came over here to spend some time with me, and I blubbered like a big baby."

"Yet here we are. Still trying to figure it out," I said.

"That was nice of you to come over tonight."

"Yeah, I think I surprised Jeanne and Tim when I asked them if they were up for a sleepover. I wanted to spend some time with you."

"How'd you know I wouldn't be out on a date?" she asked, grinning.

In one swift move, I flipped her on her back on the couch, pinning her hands above her head. "Admit that you want me."

She laughed hysterically as she squirmed beneath me. "It's no secret that I want you, Charles."

Her words were breathy and laced with need.

I thrust forward, letting her feel just how much I wanted her.

"Let's give this a try. See where it goes. No pressure. No expectations."

"Assuming we don't kill one another," she said teasingly.

"If it all blows up in our faces, then we'll be right back where we were. We're grown-ups—we can handle it."

"That's true. We'd just go back to being friends who fight," she said.

"Sure."

"Then stop torturing me and kiss me already." Her hands tangled in my hair, and I leaned down and claimed her mouth.

Her lips parted immediately, and my tongue slipped inside.

There was a hunger this time as her tongue tangled with mine, and my hips moved up and down as she met me thrust for thrust.

Grinding against my cock, all hot and needy.

A little moan escaped her lips, and I nearly came right there.

I pulled back, her wild gaze searching mine. "It's been a while for me."

She smirked as a smile spread across her face. Her hand moved to my cheek. "It's been a while for me too. I'm as eager as you are."

"I don't know about that," I said, clearing my throat as she sat forward and held her arms out.

I tugged her robe open before pushing it off her shoulders as her fingers fumbled with the buttons of my flannel. I was not a patient man, especially when it came to Violet Beaumont. I grabbed the sides of my shirt and tore it open as the buttons bounced on the wood floor beneath us. My fingers traced over her pretty pink nipples as goose bumps spread across her golden skin.

"If you knew how many times I've fantasized about these perfect tits."

"How did you know they were perfect if you hadn't seen them?" Her voice was heavy with desire.

I just stared down at her beautiful body. "I just knew. Look at you, Firefly. Prettiest girl I've ever seen."

Her breath caught as I leaned down, taking one hard peak between my lips and flicking it with my tongue. I could get lost in these tits for hours, but my dick had other ideas as he strained hard against the zipper of my jeans, threatening to tear right through the denim.

"Tell me you brought a condom," she panted.

I moved to her other breast, wanting to give them equal attention, before pulling back to look at her. "I came prepared."

I unbuttoned my jeans as she pushed up on her elbows and watched. I kicked off my shoes and shoved my jeans and briefs down my legs before pushing them out of the way. My dick sprang free, and Violet's eyes widened.

"Of course you have a perfect penis." She smiled.

"Yeah?" I asked as I stroked my cock a few times before kneeling between her thighs.

"Condom." Her breaths came quick.

"Not so fast. There's something I need to do first," I said, moving down the couch a little bit, gripping her ankles and hooking them over my shoulders. "I need to taste this sweet pussy of yours. I can't wait another second."

I buried my head between her thighs, and her fingers were tangled in my hair as I licked and sucked all that sweetness.

"Goddamn, woman." I pulled my head up. "I could die a happy man right here."

"You best not die before we finally have sex, Charlie Huxley," she groaned as she pulled my head back down.

I slipped my tongue inside, and she nearly arched off the couch as she bucked against me. I fucked her with my tongue as my thumb found her clit and I teased her relentlessly. Taking her right to the edge, and pulling back. Over and over.

"Charlie! Please!" she groaned.

I pulled back. Locking my lips over her clit and sliding a finger into all her warmth. And then a second. I pumped in and out as I sucked hard, and she cried out my name on a gasp.

Violet Beaumont coming with my face buried between her thighs was something that would forever be ingrained in my brain.

Her body shook and quaked as she yanked on my hair and ground up against me.

It was the hottest thing I'd ever experienced.

Once her breathing calmed, I pulled my fingers out and sucked off every last drop. I sat back, looking down at her lying there sated and relaxed.

Her skin flushed, lips plump and eyes hazy.

I reached down for my jeans on the floor and pulled out my wallet, where I found the gold foil packet inside.

"I want to do it," she said, taking it from my hand and tearing off the top. Her tongue swiped out along her bottom lip, and I squeezed my eyes closed as my head fell back.

"You can't look at my dick and lick your lips and expect me to keep it together," I grunted.

She rolled the latex over my length. "Maybe I don't want you to keep it together. Maybe I want you to lose yourself in me the way I just did with you."

I wanted to take my time with her. Wanted to explore every inch of that gorgeous body. But my dick couldn't be trusted. I wrapped an arm around her back and tugged her forward as I leaned back on the other end of the couch. "You're going to ride me and set the pace."

Her teeth sank into her juicy bottom lip, and I tucked her hair behind her ear.

"I can do that," she said. She pushed up on her knees, lining the tip of my dick up with her entrance. She moved down slowly, gasping at the size and squeezing her eyes closed.

"Take your time, beautiful. There's no rush."

She nodded, lacing her fingers with mine. And she moved slowly, inch by glorious inch. I tugged her head down, wanting her mouth on mine.

Needing her mouth on mine.

I kissed her, my fingers tangling in that wild mane of waves.

And she slid down farther.

My mouth never leaving hers.

She pulled back once I was all the way in, squeezing my dick like some kind of vise.

Nothing had ever felt better.

Her hands found the back of my thighs as she leaned back and slid up my cock before gliding back down. It was slow at first. My hands found her tits, and I sat forward, wrapping my mouth around a nipple.

Taking turns going back and forth as she found her rhythm.

As we found our rhythm together.

I fell back against the couch as she moved faster.

Lips plump and swollen from where I'd kissed her.

Tits bouncing.

Fucking perfection.

I gripped her hips as her head fell back.

Faster. Harder. Needier.

My hand found her clit, knowing what she needed. She cried out my name, and I thrust forward.

Once.

Twice.

And I followed her right over the edge.

Lights flashing behind my eyes as a feral sound left my mouth.

I came hard as we both continued riding out every last bit of pleasure.

Because nothing had ever felt better.

CHAPTER NINETEEN

Violet

I collapsed on top of Charlie as his arms wrapped around me and his breathing finally slowed.

"My God, woman. That was fucking incredible," he finally said.

I looked at him. "Agreed. If we only do that once, it will still be worth it."

"I thought we were taking it one day at a time," he chuckled. "You're already calling it done?"

"I'm calling it spectacular. Everyone should experience that once in their life." I bit down on my bottom lip to keep from saying more.

It was exhilarating and terrifying all at the same time.

To feel so connected to someone.

It was something I normally avoided, and God knows I'd tried to avoid this man.

But we were like two magnets, the force so strong, it was impossible to ignore.

Maybe this would be a one and done. Maybe we just needed to get it out of our systems.

But I already wanted to do it again.

He slowly shifted me off him, then set me on the couch before he moved to his feet. He was a big man. Large in every way.

He strode the short distance to the bathroom, and I assumed he was disposing of the condom. I reached for the throw blanket on the couch, suddenly self-conscious about being naked and vulnerable.

I tried to shake off the memory of crying to him just an hour ago.

I'd broken every rule I'd ever had with Charlie.

I'd cried. I'd told him I liked him. And then I'd had earth-shattering sex with the man.

I wrapped myself up in the blanket, waiting for him to come out of the bathroom and realize we'd made a huge mistake before he bailed and went home.

He strode toward me with an unreadable grin on his face.

He stopped in front of me, leaned down, and picked up his jeans.

Here we go.

He was going to explain all the reasons we should call this done.

But instead, he pulled his wallet out and took out two more condoms as he waggled his brows. He leaned down and scooped me up in his arms, and I startled.

"What are you doing?" I squealed as he cradled me like a baby and carried me to the bedroom.

He pulled back the covers and set me down on the bed before sliding in next to me. He shifted me on his chest and then pulled the covers over both of us.

"We're cuddling," he said, his voice lacking all emotion.

I laughed. "You sound thrilled about it."

"Listen. This isn't the norm for either of us, but we just said we're going to try. You attempting to act like it's already over, that's not trying. So lie here on my chest and tell me about your call with your mom, and then once we've recovered, we're going to do that again and again."

I looked at him and pushed myself up. "You want to talk while we cuddle before we have sex again?"

"Yes. And so do you. So stop being a stubborn ass and start talking."

I lay back down and breathed in his manly scent of mint and pine.

"I told you my mom is an alcoholic, and my dad is a narcissist. Great combo in the parenting department," I chuckled.

He didn't laugh. "That had to suck. You know, sometimes I think having no parents is better than having shitty parents. At least I didn't have hope of someone showing up, you know? You probably held out for more because they were there."

I'd never thought about that.

"That's very true. But it still had to be hard on you, moving around and not knowing what each day would bring?" I whispered.

"Nah. I learned at an early age to rely on myself. I don't have expectations with people. But having Harper changed me in a way. It made me want to be a better man. And being a good father is the most important job I'll ever have."

"You're such a good dad, Charlie. Watching you with Harper restored my faith in the father-daughter relationship," I said as he stroked my hair in the most soothing way. "I thought it was all a fairy tale, but you two are the real deal."

"Were there good times with your mother, or was she always abusive?"

"There were good times. That's what makes it hard. She tried. She had her heart broken, and she never bounced back from that. It made me aware at a very young age that trusting others with your heart was a really bad idea." I sighed. "But she coped by numbing herself with alcohol, which is never a good thing. So her addiction has led to a lot of toxic behavior. But she has her moments of goodness too."

"I'm sorry, Firefly. That wasn't fair to you. You deserve better."

I smiled at his words and raised my head again to look at him. "I'm very good to myself."

"As you should be."

"I'm cautious about who I trust," I said, my words hesitant.

"You don't say?" he chuckled, making no attempt to hide his sarcasm.

"I'm not that bad."

"Nah. You're cautious. And you're scrappy," he said.

"I'm not scrappy." I smacked his chest, and he tightened his hold on me.

"It's not a bad thing. You protect yourself. You don't let people in, because you don't want to be disappointed. I get that more than you know."

"What was it like being in the foster system?" I asked, rolling onto my stomach and propping up on my elbows so I could look at him. So I could look him in the eye and show him that he could trust me.

He cleared his throat. "It's not all bad, but it sure as hell wasn't all good. I was in some shitty homes. I saw things that kids should never have to see."

"Like what?" I whispered.

"Abuse. Physical and emotional. Not to me. No one ever laid a hand on me. But I kept to myself. I saw drug abuse at a young age, and I knew I'd stay far from that. But if you weren't someone who knew what you wanted out of life, you could have been drawn into it. You know, there was no guidance. No support emotionally."

My chest ached at his words, and I ran my hands through his hair. "And you knew at a young age what you wanted out of life?"

"I did."

"What did you want?"

"Freedom." He sighed. "Not to be dependent on anyone else. Not to ever be in a situation where I had to live under someone else's roof and follow their rules. I wanted to follow my own. Live in a home that felt safe, where there was food on the table and running water. A home that was clean and taken care of. A business that I controlled and worked at. Those were things I knew I wanted even as a kid."

"And you got them," I said.

"I almost fucked up with Caroline. I got her pregnant, even though we'd been safe. I'd never had unprotected sex, and she shows up at my door pregnant several months after our summer fling. She could have fought me for Harper, taken the one thing I care most about away from me. Luckily for me, she didn't want to be a mother, and I got to keep my baby girl. But that could have gone differently, as I was reminded today."

I sucked in a breath. I'd overheard some of their conversation. "Are you worried she'll be back?"

"I'm not. She's too selfish. Her fiancé doesn't want a kid from another dude. Her parents wanted her to give Harper up for adoption. But I let things go too far. I'm going to get an attorney and force the issue because I can't let her come in and out of Harper's life whenever the hell she feels like it. Not after what happened today. I'm going to need to have her put it in writing."

"Put what in writing?" I asked.

"That she doesn't want to be a mother. She's never contributed financially. She's never contributed emotionally. She doesn't get to call the shots," he said, his voice hard.

"Yeah. She's a real piece of work." I shook my head with disbelief. "I would have liked to give her a piece of my mind."

"I could tell. I appreciate the way you stepped up for Harper and stayed with her while I dealt with the mess that Caroline caused today."

"Unfortunately, it was familiar to me. The way she just showed up when it was a good time for her to do so and then wanted to put on a show. My father was very much that kind of parent."

"Yeah, it's a shame that you need a license to drive a car and to order a drink in a bar, but any selfish asshole can be a parent." He shook his head. "I should have put my foot down a long time ago."

"Well, you're doing it now, and that's all that matters. It sounds like this is the first time that Harper didn't want to be around her. So you're following her lead and fixing the situation. In the wedding business, we'd give you a hashtag for this type of behavior," I said with a laugh.

"A hashtag? What the hell does that mean?"

"You know, we do the hashtags for weddings. Like, hashtag 'here come the Cooneys.'"

He laughed and said, "'Here come the Cooneys'? I don't get it."

"Like 'here comes the bride.'" Now we were both laughing. "A hashtag can tell you a lot about a couple. Like Montana has always said that her hashtag would be hashtag 'you, me, and forever.'"

"Hmm . . . sounds very odd, but I get it. So what's my hashtag?" he asked.

"Yours would be hashtag 'hot daddy.'"

His body shook with laughter.

"And what about you, Violet Beaumont. You told me Montana's hashtag. You said it tells a lot about a person or a couple. What would your hashtag be if you ever walked down the aisle? Hashtag 'I'm going to wear the pants in this relationship'?"

"That's not bad, actually." I tipped my chin up and smiled at him. "But I don't think I'm the marrying type. The only way I'd ever have a wedding hashtag is if I felt confident enough to use the only one that I'd ever consider."

"Tell me," he said, surprising me that he wanted to hear it.

We'd just had sex for the first time. We didn't know where this was going, or if it would last longer than tonight. But he was pressing me for my wedding hashtag?

Clearly, Charlie Huxley and I have the strangest relationship.

"It's actually pretty simple, which is a shocker because I'm kind of a complicated gal." I chuckled. "But if in some alternate universe I wanted to get married, I'd insist on the hashtag 'love you, mean it.' It would have to be real. Because I've had a lifetime of not real."

"It seems simple enough. But I'm sort of baffled by your lack of interest in getting married," he said, his thumb moving along my collarbone. "You're a wedding planner, for God's sake. It's your holy grail, right?"

"Hey, consider yourself lucky. At least you know I'm not trying to lock you down." I smirked. "I believe in happily ever after for those who want it. But I don't think it's for everyone, and it's definitely not for me. But Montana was hell bent on me doing this business with her, so from a business perspective, I like it. Doesn't mean I have to do it."

"That would be like me being a contractor who refuses to fix what's broken in my house," he said over his laughter.

"Hey, I am who I am. I don't want the fairy tale."

"But you have a hashtag," he said, arching a brow when I looked up at him.

"I have a hashtag because my partner insisted that we pick one. Montana is a real stickler when it comes to the wedding planner rule book."

"So I'm guessing you don't plan on having kids?" he asked, as if he was trying to figure me out.

"I don't particularly care for most kids. But I adore Harper. She's not a normal kid, though. So sure, if I could have a couple Harpers, I'd be fine with it. But what if you get one of those hellions like Denise Quigley?"

He roared in laughter, and my head bounced on his chest. "She's a real piece of work. But I blame her mother. She's been taught that behavior."

I pretended to shiver dramatically. "She's a lot. I wanted to call her out so bad for what she said to Harper a while back. I tend to hold a grudge."

"I get it. When you love someone and you see them hurt, it doesn't go away. That's what I felt today with Caroline. She hurt Harps, and I won't stand by and allow her to do it again."

"Hashtag 'here comes Papa Bear,'" I said as he flipped me on my back and tickled me.

"Hashtag 'do you want to have sex again, Firefly?'"

"Oh, that's clever, Charles. Hashtag 'one more orgasm before we call this done.'"

He rolled his eyes. "Hashtag 'one day at a time, you smart-ass.'"

"Fine. Have your way with me, because tomorrow we might hate each other again."

"I never said I stopped hating you." His voice was all tease as he nipped at my bottom lip.

"Hashtag 'samesies, Charles!'" I said over my laughter.

And then he kissed me.

He really kissed me.

And I forgot that I was supposed to be careful.

Because at the moment, it was far too easy to get lost in this man.

So I'd allow myself tonight, and then I'd get my shit together tomorrow.

But tonight . . . I was going to enjoy every minute.

Because the good stuff in life never lasted long.

CHAPTER TWENTY

Charlie

I'd gotten a call first thing in the morning from Will that had both Violet and me throwing on our clothes and hopping in my truck. We'd spent the night together, and that was not something I'd done in a very long time.

Not since Harper was born.

But we'd raced over to her house because Will said it was an emergency. And the three of us were now standing in her backyard, staring down at a gaping hole beneath where the deck used to be.

"What does this mean?" She ran her hands through her hair, and I had a flash of that wild mane of blond waves spilling all around her shoulders while she rode me into oblivion last night.

Will shrugged. "We were going to start rebuilding the deck this morning, and by chance I took a look before we started, and lo and behold, there was a hole. I poked a broomstick in there, and this big-ass groundhog came running out. He took off into the tree line."

"So a groundhog was living beneath my house?" she said, shaking her head with disbelief as we all stared down at the gaping hole beneath her deck.

"Yep. Welcome to wildlife in Alaska," I said.

"Trust me, I already deal with Clifford Wellhung staring into our window at the office. But come on, now I've got to deal with a freaking groundhog? Can you just close the deck up and hopefully he's gone?"

"I wish it were that simple, Violet. I know you were planning to move back in this week. But I used the flashlight down there, and I'm afraid he's chewed through some of the electrical wiring and possibly the pipes that run to your laundry room." Will scratched the back of his neck as if he was nervous about telling her.

"That fucker is eating my house?" Violet shrieked.

"I think he's been at it for a while, and we just didn't notice. I should have closed that area up," he said.

"It could have happened to anyone," I said. "You weren't checking the backyard, because you've been focused on the interior. But we've got to make sure that we get everything repaired before we close it up. We'll have to build a wood box around it so he can't get in there at night while we're getting this repaired. And then we'll get the deck back on and secure the area around it."

"And how long will all of this take?" Violet asked as she crossed her arms over her chest.

"Probably around two weeks," Will said. "I'm real sorry about this, Violet. But if we don't fix this now, you could end up having another flood and all sorts of issues with the electrical. I already talked to the guys, and they all agreed to work the next two weekends to get this done for you. Everyone feels real bad about it."

Her features softened. I was learning that Violet Beaumont had a hard outer shell, and rightfully so. But beneath was a very warm, empathetic woman who cared a lot more about the people in her life than she let on.

"You don't need to do that. As long as the old ball and chain over here will let me keep staying in the guesthouse, it'll be fine." Her gaze locked with mine.

"Not a problem. We'll get it done and get you moved in as soon as we can," I said, trying to play it cool when the truth was—I was relieved she wasn't leaving yet.

We lived in a small town. Her house was not far from mine. But I liked knowing she was in my backyard most days.

I liked waking up to her being there for breakfast.

I liked how much time she was spending over at the house with me and Harper.

And that was saying a lot because I normally hated people coming into our space.

"And how do we get Chompers the groundhog to stay away?" she asked as she pushed some dirt around with the toe of her shoe.

"I'll build a box today to go over the area when we leave at night," Will said. "It'll keep him out, and he'll eventually move on."

"Sounds like a plan. I've got to get out of here, but if you need anything, let me know." I clapped him on the shoulder. "Thanks for catching this and getting it fixed."

"What's going on here?" Will chuckled as he waved his finger around in front of me. "Is Charlie in a good mood?"

I rolled my eyes, and Violet laughed.

"He does seem to be chipper today," Violet said with a smirk. "Maybe it was all the birthday cake he ate yesterday at Harper's party."

"Yeah, it must be the cake." I winked at her.

"Nah, there's something happening here," Will said, a wide grin on his face as he motioned between us. "I'm picking up on something."

"Well, how about you start picking up this mess from the groundhog and mind your own damn business," I said, trying to act annoyed but unable to hide the humor from my voice.

"See, he's still plenty grumpy." Violet bumped me with her shoulder.

"I don't know. He seems pretty happy to me," Will said with a laugh, and I shot him the bird.

"I'll call and check in with you in a few hours. I've got to drop this one off at some liquor lunch and then go pick up Harper from the McAffreys'."

"What's a liquor lunch?" Will asked.

"It's a boozy brunch, not a liquor lunch," Violet said over her laughter. "Me, Monny, and Blakely do these once a month. Mimosas and yummy food."

"I like the sound of that," Will said as we walked toward the door.

"Fix the wiring and the pipes, and then you can have a boozy brunch," I said as we walked outside.

"Are you freaking out?" Violet whispered once we got in the truck.

"About the groundhog?"

"No. About Will being suspicious about us." Her gaze searched mine.

I turned to look at her. "I don't give a shit what anyone thinks."

"I just don't want that to freak you out."

"Do I look freaked out? You're the one who looks freaked out. What's going on?"

"I just. You know. I don't know. We don't know." She threw her hands in the air. "I don't know what this is, Charlie. I'm not good at this."

"I haven't had a relationship in a very long time. I'm not fucking good at this either, but I'm also not freaking out."

"Why?" she asked as I pulled down the driveway and headed toward the Brown Bear Diner.

"Because we're friends no matter what. Because last night was fucking amazing. Because I like you." I cleared my throat, because that was a lot for me.

I pulled into the parking lot at the diner and put the truck in park.

"I'm a really good lover, aren't I?" she said. "I'm kidding. Last night was—amazing."

"Was that so hard?"

"That's what she said!" she said with a laugh. "And no, that wasn't so hard. It's just—I don't want to mess anything up, you know?"

"Hey. One day at a time. Go have some fun with the girls, and Harper and I will pick you up when you're ready."

"You don't have to do that. I can walk home," she said as she unbuckled herself.

"Stop being stubborn, Firefly. We're picking you up. Just text me when you're ready."

"Fine. I'll text you." She glanced around before lunging herself at me and kissing me. "Thanks for the ride, Charles."

I laughed as she got out of the truck, and I watched her walk inside.

What the hell was wrong with me?

I actually was in a good mood.

And that little blond smart-ass was the reason for it.

I left there and went to pick up Harper, who talked nonstop the whole way home about her birthday party.

About the pink balloons and the cake.

I knew we needed to have a conversation about Caroline, and I just wasn't sure how to bring it up.

"I'm glad you had a good party, baby girl." I helped her out of the truck, and we walked into the house.

"Is Violet home?" she asked.

"She went to meet Montana and Blakely for brunch. She'll be back later."

She sat down on the couch, and I made my way over to sit beside her.

"I wanted to talk to you about what happened yesterday with Caroline."

"I don't like that my mama just comes to see me on my birthday. She's a stranger. And remember, you told me about stranger danger, Daddy."

I nodded. "I understand that, and that's why I wanted to talk to you. When your mom left when you were a baby, I didn't really know what I was doing. And she came up with this idea to come visit you once a year on your birthday, and I agreed to it because I thought it was the right thing. I didn't want to rock the boat, and I was just happy that I got to have you with me every day, you know?"

"I always want to be with you. You're my favorite person, Daddy."

"You're my favorite person too, Harps." I tucked her long hair behind her ear. "But I didn't know what the right thing to do with your mom was, but I want to do what makes you happy."

"I don't need a mama because I have the best daddy around." She shrugged, her eyes wet with emotion, which told me this was something that had been weighing on her. "I don't want to see Caroline because I don't know her, and I don't like that she feels like a stranger."

"That's fair. I told her that I didn't think this was a good idea anymore. I wanted to make sure that's what you wanted. And if you change your mind and you want to know about her, or you want to see her, you just tell me, okay?"

"I will. I had fun with Violet yesterday. She made my party so special. I think she might be my best friend sometimes." She shrugged, and I chuckled at how not smooth she was about the change in conversation. My daughter was done talking about Caroline, and I got the message loud and clear.

"Yeah. Violet's good people, isn't she?"

"I like that you two pretend that you don't like each other but everyone knows that you do." She chuckled.

"She's pretty easy to like."

"Is she your girlfriend, Daddy?" she asked, smiling up at me with those rosy cheeks and that toothless smile.

"I don't know what she is, Harps. We're good friends and I like her," I said, feeling like a teenager being questioned by a parent.

"I think she likes you too." She climbed on my lap. "Sometimes when she's here it feels like we're a family. I like it."

Fuck. Was I messing things up by bringing Violet into Harper's life, when I didn't know where this was going?

"Friends can be part of your family too, right?" I asked.

"Do you think we'll still see Violet all the time when she moves back to her house?"

"Well, her house is going to take a little longer than we thought," I said, trying to hide the smile from my face. "She had a groundhog do some damage underground."

Her mouth fell open. "A groundhog ate Violet's house?"

"Well, I'd say he ate enough to keep her here for a few weeks." I rumpled the top of her head, and she giggled.

"Lily does her mama's makeup, and I wanted to see if I could do Violet's makeup with that makeup kit you got me for Christmas."

"I don't know what Violet's plans are after brunch, but you can practice on me if you want."

Her mouth dropped open, and she clapped her hands together. "I'm going to make you the prettiest daddy in Blushing!"

"Oh boy. Lucky me."

The shit I did for my little girl was not something I'd ever seen myself doing.

But seeing her smile was worth whatever torture she was about to put me through.

"I'll go set things up in my bathroom!" She jumped to her feet.

"I'll be in there shortly. I need to take care of a few things real quick. Give me five minutes." I pulled out my phone and scrolled through my contacts and found the name of a high school friend of mine, Logan Hawkins. She was an attorney now, and I'd just renovated her home last year, and she had a reputation for being a shark in the courtroom. I sent her a quick text.

Me: Hey, Logan. I may need some legal advice regarding Harper's mom and my custody rights. I wondered if this was something you could help me with.

Logan: Of course. This is what I do. Let's set up a meeting for tomorrow morning. Can you meet me at my office at 11am?

Me: I'll be there. Thank you.

Logan: Of course. See you tomorrow.

I made my way down the hallway toward Harper's bathroom.

"Ready for your makeover, Daddy?"

"As ready as I'll ever be, baby girl."

I glanced over at the container of glitter shadow and groaned.

Because I'd just agreed to let her make me sparkle like a fucking disco ball on New Year's Eve.

CHAPTER TWENTY-ONE

Violet

"Okay, ladies. Last round," Delilah said. She owned the Brown Bear Diner, and she was one of my favorite people in town.

"How does a boozy brunch of bottomless mimosas have a last round?" I asked before falling back in the booth in an eruption of giggles.

"That's a brilliant question," Montana said, her words slurring.

"And why are we the last people in the place?" Blakely hiccuped.

"Because dinner is starting in an hour. You ladies managed to drink more mimosas than the entire restaurant put together." The older woman smirked.

"But aren't you glad you listened to me about offering boozy brunch once a month? And then we moved it from boozy brunch to liquor lunch. It's an all-day affair." I tipped the last of my champagne and orange juice back.

"I am. Even if just to see you three in here acting like fools, it's worth it." She winked. "I need to get back in the kitchen to help with the transition to dinner, so take your time finishing up, but the mimosas are done."

"I'm texting Myles to come get me. Do you two need a ride?" Montana asked as she typed out a text on her phone.

"I'd love a ride," Blakely said.

I chewed on my fingernail. "Charlie said he'd come pick me up. Do you think I should text him?"

"Well, you did have sex with the man three times last night, I'd say you should let him pick you up." My best friend fell forward in laughter, and I rolled my eyes.

"Thank you for announcing it for the whole restaurant to hear." I sent a text to Charlie that I was done, but happy to walk home.

"No one is here but the three of us." Blakely hiccuped once again. "And I love that he doesn't want a one and done with you. Our little Vi is growing up."

I flicked a piece of pancake at her. "We're just taking it one day at a time. It'll probably be over by tomorrow."

"Why are you so doom and gloom about it? You know you like him," Blakely said, her brows arched.

Montana sighed dramatically. "She doesn't want to like him. Because if she likes him, he could hurt her. She's been let down by one too many people in her life."

"Thank you, Sigmund Freud, for sharing the inner workings of my psyche." I rolled my eyes. "I just don't like to expect things from people. I prefer to count on myself."

"I've never let you down, have I?" my bestie asked.

"No. But you're a woman. And a rare gem." I smiled as I reached for my water.

"And it took you the entire first year in college to finally put your guard down with me. Not everyone is going to let you down." She leaned her head on my shoulder before continuing. "I just love you so much, and I want you to know how easy it is to love you."

"Oh boy. Someone has had one too many glasses of bubbly," I said over my laughter.

"I've never let you down either, have I?" Blakely asked, her eyes wet with emotion now.

"Do not start crying. Why are you both getting weepy? I'm not upset. And no, you haven't let me down. You two would be in the small group of humans I love who are not assholes."

"There's a lot of us out there, Vi." Montana sat up, and tears ran down her face. "You just have shitty parents and an asshole sister. And a bad track record of ex-boyfriends. But otherwise—"

"Otherwise, what? That's kind of a lot. And stop crying. You're making things weird." I wiped her face with my napkin just as Myles walked in.

"Oh boy. Someone is three sheets to Emoville," he said, winking at his girl.

"Emoville. You stole that from me," I gasped.

"Hey, I'm hip on the wedding lingo. What can I say?" He shrugged. "Why are they both crying?"

"Cheap champagne and childhood trauma. You know, girl stuff." I glanced up as the door opened, and Harper came running toward our table.

"Vi, I got to do Daddy's makeup! Wait till you see him." She climbed right up on the booth and wrapped her arms around my neck. "I missed you."

She missed me.

I missed her.

"I missed you too, Harps." I hugged her tight as my gaze moved to the large man walking toward the table.

Broad shoulders. Long legs closing the distance. And that's when I saw it.

Blue glitter covered his eyelids.

Dark blush was on the apple of his cheeks.

And his hair was pulled back into two tiny pigtails on top of his head.

"What the hell is happening here?" Myles gaped at him.

"Hey. Earmuffs, dude. Harps is sitting right there," Charlie grumped.

"So, calling you out for looking like you're about to step onto a Broadway stage is offensive to Harper?" Myles asked.

"No. You can't say 'hell' in front of a kid," Harper said, shaking her head at him.

"Oh, shit. I'm sorry. I didn't know 'hell' was a bad word." He shrugged.

"I think 'shit' is worse," Blakely said, and the table erupted in laughter.

But my eyes never left the gorgeous man standing in front of me.

Yes, I had a good buzz going from the bottles of champagne we'd consumed over the last few hours.

Yes, I was still floating on air from the orgasms I'd received last night.

But none of that had anything to do with the reason that I was salivating as I took him in.

It was the glitter and the hair and the fact that he'd let his daughter give him a makeover simply because it made her happy.

Charlie Huxley is a good man.

A really good man.

I didn't know many, and he was showing me that they still existed.

"I think you look great," I said as Blakely and Montana looked at me and chuckled.

"Oh, she's got it bad," Montana said as she slid out of the booth and wrapped her arms around Myles.

"What do you got bad, Vi?" Harper asked.

"Nothing. Ignore them. I'm happy to see you guys, that's all."

"Well, dude," Myles said, "I'm not going to lie to you. I love that you're a good dad, but this whole look is a bit alarming. No offense, Harps. You're cute as hell. Oh wait. I can't say that. You're the cutest kid I know. But your dad looks a little strange with that hair and all the glitter."

"I'll give you a makeover next, Mr. Myles," Harper said through her giggles.

"I think that's a great idea," Charlie said with a look at his friend.

"I get it. She's impossible to turn down." Myles winked at Harper as we slid out of the booth together.

"Tell me about it." Charlie took Harper's hand, and then he did the most unexpected thing of all.

He reached for my hand too.

He interlocked our fingers, and I looked up to see my friends watching and smiling.

Normally this type of public affection would freak me out.

Maybe it was the buzz still coursing through my veins.

Or maybe it was just the man who was holding my hand.

But I liked it.

I liked it a lot.

We all said our goodbyes, and Charlie opened the passenger-side door for me before he helped Harper into the back seat and got her buckled.

As we drove home, Harper told me all about doing her father's makeup.

"He yelped out when I put the ponytail in his hair, Vi. He was being a big baby," she said over her laughter.

"Hey, you pulled my hair really hard," he huffed as he glanced over his shoulder at me and smirked.

"Maybe you have a sensitive scalp." I reached over and tugged on one of his pigtails.

"Ouch!" he said dramatically.

"Listen, I give you credit for leaving the house like this. That's a loyal daddy right there." I chuckled.

"Would your daddy not leave the house like this?" she asked.

The question was so innocent, yet it was a sore subject for me.

"No. My dad wasn't big on that kind of stuff."

"What's he like?" she pressed.

"Not everyone likes to talk about their families, baby girl," Charlie said as his hand found my thigh and he squeezed it.

"No. It's okay. I don't mind talking about it." I shrugged, placing my hand over his. "My dad left when I was a baby, and we don't have a great relationship now. But I have siblings that I'm close to, so I see him at family events, and he'll be here for my sister's wedding in a few weeks."

"He sounds like Caroline," Harper said. "Daddy's not going to make me see her anymore. If it makes you sad to see your dad, maybe you shouldn't see him anymore."

I never actually considered that. I was usually feeling wounded that I wasn't included. But she was right in a way—being around him did not make me feel good. It made me feel unwanted.

Unloved.

And that wasn't healthy for anyone.

"You're awfully smart for a seven-year-old," I said.

"Daddy! Vi's the first person to call me a seven-year-old. I'm not six anymore. I'm seven. And I am really smart. Super smart." She giggled as we pulled into the driveway and Charlie opened the garage.

Harper ran inside because she wanted to go set up her makeup for me to get a makeover next. Once we stepped into the house and Harper took off down the hall, Charlie stopped me. My back was pressed to the door, and he placed a hand on each side of me, caging me in.

"Your dad is an asshole, Firefly."

I nodded and smiled, because this man just somehow knew what I needed to hear.

"I know. And maybe Harper's right. Maybe I shouldn't be so accessible to a man who hasn't treated me well." I tipped my chin up.

"Well, you've probably spent a lot of time guarding yourself from others because of your relationship with him. When the person you should have been guarding yourself from all along was him. Other people might not let you down, you know?" He leaned forward and kissed my cheek.

It was sweet. Intimate in the strangest way.

Not sexy. Not passionate.

But there was a connection. An understanding.

"I've never thought of that."

"Listen, I've been guarded my whole life, so I'm not one to talk. But I'm just saying, you're all kinds of magic, Violet Beaumont. And I don't think that man should be the reason that you don't trust the rest of the world. He's the one who doesn't deserve you."

"What happened to the man who doesn't like to speak? I feel like you could be my therapist lately." I chuckled.

"I'd like to be a lot more than that," he said, his voice gruff as he whispered against my ear, his lips grazing the sensitive skin there as he spoke. "I'd like to strip you naked right here, turn you around, and fuck you senseless against this door. But I've got a little girl counting on me, so that'll have to wait."

My breaths were coming fast, and I searched his gaze when he pulled back. "You're an asshole, Charlie Huxley. Now I'm all flustered."

He took a step back and laughed. "Good. I wanted to make sure I hadn't run you off just yet."

"One day at a time. And we've made it through the first one, and I'm still here. How about you?"

"Me and my dirty thoughts aren't ready to run yet, Firefly." He grinned at me, and I chuckled, because the blue glitter was sparkling in the light shining down on him.

"I'm ready for you, Vi!" Harper shouted as she came running down the hall and took my hand. I glanced over my shoulder and found his heated gaze watching us.

"See you later, Charles," I said with a smile.

"Count on it."

I chuckled as I followed Harper down the hall.

I liked how I felt when I was here.

When I was with them.

Like I belonged.

It was equal parts exciting and terrifying.

CHAPTER TWENTY-TWO

Charlie

I dropped Harper at school and made my way to Violet's house to see how the deck was coming along. She'd stayed for dinner last night, but she'd left shortly after because the reality was, I still had a daughter to take care of.

We both agreed that we needed to figure out what this was before we started having sleepovers in front of Harper.

I'd never had a woman stay the night at my home, and I never thought I'd consider it.

But Violet was different.

All-consuming.

She'd come by for breakfast this morning, even though her oven was fixed.

She'd come over and cooked Harper and me breakfast.

We'd traded some sexy texts last night, and I was going out of my mind.

I wanted her in my bed.

I'd gone long stretches without sex many times over the years, but now that I'd been with Violet, it was all I could think about.

"Hey, boss. I thought you were working over at the hotel job today," Will said as he wiped his forehead with the sleeve of his shirt.

I nodded at Jason and Kory, two of our workers, as they continued laying out the planks for the deck.

"I have an appointment this morning. I just wanted to see how it was going over here. I'll be at the hotel all afternoon."

"That groundhog sure did some damage. I got a good look at the wires and the pipes, and he was awfully busy down there." Will chuckled. "I've got James coming to fix the wires this afternoon, and we'll get those pipes replaced this week."

"All right. That sounds good. Have you seen the groundhog around this morning?"

"Nope. I had things really fortified last night, so he probably figured out that we're onto him."

I glanced around. She had a nice piece of land, and the tree line wasn't too far off. We'd just need to make sure everything was closed up well.

"Okay. Thanks for getting this done. I appreciate it."

"No problem. I like it over here more than the hotel anyway." He shrugged. "It's quiet, and Violet always brings us treats when she stops by."

I snorted. "You're so easy."

"And you aren't?" he said. "I see the way you look at her. We all know there's something going on there."

"Everyone in town is talking about it," Kory said from a few feet away.

"I thought you guys were construction dudes. I had no idea I'd hired a bunch of gossipy schoolgirls."

Jason laughed. "Glass houses, boss. I heard you were at the Brown Bear Diner wearing pigtails and glitter yesterday."

This fucking town.

There were no secrets.

"Yeah, well, when you have a seven-year-old daughter, you come talk to me about how difficult it is to say no to her."

"From what I can tell, she isn't the only one you can't say no to." Will smirked, and I gave him the finger.

"Just get back to work. I've got a meeting, and then I'll be over at the hotel the rest of the afternoon if you need me."

I drove the short distance over to Logan Hawkins's law office.

Her assistant led me into her office as soon as I arrived, and I whistled at all the custom built-ins. "Nice office."

"Yeah, it's nice when the guy before you has it all done before he retires." She laughed and motioned for me to take a seat. "So tell me what's going on with Harper's mom."

I filled her in on our arrangement, and she listened intently, taking notes and nodding.

There was no judgment at all when she looked up at me.

"Okay, so I understand your concerns. She has clearly abandoned her child, as showing up one day a year is far from anything close to being considered a parent. She hasn't paid child support or contributed in any way to Harper's needs," she said, tapping her pen against her desk. "But I'm not going to lie to you, Charlie. It's complicated."

"How so?"

"Well, Alaska law does not allow the court to terminate one's parental rights. The court can restrict access, but it's not like she has access anyway, so it's an unusual situation."

"I'm just trying to do the right thing by my daughter. She was uncomfortable on her birthday, because Caroline feels like a stranger to her. And I get it. I wouldn't like that either." I scrubbed a hand down my face. "But I don't know how to handle the situation. I don't think she should just be able to show up once a year when it's convenient for her. I think I sort of went along with it all these years to keep the peace, do what I thought was best for Harps. But now it feels strange when she shows up. We have a life now, and it doesn't involve her in any way, shape, or form."

"Yep. I get that. We have a few options," she said as she reached for her coffee mug and took a sip.

"Okay. Let's hear them."

"We could get a court order for child support and back child support and force her hand."

I immediately interrupted. "No. I don't want money. Her family has a lot of it, and I don't want this to turn into a pissing match on who has more. Because I'll lose. This isn't about the money. There's nothing more important to me than supporting my daughter and providing a good home for her. I'm happy that I can do that on my own. This is about the emotional effects of a woman showing up once a year and calling herself a mother. It was fine, until it wasn't. The minute my daughter was not okay with the situation, I felt the need to do something about it."

"Okay. So we're not looking for any financial support."

"We are not," I said adamantly.

She put her hands up. "Okay, got it. The goal is to just stop with the once-a-year visits. We aren't looking for a relationship or any support. So we could press her and force her hand."

"How would we do that?" I asked.

"You know, it's all risky, Charlie. Because if by chance we press this and she in turn decides that she wants to be a mother, we could be opening a can of worms. She could fight back."

I nodded. My stomach twisted at the thought. But I knew in my gut that this woman just didn't have it in her. She was far too selfish to want any sort of custody.

"I get that, and it makes me uneasy. But I'm fairly confident that she doesn't have any interest in being a parent."

"Okay, so we can test the waters. We could file a dispute about her visits, point out the fact that she has abandoned her child and has not been there emotionally or financially. We can mention the emotional toll her visits are taking on Harper, as they don't know one another. We can put a bunch of legal jargon in there and suggest that she either step up to the plate or relinquish her parental rights."

"Is that a thing?"

"A parent in the state of Alaska can voluntarily relinquish their parental rights to their child in writing and sign it in the presence of a court. So if you feel confident that she will not bite at the opportunity to step up, then I would say this is your best shot to get her to relinquish her rights."

I sighed. This wasn't something I'd ever set out to do. I didn't even know Caroline well when she got pregnant. It was a whirlwind relationship. We were young. But I'd been okay with the arrangement up until now, and I wasn't looking to pick a fight. I just wanted my daughter to be happy. And seeing the toll this last visit had taken on her, and the shift in her attitude about seeing Caroline, I felt like my hands were tied.

But there were risks, and that was terrifying.

"Can I have a little time to think this over?"

"Of course. And keep in mind, we could serve her and she could choose to ignore you." She shrugged. "But, we could also take her to court, prove that she's abandoned her child, and try to go that route. That would drag everyone through it, though, so you'd have to be committed. The letter seems like the best option, if you aren't looking for a big fight."

I nodded. "I'm not. I just want to do the right thing."

"All right. Take all the time you need, and I'll be here when you're ready."

She stood and came around her desk, extending an arm. "You're a good dad, Charlie. Harper is lucky to have you."

"I'm the lucky one."

"Let's see if you're saying that during her teenage years." She chuckled. "I really tortured my parents."

"I highly doubt that." I smirked. "I've heard that I'm going to be in for it. But my baby girl has always been different. She's a special one."

She clapped me on the shoulder. "Well, the apple doesn't fall far from the tree, my friend. We'll talk soon."

I left her office and was sitting in my truck, unsure about what to do, when my phone vibrated.

Firefly: How did the meeting go?

Me: I don't know. It's complicated. I don't have a fucking clue what to do.

Firefly: Where are you?

Me: Parking lot at Logan Hawkins' law office. Why?

Firefly: Stay put.

I didn't know what she was up to, but I did as she asked, because I was still trying to figure this shit out.

What if I picked a fight and lost?

What if her parents decided to throw money at the situation and tried to take Harper from me?

Was that even an option?

Logically I knew that couldn't happen. I'd been her only parent since birth. But money could be a powerful tool, and the thought made me sick to my stomach.

There was a knock on the passenger-side window of my truck, and I startled.

I unlocked the door when I saw Violet on the other side.

"Hey. It sounded like you needed to talk things out."

"I thought you had a meeting with the tent people this morning for your sister's wedding?"

"And they'll still be there when we're done. It's fine, I promise. Tell me what happened," she said, turning her body to face me.

I filled her in on the different options I'd learned about, including the one I was leaning toward—the letter, in hopes of her relinquishing her rights voluntarily.

"That does sound like the best option. What are you hesitant about?"

I blew out a breath. "You know, the day Harps was born, I was terrified. Fucking terrified. I didn't know how to be a parent. Hell, most days I'm just making it up as I go, you know? So who the fuck am I to tell someone they shouldn't be a mom?"

"Who the fuck are you?" she asked. "You're Charlie fucking Huxley, that's who. You're the best dad I've ever known. The dad who gets his hair and makeup done just to see his daughter smile. The dad who asks how to make pink pancakes because he knows that's what his little girl wants. The dad who shows up every single day for Harper. You know what a parent is, Charlie. You're the hashtag." She smiled.

"What hashtag is that?"

"Hashtag 'love you, mean it.' You show it. You feel it. And you live it." She took my hand in hers. "And Caroline is not it. And your daughter is telling you that she's uncomfortable with the situation, so you're trying to fix it the best way you can."

I nodded. "Yeah. I guess there's this fear that she'll push back. That she'll let her ego get involved and fight for Harper just for the sake of winning and not losing."

"I get that," she said. "And I don't know all the different legal things that can happen in a custody battle like this. But I know what a good parent looks like, and I'm looking at him. Caroline is not a parent. Hell, she's not even a friend. She doesn't call and check in. She shows up one day a year. That is not a woman who seems like she would want to fight to be a mother. But I also understand being scared, because you have something to lose."

"I have everything to lose," I said as a deep pain settled in the middle of my chest.

"So then, there's your answer, Charles." She moved across the seat and climbed onto my lap. She placed a hand on each side of my face as her gaze locked with mine. "There is too much at risk. So maybe when she calls once a year, you change the way things happen. You don't let it happen at Harper's party. You tell her how it's going to go down."

"But Harper doesn't want to see her at all," I said, shaking my head.

"You explain to Harper next year when the time comes that you are setting ground rules with Caroline. About when she can visit and what an age-appropriate gift looks like. You can be honest with her about some of this, you know? She'll appreciate how hard you're trying. And if she doesn't want to see her, you go with her to a public place, and Harper can tell her that, and you go from there. She left immediately when she felt rejected at the party. She won't keep coming back if she feels unwanted. She's a complete narcissist. When it doesn't serve her, she'll stop showing up."

I thought it over, and she'd made a good point.

The risk was too high. The possibility that she could push back, even though it was highly unlikely, was still possible.

As much as I wanted this to go away, the worst-case scenario forced me to reconsider doing this.

I'd never had someone I could talk to about Harper.

But Violet Beaumont was not just a woman I was painfully attracted to.

She was not just a woman who got under my skin when she argued with me.

She'd become more than I'd realized.

She'd become someone I relied on.

Someone I trusted.

Someone I thought about when I wasn't with her.

Someone I wanted when I was with her.

"Okay. That's what I'm going to do. I appreciate it." I tucked the hair behind her ear, my large palm covering the side of her neck as my thumb stroked her jaw.

"'Okay'? You're actually listening to me?"

"Yeah. I agree with you on this. I didn't know what to do, but you're right, the answer is clear. There's too much at risk. I need to ride it out."

"I like agreeable Charlie."

"Don't get used to it. He doesn't come around often," I said as I tugged her closer, grazing my lips against hers.

"I think you're a lot softer than you let on, Charlie Huxley." She nipped at my bottom lip.

"Nothing soft here, Firefly." I thrust forward, letting her know just how much I wanted her.

"Take me home and show me."

"Yeah? You don't have to get back to work?" I asked.

"I do. But right now, I just want to be with you."

I attempted to pull the seat belt over both of us, because I wanted to keep her right here and drive home as fast as possible.

She laughed. "I'm not sitting on your lap while you drive."

"Fine. Buckle up, Firefly. That's all I needed to hear."

She was still laughing as I pulled out of the parking lot.

I couldn't get her home fast enough.

CHAPTER TWENTY-THREE

Violet

The last two weeks had gone by in a blur, since we'd been swamped at the office, and I'd spent all my free time with Charlie and Harper.

"Monny is still at her meeting?" I asked Blakely.

"Yep. She said she'd be in around lunchtime."

"But you're all glowy and floaty this morning," she said. "Very un-Vi-like. You have a meeting with your stepmonster and Velveeta, yet you aren't spewing venom."

I dipped my hand in the candy jar, reaching for a handful of Skittles. *The breakfast of champions.*

"Well, two weeks after Chompers the groundhog from hell attacked my pipes and electrical, I'm finally moving into my house this weekend, and that's exciting."

"Nice try. You've known you were moving all week. I think you like being in a relationship. You're less bitter. More content," she said, dodging the Skittle I launched at her head.

"I'm hardly in a relationship. It's a day-by-day thing." I shrugged.

"It's been two weeks of your whole 'one day at a time' thing, so I'd say things are going well. Did you have breakfast over there this morning?"

"Yes. His oven is better than mine."

She roared in laughter.

"Violet Delphinium Beaumont," she said as she walked toward me and placed a hand on each side of my face, "it's okay to be happy."

No. She. Didn't.

She knew I hated my middle name.

My mother was clearly bitter about my father leaving her, so she'd tortured me with an over-the-top name.

"For the record, being happy tends to be the kiss of death. I'm not happy. I'm just—fine. Now if you don't mind, I need to go meet with Velveeta and Pissy."

She laughed hysterically as I marched to my office.

She was right. I'd been in a ridiculously good mood lately.

I'd fallen into a routine with Charlie. I wasn't spending the night at his house, because we didn't want to confuse Harper.

Actually, he wanted to talk to Harper about our relationship.

I was the one who was hesitant.

Who knew what would happen after I moved back to my place. I wouldn't be living in their backyard. What if we realized it had just been a convenience thing?

I would never risk turning Harper's world upside down, when she had a good thing going with just her and her dad.

I wouldn't be the person who let her down.

Speaking of letdowns, I clicked on the link, and there they were.

All three of them.

My father. Missy. Velveteen.

"Violet, it's so nice to see you," my father said. "You're looking well."

"Thanks. Nice to see you." I fiddled with my paperwork because Missy's eyes were assessing me as they always did.

"The wedding is literally right around the corner. Are you sure you have everything handled?" she asked.

So much for a friendly greeting.

"This is what I do for a living, Missy. I assure you, we've got everything covered. I'm just waiting on you, Velveteen, to choose between the two floral arrangements I sent you."

"And this is where I tap out. I just wanted to say hello," my father said as he waved at the camera. He always appeared slightly nervous around me. Maybe it was guilt or shame, who knows.

Missy waved him off and I said a quick goodbye as he left the screen.

"I like them both—could we combine the arrangements?" my sister said.

"I don't think that would look good," Missy blurted out, arching a brow at the screen as if she was waiting for me to back her up.

"I like them both a lot, too, and they actually complement one another." I paused, taking a breath because it pained me to say my next words. "But I agree with Missy that combining them would be tough, because it might be too much color in one arrangement. But what about using both, and placing them at every other table? I think it would be really beautiful."

"Oh, I like that idea." Velveteen looked to her mother.

"I think it's tacky. They should be uniform. This isn't a barn wedding," Missy hissed.

Do barn weddings have multiple floral arrangements?

"Actually, it's very trendy. The two arrangements coordinate well. The last couple to use this style was Harry Simon and Bailey Clark." I had to contain my smile, because I knew this would stick it to Missy and have Velveteen salivating. They were a Hollywood power couple who'd put our town on the map. They were also the reason my sister wanted to be married here. "Their wedding was featured in *People* magazine, so I don't think anyone would call their reception tacky."

"We're doing it. I want all the bells and whistles," my sister said.

"Fine. And you've made sure everything is set for the accommodations, right?" my stepmother asked.

"Mom. She's already told us that she's checked on all of that. The wedding party is booked at the hotel, and so are we."

It was a rare moment where my sister was standing up for me, so I'd take it.

"I'm just double-checking. Remember that time we all met in New York for New Year's, and Violet hadn't booked her hotel room?" My stepmother gave me a pointed look.

"Ahh . . . yes. I recall that trip well." I cleared my throat. "I was in college, and I thought you were booking my room, Missy. As you'd booked all of my siblings' rooms, I'd assumed I would be sharing a room with them."

It brought me back to a place that I didn't like.

That feeling of being rejected.

Of not fitting in.

Of being hyperaware that I was an outsider in this family.

I fucking hated that she had the power to make me feel this way. No matter how confident and self-assured I was, there was still this little girl inside me who remembered that pain too well.

She shook her head, as if my argument made no sense. "We got a room for the girls and a room for the boys. They were much younger than you. You were an adult and responsible to book your own room. Luckily they had one available, or you would have messed up the whole trip."

Yes. The pricey hotel room had maxed out my credit card.

"That's what happened?" Velveteen said. "She's only a year older than me, Mom. I never knew that was the issue. I thought she hadn't told you she was coming."

Plot twist. Your mother is a real biatch, Velveteen.

"I was always coming. But it was a long time ago, and we've all moved on." I met Missy's gaze, and she quickly looked away. "You're welcome to call the hotel and double-check your accommodations for yourself."

"I think we're good to go, Violet," my sister said, her gaze softer now. "I appreciate you handling all of this so I can focus on the honeymoon."

"She's getting paid to handle all of this. It's actually her job," Missy said without taking so much as a breath before insulting me. "It's how she makes a living."

"Thank you, Velveteen. I'm happy to plan your wedding. And yes, Missy, this is my job. My business, that I've built with my partner from the ground up. And we also charge for weddings, which I've obviously waived the fee for your wedding, as Velveteen is family. So, just to be clear, I'm not getting paid to plan this wedding."

My stepmother looked startled that I'd called her out. I wasn't someone who held back normally, but my discomfort with my father and his wife had always left me more withdrawn than I'd usually be.

And I was over it.

I was an adult.

A successful adult who was living her best life.

"It's what family does for one another," she said, her voice quieter now, as her daughter gaped at her.

"I couldn't agree more. Sort of like booking a hotel room for *all of your children*. Leaving one to fend for themselves would be cruel, right?"

Her eyes widened, but she didn't speak.

"Yeah. That's what I thought." I turned my attention back to my sister. "Everything is covered. I'll let the florist know about your decision for both arrangements."

"Thank you, Violet," Velveteen said. "And did you hear from Ralph's family finally?"

"I did. They weren't able to get a room at the same hotel that you're staying in because it's all booked up, but I found them a place nearby, and I made sure they secured the rooms." I forced a smile, because trying to manage Ralph's family was like trying to manage a pack of wild coyotes.

They were unresponsive, and when I finally did reach them, they'd always say they'd get back to me with a decision soon.

And weeks would pass.

Maybe they weren't happy about the wedding.

Maybe they were just attentionally challenged, like their attentionally challenged son.

"Thank you for making sure they were covered," she said.

Missy had gone completely silent. *Maybe I should put her in her place more often.*

"Not a problem. I'm sure we'll be talking a lot over the next two weeks, so just keep me posted if anything comes up, and I'll do the same," I said. I looked up to see Charlie standing in my doorway.

I tried hard to keep from smiling so big I'd give my excitement away.

"Bye, Violet." Velveteen waved and Missy forced a smile, and I said a quick goodbye and ended the Zoom.

"What's going on here?" I said, arching a brow. "Did I violate a parking rule at the house? Set off a fire alarm? Step on a flower bed?"

He chuckled. A sexy-as-hell grin spread across his handsome face. His jaw was peppered in day-old scruff, and his blue eyes were darker than normal. "Nah. I thought I'd take you on a lunch date. Just you and me."

"You want to go on a date with me, Charles?" I said, trying to play it cool as my heart raced at his words.

We spent so much time together. Usually, it was the three of us, which I loved.

When we actually got time alone, we were all over each other and trying to sneak in a quickie.

"I want to go on a date with you, Firefly."

"Okay." I sucked in a breath. "Let's go eat lunch."

I grabbed my purse and moved toward him. He held out a hand and intertwined his fingers with mine.

"You're really pulling out all the stops." I chuckled. "You know I'm a sure thing, right?"

"Doesn't mean I don't want to hold your hand," he said.

Blakely's eyes widened when we came around the corner just as Montana walked through the door, and she beamed at us.

"Where are you off to?" she asked.

"I'm going to lunch." I tucked my teeth between my lips.

"I'll bet you are." A mischievous smile spread across her face. "Have fun, you two."

Charlie opened the passenger-side door of his truck, and I slipped in. The man was always a gentleman, even when he was annoyed with me. But today he seemed a little nervous. Like he had a secret.

"We aren't going to the Moose Brew?" I asked as he turned in the opposite direction.

"Nope."

"Charles, are you taking me to your house for a little afternoon delight?" I asked, wondering if he'd just used the lunch date as a way of getting me out of the office. Though he knew me well enough to know that I'd have sneaked home with him without hesitation.

"Are you always this impatient?" he asked over a chuckle. "Actually, I already know the answer to that. You're the most impatient woman I know."

"Yet, you can't seem to stay away from me," I teased.

"Guilty as charged." He pulled into the driveway at my house.

There were no work trucks there, which was a first.

"Where is everyone?" I asked.

"We wrapped up a day early. I wanted to bring you here to show you."

It was sweet.

Thoughtful.

My heart thumped rapidly in my chest.

Threatening to explode.

I wasn't used to surprises, but Charlie Huxley was feeling like one big surprise lately. He'd convinced me to stay away from the house this week, as he didn't want me to see things until they were done.

We both made our way up the walkway, and I stopped him at the door. "Why do you seem nervous? Did you not hang the new light fixture in the laundry room that I left in there?"

"You mean the one you changed for the third time?" One side of his mouth turned up in a crooked smile.

"Yep. That's the one."

"Find out for yourself." He pushed the door open.

My mouth fell open, because all my furniture had been moved back in. We were supposed to do that this weekend. I'd had it all in storage.

"When did you do this?" I just stood there, moving my head slowly and taking it all in.

"I had the guys bring it all here over the last two days. I remembered how you'd had it set up, and Montana met me here early this morning to help me get it all arranged just right."

"She said she had a meeting." I shook my head with disbelief because it looked so good with the new floors, the farmhouse chandelier hanging above, and the area rug that I'd purchased a few weeks ago.

"She did. She was meeting with me." He laughed, but I could hear the hesitation.

This was why Charlie seemed so nervous.

"Were you nervous that I wouldn't like it?" I turned to face him.

He didn't even deny it. "No. I've just never done anything like this for anyone. I mean, aside from Harper."

I took his hands in mine. "No one's ever done anything like this for me before, so thank you."

I stood up on my tiptoes and kissed him.

When I pulled back, he smiled down at me. "Come on. Let me show you your new home."

I nodded.

Because as much as I wanted to pretend that I was fine.

This was so much more.

I. Was. Happy.

For the first time in my life, I was really happy.

CHAPTER TWENTY-FOUR

Charlie

I'd never been a romantic guy. The few women I'd dated before I had Harper had let me know that.

But home renovations were my thing, and I wanted to make this perfect for Violet. She'd worked hard to buy her first home, and then having it flood shortly after had been upsetting, to say the least.

So I'd asked Montana to help me first thing this morning, and we'd spent several hours pulling it all together to surprise her.

All the guys had shown up to help me get the furniture in the right places. Montana then directed us about where to put everything, and where to hang everything as well.

"Charlie," Violet whispered when she saw the chandelier hanging over the kitchen counter.

Yes, she'd changed her mind multiple times, and I'd hung the second one two weeks ago. But then last week she'd sent me a photo from an antique store of yet another chandelier. She said that she'd never seen anything in her life that was more perfect for the kitchen. I'd of course acted annoyed and told her we were done hanging light fixtures, and she hadn't purchased it. But I'd gone down the next morning and bought it for her and hung it up yesterday.

"I hope that's still the most perfect chandelier you've ever seen for the kitchen, because I swear I'm not changing it again." I chuckled.

She lunged herself at me and wrapped her arms around me. Her body started shaking, and I realized she was crying.

"Hey, it's a chandelier. It's not that big of a deal. I agree it's perfect for the space."

She pulled back and swiped at her tears. "That was really nice of you. Really, really nice of you."

"Maybe we're both nicer than we think. You did blow up a couple hundred balloons for Harper's birthday."

She smiled and swiped at her cheeks. "Damn straight. I don't know if you know this, but Denise Quigley is still talking about that birthday party."

I laughed. "Yeah, I heard you and Harps whispering about it last night."

"Hey, Denise Quigley knows the truth. Harper Huxley had the best party in town."

I shook my head as she walked around the island to check out all the details. She'd seen a lot of the finished work, but with everything moved in, it felt more like a home.

"I love this green range so much. The brass hardware just gives it such a vintage vibe. It just all looks so good put together."

"You've got a really good eye. I think you could easily flip homes for a living if you weren't busy planning weddings," I said.

"Coming from Charlie Huxley, that's quite a compliment. I know how particular you are about your finishes." She paused at the built-in banquette. "Oh my gosh. You put the cushions on. How good does this look?"

"Gorgeous," I said, but I was looking at her. Not the banquette. I'd seen enough of that already.

She took her time going through the space, admiring the built-ins in the family room. Taking in the sconces and light fixtures. She was thrilled with the way the guest room had come together with the shiplap on the walls and the curtain panels she'd picked for the space. She paused in the laundry room and squealed when she saw the light fixture that had been moved in there, along with the custom cabinets I'd built and painted a sage green for her. She reminded me how much she loved the wainscotting in the bathroom, because it looked perfect with the vintage vanity she'd found, which we'd added a sink to.

Her home could easily be featured in a magazine. It was detailed and stylish and very unique.

She'd poured her heart into every inch of the design, and it showed.

I'd been the dick who was annoyed by all the changes, but in the end, she'd been spot on with everything.

"All right, the last thing to see is my bedroom." She winked, which made me laugh.

I wrapped my arms around her, putting her back to my chest as we walked toward the door.

"Open it."

She pushed the door open, and she laughed. "What in the world is this?"

"The balloon fairy must have come to welcome you to the neighborhood."

"Charlie," she said, pushing out of my embrace and kicking a few balloons as she laughed some more. "This has to be three hundred balloons in here."

"It's two hundred and ninety-eight," I said dryly. "Two popped on the drive over."

"When did you do this?"

"I stayed up until three a.m. blowing these damn things up. And you had sexted me some dirty message before you went to bed, so I got stuck doing these with a bad case of blue balls. And you weren't kidding about the scars on the fingers. Tying this many balloons is a huge pain in the ass." I held out my hands to show her my blisters. "I've built custom wall systems that left my hands in less pain than these damn balloons."

She ran her fingers over my hands, soothing in every way. "Balloons are no joke. That fairy must have thick skin, huh?"

"I had to hide them from you and Harper, so I loaded them into the truck in the middle of the night."

"With a bad case of blue balls." She had a goofy smile on her face.

"I'll live. It's worth it to see you smile like this. I wanted you to know that the fairy showed up for you too."

"You're full of surprises, Charles." She sighed. "And I think we should rectify this whole blue balls situation."

Before I could respond, she dropped to her knees right there in the middle of a pile of a couple hundred green and peach balloons.

"You don't need to rectify anything." My voice was already gruff at the sight of her down on her knees. "I'm fine."

But she was already undoing my belt and unzipping my jeans while looking up at me with this heated gaze like she wanted this as much as I did.

She had my briefs down in a matter of seconds, and my dick sprang free, already rock hard.

"Fuck," I grunted as she circled the tip with her tongue and her hand wrapped around the base, stroking me a few times.

She looked up at me one last time before she wrapped her lips around me and took me in.

Inch by glorious inch.

Her lips gliding up and down my shaft as she took me deeper.

Fuck me. Nothing had ever felt better.

Her tongue swirled around as my tip hit the back of her throat.

My hands tangled in her hair as I groaned and moaned with every movement.

Harder.

Faster.

My eyes fell closed as my hips bucked into her mouth and she met me thrust for thrust.

I tugged at her hair because I couldn't hold on for another second.

I was there.

So fucking there.

"Violet," I shouted in warning, but she just kept going.

A guttural sound left my mouth as I went over the edge, coming harder than ever before.

And she stayed right there.

Taking every last drop.

My breaths were coming hard and fast, and I stroked the hair away from her face until my breathing slowed.

She pulled back, making a popping sound as my dick left her lips. She wiped her mouth with the back of her hand and smiled up at me, and I swear I'd never seen anything sexier.

"That was fucking amazing," I said, my voice gruff.

"Blue balls all gone?"

"You found the cure, baby." I chuckled, pulling her to her feet.

"Thanks for doing all this," she said as I tucked myself back in and buttoned my jeans.

I scooped her up over my shoulder fireman-style, catching her off guard. I tossed her on the bed and hovered above her. "You don't get to do that without me returning the favor."

"You kind of rebuilt my house and moved me back in. I'd say we're more than even, Charles," she purred.

"Not even fucking close. Lift this skirt up. Now," I demanded as I pulled her booties from her feet and tossed them on the floor. She had her skirt hiked up, and I reached down and tore away the scrap of lace in one swoop.

She gasped. "Did you just tear my panties?"

"I sure as fuck did." I smiled down at her. "I just watched you take my cock between your lips over and over. We're not going anywhere until I bury my face between these thighs and you come on my lips."

Her eyes widened. "For a man of few words, you sure say the right ones."

"I'll replace the panties. Spread those legs for me, baby."

She did as I asked, her chest rising and falling. I was already hard as steel again. I licked from one end to the next before I devoured every inch of her. Licking and sucking as she writhed beneath me.

"Charlie, Charlie," she panted as she tugged at my hair.

I slipped my tongue inside, knowing just what she needed. She bucked against me with a fury.

Her thighs tightened around me.

A gasp left her mouth, and her body quaked.

And she went right over the edge as I licked every drop that she gave me.

I couldn't get enough.

I lifted my head and smiled at her as I climbed up next to her and pulled her onto my chest.

"You really are a cuddler, aren't you?"

"I don't get to do this often, because you never sleep in my bed," I said, because I loved giving her shit. But the truth was, I wanted more.

She pushed up on her elbows and looked at me. "Do you want me in your bed, Charlie Huxley?"

"I do."

"When Harper's at school?" she asked.

"No. I think it's time to tell Harper that we're dating." I tucked her hair behind her ear.

"Why?"

"Because I'm fucking crazy about you. And I know it's scary. This is not the norm for me. But I'm not running from something good just because I'm scared. Can you say the same?" I asked.

"Maybe I'm fucking crazy about you too," she said, smiling.

"So we'll talk to her, and that way we won't have to sneak around. I am allowed to date, you know. I'm a grown man."

She chuckled. "If you tire of me, I'm not giving Harper up."

"Why would you say that?" I asked. "I won't tire of you, Violet. It's not my style. I want this. I haven't wanted this for a very long time. But I do. And I want you to trust it. To trust me. To trust what you're feeling."

Her gaze was wet with emotion. She put her hand on her heart. "I'm feeling so much, and it terrifies me."

"I know it does. But I promise it'll be okay. You've got to trust in something, Firefly. Not everyone is going to hurt you." I'd never spoken to a woman like this before, but I'd never had a connection with a woman like this before.

We were more alike than we wanted to admit.

Both of us so guarded.

But I didn't want to guard myself against her.

She made me feel things I didn't know I could feel.

"I know you don't want to hurt me, Charlie," she whispered. "And I don't want to do anything to hurt you or Harper."

"Then don't run. That's the only thing that will hurt us. Just stay right here."

She looked down at me. "Okay. I'm going to stay right here."

"So, we're doing this." I tugged her back down on my chest. "It only took thirty-five chandelier changes and four hundred balloons, and she's finally agreed to stay."

Her body shook with laughter.

"You're hilarious," she said.

"Tell me how the meeting with Pissy and Velveeta went," I asked.

Her head shot up. "Wow. You are definitely Team Violet."

"Damn straight, woman."

She settled back down on my chest and told me all about her call. About the comment Missy had made about the hotel room in New York when a family vacation had been planned, but she was expected to pay for herself while her other siblings were paid for. I was appalled at the way they'd treated her.

I fucking hated them for doing that to her.

I could picture a young Violet, all stoic and brave, acting like her shield would protect her, but I knew she probably went home and cried alone that night.

I was enraged on her behalf.

"It felt good to remind her of how it all went down," Violet said.

"You aren't one to usually hold back. What is it about your family that's different?" I asked.

She tipped her head up to look at me. "I think that as a kid, I just felt like I didn't fit in, and I probably thought it was due to something I'd done. I don't know. I figured my dad rejected me because there was something wrong with me." She sighed. "But now that I'm older, I realize it has nothing to do with me. I was a baby when he left. And I sure as hell am not going to apologize for being born."

"Damn straight. I'm guessing your stepmom just resents the fact that he had a family before her. But I can't imagine turning my back on Harper just because I met someone else. There's nothing that would ever make me walk away from my baby girl," I said.

She nodded. "Yeah. Seeing the way you are as a father has really opened my eyes. He's not the victim in the situation. He's a weak man who hasn't stepped up for me. I don't respect that. And I don't need to try to make something work when it's terrible. What am I even fighting for? They can take me or they can leave me. I don't need my father's love to survive. I've survived a long time without it."

"Trust me when I tell you, it's his loss."

"The tricky part is that I have siblings that I love. And they have a different relationship with my father and Missy, so it makes things a little more complicated."

"I get that. But you can have boundaries for what you'll tolerate," I said.

She smiled. "I can't believe we're talking about this stuff. Especially after the orgasms."

I laughed and said, "I'm glad you're sharing this with me."

"It's a lot, Charles. But we're not talking about them anymore, because today is a happy day. Especially after this epic surprise." She blew out a breath. "So, you either need to feed me now, or I'm going to get up and ride you like a stallion."

"Can I take both?" I asked.

"Good answer." She laughed as she moved on top of me.

My fingers interlaced with hers, and it was on the tip of my tongue to tell her how I felt.

I am in love with Violet Beaumont.

But it wasn't the time to tell her just yet.

CHAPTER TWENTY-FIVE

Violet

"Well, I've received twelve calls from Missy Beaumont today while you two have been over at the venue mapping things out." Blakely pursed her lips. "She's a real piece of work, Vi."

I chuckled. "Oh, trust me. I have years of therapy that supports this statement."

"She is so impatient. She asked me if you'd checked the hotel reservation four times. I assured her you have checked. What is her deal?" she grumped, which was rare because Blakely was never in a foul mood. But no one knew more than me how difficult Missy could be.

"That's on brand for her," I said, my voice light and unaffected. Something had shifted in me, and I was reacting differently to my family.

The phone rang, and Blakely groaned. Montana offered to answer, but I reached over the counter and grabbed it.

"The Blushing Bride. This is Violet, how can I help you?"

"This is Missy. I'm glad you finally decided to show up to work. I've tried your cell phone several times as well. My daughter is getting married in a few days, and I need you to be responsive."

I leaned against the desk. "I've been at work since seven this morning. I'm trying to plan my sister's wedding, so my phone is off when I'm working with contractors to get the venue mapped out. What do you need, Missy?"

"I need to know that the hotel has been confirmed," she hissed.

"I told you the hotel was confirmed on our last call. Blakely told you the hotel was confirmed each time you've called today. We are busy trying to get things ready over here. I'm a wedding planner, not a travel agent. Go ahead and call the hotel yourself, and please stop calling the office with ridiculous questions. We've got a lot on our plates," I said, glancing down at my fingernails and realizing I'd need a manicure before the wedding.

"I thought you handled this stuff?"

"I was just kind enough to do it for you, because you're family by default. But we don't normally handle travel arrangements, nor do we allow clients to harass us after we've assured them things were handled. So this whole back-and-forth ends now. Velveteen and I are in contact daily. Unless you're calling with a question that hasn't been answered, go ahead and email me, and I'll get back to you when I can." I reached for some Skittles as Montana and Blakely stared at me with wide eyes.

"Fine. I'll call the hotel myself."

"Wonderful. I'm sure they will love that. Have a good day." I ended the call.

Damn. That felt good.

"I mean, I'm used to this side of you, but just not with your family. It's about damn time." Montana wrapped her arms around my neck. "Proud of you, Vi."

I was proud of me too.

"Thank you. If she calls again, just say you will forward it to my voice message." I reached for a few more Skittles. "Okay, we've got lots to do to get ready for this wedding. I'm heading over to the florist to look at the samples she put together, and then I've got a Zoom meeting with the DJ that Ralph picked."

"DJ Daddy O?" Blakely asked. "It's his fraternity brother, right?"

"Yes. I asked for samples, and he had nothing to share," I said. "I have a feeling this is his first wedding. I've addressed my concerns with both Ralph and Velveteen, and they want to stick with the plan."

"There are so many red flags here," Montana groaned. "I'm going to just follow up on the delivery for the tables and linens and stop by the bakery to make sure the cake is all set."

"I'll call and check on the catering staff," Blakely said. "And I will confirm with the hair and makeup team as well."

"Damn. We're good. A well-oiled machine." I winked before grabbing my purse and making my way out the door.

Clifford was lying in the grass across the street, the sun shining down on him, and I chuckled. I'd never thought this place would feel like home, but now even a giant moose lying in the grass felt normal.

I loved it here.

Blushing, Alaska, felt like home.

I made my way to Blushing Blooms.

"Violet, I'm really glad to see you. I just hung up with Missy. She's your mother?" Charlotte asked, and I didn't miss the hesitation in her voice.

"No. She's married to my father." I cleared my throat. "Why is she calling you?"

"She said they want to change the color of the arrangements." Her voice was shaky, and it was clear that she was panicking. "I just don't have the colors that she wants in stock. We're too close to the big day. I've already got my team lined up to knock these out on Friday afternoon and deliver them to you first thing Saturday morning."

I groaned. Missy had always been a thorn in my side, but throw in her daughter's wedding, and she was intolerable. "We aren't changing anything. She's clearly just getting anxious about coming here, as she's been calling our office all day too."

"Normally I would have told her that she'd have to go through you, but with her being a family member, I wasn't sure how to handle it."

Welcome to my life.

"We're good with what we already have planned," I said, and she led me to the refrigerator in the back to show me all the blooms that had just arrived.

"Like I said, we already have everything here and ready to go." She shrugged.

The white hydrangea and peach ranunculus mixed with all the greens were going to be beautiful. The second arrangement was of peach roses and white gardenias with the same greens and would complement one another perfectly.

"This is going to be gorgeous. I am curious, though—what did she want to change the arrangement to?" I asked.

"Red roses and purple tulips."

"But the wedding colors are peach with sage-green accents."

"Yep. That's why I was a little thrown," she said, which made me laugh.

I sighed. "All right. If you get any other calls from her, you can just ask her to call me. I'm sorry about the confusion."

"You're a saint doing this job, you know that? I don't know how you deal with all the bridezillas of the world," Charlotte said with a laugh. "And the mother of the bridezilla might be the worst in this case."

I laughed. "You aren't wrong. This job definitely keeps us on our toes. But I love it too."

"I saw you, Charlie, and Harper when I was leaving the diner last weekend. It was nice to see that man smiling. Keep doing whatever you're doing to him." She winked.

Normally I would have corrected her. Deny that anything was going on. Insist it had nothing to do with me.

But I didn't do that.

My chest puffed up with pride, and I smiled. "I think we're both smiling a lot lately."

It was true.

I wasn't overthinking things anymore.

I was just living, and it was really nice.

I waved goodbye, and on my walk back to the office, I glanced at my phone to see I still had an hour before I had to meet with DJ Daddy

O. I decided to stop by the hotel to see Charlie. We did this often, stopping by just to say hello.

"Hey, Will," I said when I stepped inside and took in the large entryway that Will was painting. "Now you get to spend your days over here."

"Yeah. I preferred it at your place. It was a lot quieter, and no one brings us treats over here," he said.

I chuckled. "I could still bring you treats."

"How's the house? No sign of the groundhog?" he asked.

"The house is perfect. I love it. Every detail just makes it feel like mine. And Chompers the groundhog has been caught on my Nest camera a few times lurking around, but you fortified that deck so well, he's got nowhere to go," I said, acting all tough, when the truth was I felt bad that he'd lost his home. Even if he pissed me off. So I was putting fruits and vegetables and a little dish of water out near the tree line for him.

Will stopped painting and smirked at me. "Really? Charlie tells me you're feeding that bastard."

"Charles is such a traitor!" I threw my hands in the air.

Will was laughing hysterically now as he shook his head. "Hey, don't shoot the messenger."

"Fine. I'll go to the source. Where is he?"

"I don't know. I think he was heading toward the office last I saw him," he said.

The place was coming along, and it was a big project. I rounded the corner to where the front desk was, the whole place still under construction. There was an office behind the desk, which I knew because Charlie had pulled me in there last week when I'd dropped off lunch for him, and we'd sneaked in a daytime quickie in the closet.

They were getting ready to paint, so the window looking into the office was lined with paper. I heard voices and froze once I realized one of them was a woman's voice.

I came to a stop, craning my head just enough to peek through the crack in the door.

Why was the door practically closed?

They had their backs to me as they sat close together. The woman turned her head slightly, and I saw her profile. Long dark hair and a big smile on her face as she looked at Charlie.

And damn it on everything, Charlie turned and smiled back at her.

"I feel really good about this, Charlie." She placed a hand on his shoulder, and my heart sank.

And then I saw the flowers sitting on the table between them.

A big bouquet of pink roses.

My God. Was he courting this woman in broad daylight, all while pretending to be crazy about me?

"I do too. I'm so glad you came by so we could figure this shit out. We can move forward now."

Fuck Charlie and the hot brunette who was swooning all over my man.

I should have expected this.

I whipped around in a fury, knocking into the ladder to the left of me. It made a loud scraping noise, but I didn't care. I was already moving.

Why the hell had I even come here?

"Hey, Firefly." Charlie's voice came from behind me, and I whipped around to face him.

"'Hey, Firefly'?" I shouted. "No. No, Charles!"

And I was moving again.

I needed to get out of here.

But of course I couldn't make a graceful exit. I tripped over the drop cloth, and my arm overcorrected and I knocked a can of paint off the counter.

I saw the white liquid oozing as the lid sprang loose.

But I didn't stop.

I heard Will shouting to me as I sprinted past him, asking if I was all right, but I beelined for the door.

I practically ran down the street because I couldn't get back to my office quick enough.

I didn't feel right.

My heart was racing. There was a lump in my throat.

I didn't ever cry in public.

I'd lost it in front of Charlie.

Charlie, the man I was crazy about.

Charlie, the man who'd been so good to me.

But I'd been let down by the people who were supposed to care about me my entire life.

Every insecurity I'd ever had flooded my mind at once.

He's going to leave me. He's found someone else. Someone better.

Charlie Huxley had the power to hurt me, and that alone was terrifying enough.

I pulled the door open, and Blakely was on the phone, and I saw the way her gaze widened as she took me in.

I could see the concern, but I shook my head and hurried down the hall, stepping inside my office before slamming the door.

I will not cry.

I will not cry over a man.

Hells to the no.

The first tear broke free, and my bottom lip wobbled.

My office door flew open, and there stood Charlie Huxley. He was holding those goddamn pink roses.

What did he do, take them from her?

"Get out!" I shouted.

He smirked. "You jealous, Firefly?"

"Stop calling me that. What do you call her? Ladybug? Hottie-Pants?" I sniffed as he set the flowers on my desk and smiled at me like the whole thing was hilarious.

I picked up the bouquet and chucked it at his head.

He caught it, of course, because the man had unusually good hand-eye coordination.

"I'd be pissed off at how ridiculous you're acting if I wasn't in such a good mood," he said, setting the flowers back down on my desk.

"You'd be pissed off? You don't see me tucked in a cozy closet with the door closed, handing a man flowers and fawning all over each other!" I shouted.

"It's an office, not a closet, and the door wasn't shut. But we did need some privacy, so I had it cracked open." His lips twitched the slightest bit before turning up in the corners.

Did he seriously think this was funny?

"I'll bet you did. I can't wait to hear the nickname you call her." I arched a brow in challenge.

"I call her 'Logan,' because that's her name. Logan Hawkins, the attorney that's helping me with my custody stuff for Harper."

My breath caught. "Logan Hawkins is a woman?"

Why did my voice sound more like a squeak now?

"Yep. And she's married to a good friend of mine, Jonas Hawkins," he said.

Shit. Shit. Shit.

I'd overreacted, per usual.

"Oh. Well, she seems lovely. Are these flowers for me?" I reached for the bouquet, even though half the petals had fallen off, but I pretended not to notice as I brought them to my nose, trying to play off the fact that I'd just freaked out over nothing.

"Why the hell did you storm out of there? What did you think I was doing?"

"I thought you were having an affair." I sighed, setting the mangled flowers on the desk. "Well, no. Logically, I knew that wasn't your style. Even when I was storming out of there."

"Need I remind you that you're the one who barely acknowledges that we're dating. I'm the one who wants to make this relationship public. I'm the one that wants to take things further. Yet you think I'm cheating on you? For fuck's sake, Violet. Make up your goddamn mind about what you want," he hissed.

I blew out a breath. "I have told people that we're dating. I'm quite proud of it, actually. I just overreacted."

I searched his gaze for understanding.

And as usual when it came to Charlie Huxley, I saw it.

The man just got me.

CHAPTER TWENTY-SIX

Charlie

This woman knew how to piss me off.

But it only drew me to her more.

Because I understood her. I understood her passion. Her fear. Her need to protect herself.

And goddamn, I loved how quickly she could adapt and realize she'd misread a situation.

"Tell me why you overreacted." I moved around her desk and bent down in front of her, reaching for her hands.

She looked away before turning back to meet my gaze. "I just saw you in there with her, and I freaked out. I assumed you wanted her. I'm so conditioned to think something good is going to go bad."

"And why would it matter if we're nothing serious, like you keep insisting? Why would you be that worked up? You can't stand me most of the time, right?" I pressed.

This shit needed to stop. I was all in. I knew she was all in.

The last few days had been great. Harper knew we were dating. But Violet was still holding back.

"I can stand you, Charles." Her eyes watered. "I can more than stand you."

"Yeah? Because I'm done holding back. I don't want anyone else. I want you and only you. Even if you just made a scene and knocked a gallon of paint over. I still want you."

She nodded and slowly released a breath. "Charlie."

"Yes?" I chuckled because she was being serious, which was out of character for her.

"I love you, Charlie Huxley. And I've never said that to a man. But I love you." A tear ran down her cheek. "I really do."

"I love you too, Firefly. I have for a while now." I used the pad of my thumb to swipe the tears away.

"Then why didn't you say it first?" She gripped my shirt in her hands.

"Because I thought you would run."

"Why would you think that?" she chuckled, not hiding her sarcasm. "I saw you with Logan, and I just thought the worst. And then a sharp pain hit my chest. I was afraid I'd lost you. I just found you, you know?"

I scooped her up off her chair and sat down, then pulled her onto my lap. "I'm not going anywhere. I waited a long time for you, Violet Delphinium Beaumont."

"I'm going to torture Montana for telling you my middle name," I said over my laughter.

"I looked at your driver's license. That's quite a mouthful."

"So are you," she said with a grin.

"Such a filthy little flower."

"A filthy little flower that you happen to love."

"I do. And I don't use those words lightly. They mean something to me," I said.

"Hashtag 'love you, mean it.'" She smiled.

Her words hit me right in the chest. Words I never thought I'd hear her say. Words she'd insisted she didn't believe in. And here she was, putting herself out there.

For me.

With me.

"We're officially a hashtag, Firefly," I said, wrapping my arms around her tighter.

"Wait. Why was Logan there, and why were you bringing me flowers? And why were there two bouquets?"

"You're a very observant woman." He chuckled. "Caroline reached out to me. She was upset about her visit to Blushing, so she told her fiancé about it when she returned home. He agreed that it wasn't fair to Harper to have her showing up once a year. She also doesn't want to risk me coming after her for any back child support, which I'd never do, but her fiancé is apparently concerned about it."

"Of course they are." Violet rolled her eyes. "The nerve of these people."

"Anyway, her parents got involved because they don't want to be responsible for college tuition for a child they don't know." I shook my head. "As if I'd ever let my girl go to them for anything. Not fucking happening. I don't care how much money they have."

"Agreed. I'd walk around naked and sell everything I own before I'd let her go to them for anything," she said.

"I could get on board with that." I nipped at her earlobe.

"So what did she say. What's the solution?"

"She wants to relinquish her parental rights. It's got to be done legally and aboveboard, but seeing as all parties agree, there's no issue. I called Logan, who then talked to Caroline and her family attorney. She stopped by my office to fill me in. Caroline's father has a judge friend, and he's going to oversee this next week. We'll get it all finalized shortly after, and they'll send over the paperwork."

Violet wrapped her hands around my neck. "That's amazing. I'm so sorry I ruined the moment."

"Nah. I'd already gone to grab the flowers for you and Harps, when Logan called and said that she was on her way over to talk to me, so I hurried back to the hotel. But this might be the best day of my life." I shrugged as I tucked her hair behind her ear.

"Yeah. You got sole custody of Harps. It doesn't get any better." Her smile spread across her face, which made my chest hurt.

"I got sole custody of my baby girl, and you told me you loved me. I'd call today a win."

"And you told me you love me."

"I did."

"Wait till you meet the in-laws this weekend. You might regret those words," she said with a chuckle.

"I don't scare easily. I stick. So get fucking used to it already."

She smiled. "Okay."

There was a knock on the open door, which I hadn't closed behind me. "I'm so sorry to interrupt," Blakely said. "But DJ Daddy O called because it's time for your Zoom, and he's going to happy hour in a little while, so he needs to start your meeting as soon as possible."

Violet groaned. "Shit. I forgot about him. I need to get on a Zoom."

I pushed to my feet and set her down on the chair. "I'll see you after work."

She stood and lunged at me, kissing me hard. "I love you, Charles."

Damn. I liked the sound of that.

"I love you too."

"Oh my gosh. All the swoons," Blakely said as she stood in the doorway watching us.

I made my way to the door and winked at her. "Hashtag 'all the swoons.'"

Blakely chuckled and fanned her face as I made my way back to work.

"So Caroline won't be coming on my birthday anymore?" Harper asked over a mouthful of noodles. I could see the relief on her face, and I was grateful that her mother had chosen to do the right thing.

You can't be halfway there as a parent.

It was an all-or-nothing gig, and her mother had never been all in.

But I would always be grateful that she'd come to me and given me the choice to be a dad.

"Right. She's going to get married and start her own life. Because we have a good thing going on our own over here," I said.

Violet was just smiling at my daughter as she twirled her noodles around her fork.

"And I'm happy that even though Violet moved back to her house, I still get to see her every day," my daughter said.

"I told your daddy something today. But he doesn't know that I actually said it to you first," Violet said.

"What did you tell him?"

"I told him that I love him. But I told you I loved you first." My girlfriend chuckled.

"But I knew you loved Daddy when you told me you loved me. And he loved you then too." Harper pushed out of her chair and climbed onto Violet's lap. "You're not just my best friend, Vi. You're my family. We're a real family."

I'd worried so much about doing this right. About being careful with how we involved Harper.

But she'd been involved from the minute Violet moved into our backyard.

From breakfasts and long talks and balloon arches.

She'd been a part of this family before she and I were smart enough to figure out how we felt.

My daughter didn't need protecting from anyone.

She saw the best in people.

She was open to love.

I just turned and watched my two girls hugging in the chair beside me.

This was what it felt like to be happy.

Everything I needed was right here in this kitchen.

And I was going to do everything I could to hold on to them.

CHAPTER TWENTY-SEVEN

Violet

The morning had started out gray as rain clouds hovered above.

I was convinced that Pissy Missy had brought the doom and gloom with her to Blushing, Alaska.

But the last two days had been tolerable because Paris, Huntington, and Brenton were here. They'd met Charlie and Harper, and we'd all stayed up late last night talking before Charlie had to get his little girl home and in bed.

I was shocked that Missy had actually agreed to let them stay with me. Even though they were grown adults, she'd always been a helicopter mom on steroids the way she tried to control everything they did. My brothers stayed in the guest room, and Paris slept with me.

I'd invited my father over to see the place, but he declined because he felt obligated to follow his wife around while she barked orders at everyone she encountered.

A tinge of something crossed through me when he showed no interest in seeing my first home. The one I'd purchased all on my own. The one I'd renovated to make it everything that I wanted.

But that tinge left as quickly as it had arrived.

I'd come to realize that people show you who they are. I'd just chosen not to believe my father.

He may be a giant asshole, but he is a consistent asshole.

I didn't need to wonder what he'd do anymore, because I already had the answers.

He'd shown me over and over again.

And just like Harper's mother was a stranger to her—my father had always been a stranger to me.

Of course my siblings had all gushed about the place, and I didn't mind hearing them go on and on about it at the rehearsal dinner last night. My dad had congratulated me, and per usual, he shot me the same old guilty look he always did when he was around me.

But that was his burden to carry, not mine.

And now that I didn't have to try to fix things, it was a hell of a lot easier.

I'd been over at the venue all day, while my siblings went and explored downtown Blushing before heading back over here to get ready.

The Blushing Inn was a charming wedding venue that we'd designed to fit our needs. The outdoor space was unbelievable, with views of the water and plenty of space to accommodate weddings of up to three hundred people.

We had an area for the bride and her wedding party to get their hair and makeup done, as well as a very cool room for the groom and his groomsmen to get dressed and have cocktails while they waited for the ceremony to start.

Velveteen hadn't asked me to be in her wedding party, which didn't surprise me. I was the wedding planner, after all, so I'd be busy making sure everything went off without a hitch. But the truth was, we weren't close, so I wouldn't have expected it.

Paris had been furious about it, thinking she at least should have extended the offer, and if I was too busy with planning the event, I could have backed out.

But I was exactly where I wanted to be today.

Busy overseeing the chaos.

Because I'd stopped in the room with Velveteen and her mother, and the tension was so thick I couldn't get out of there quick enough.

"Take me with you," Paris pleaded as she followed me into the hallway, laughing.

"Get back in there and do your job." I pointed at the door, making no attempt to hide my smile.

"Ugh. I can't wait until you are off duty and can have a cocktail with me. You promise you're going to be off the clock at the reception?"

"I promise."

"And Charlie and Harper will be here too, right?" she asked.

"Yes. They'll be here." I blew her a kiss just as Missy whipped the door open and growled at Paris to get back in there.

The rest of the bridesmaids sat silently on the pink velvet sofas and sipped their champagne.

That room was not giving off good wedding vibes, but I couldn't control what went on in there.

I came around the corner and found Montana's father, Daniel, in the kitchen with his crew, getting everything prepped and ready. He was the best chef in town, and he catered most of our weddings.

"Smells delicious," I said, snatching a carrot stick from the trays he had out on the enormous kitchen island.

"Yep. It's going to be damn good." He leaned forward, keeping his voice low as he said the next statement. "Man, that stepmother of yours makes me want to dip my work boot in her soup."

I laughed loudly. Daniel Kingsley was a good man. A kind man.

"Keep your boots on, please." I winked before grabbing one more carrot. I was walking out toward the living area when Montana called a 911 in my headset. Blakely was also on the call.

I held one hand over my ear as I walked. "I'm here. What's up."

"Uhhhh . . . come outside, please. I'm to the left of where the ceremony will be held."

"Don't tell me it's raining," I said. We needed the weather to cooperate just for the ceremony. In case it rained and we had to make some changes, we had a backup plan to move the guests to another tented area we'd put up. I'd made the judgment call to move the ceremony to the tent, but my sister and her mother had refused the idea.

Velveteen did not want to get married under a tent. She loved the open green space with the water in the distance. I agreed that the outdoor option was prettier, but I also knew that getting soaked in the rain would be a disaster.

"I'm on my way," Blakely said, and she sounded like she was running.

When I turned the corner, my mouth fell open. Ralph's brother, Robby Parker, was lying in the grass, passed out and stark naked.

Montana's eyes were wide as she gaped at me, just as Blakely came jogging up behind me.

"Oh." I covered my mouth with my hands to keep from laughing.

"'Oh'? I mean, the man isn't budging." Montana threw her hands in the air. "I've yelled his name, and I used this stick to poke him a few times."

"Is he dead?" Blakely asked, just as a loud snore escaped Robby.

"That's a good sign that he's still alive," I said with a laugh.

"I mean, he's just putting it all out there," Montana chuckled. "We can't move him with his—johnson on full display."

"I'd say that's a little johnson," Blakely said, smirking.

I glanced over near the reception tent to see a pile of linen napkins on the cart where they were setting things up. I hurried over and grabbed a napkin before tossing it over Robby's "little johnson."

Then I leaned down near his head and shouted in his ear. "Robby Parker, wake your ass up."

"Ma! Don't turn the hose on me," he grumped before one eye opened and he met my angry gaze.

"I'm not your mama, Robby. But it is my sister's wedding day, and you will wake your naked ass up and go get dressed right now, or I swear I'll have no problem turning the hose on you."

Robby sat up, glancing down at the linen napkin on his crotch. He just chuckled like this was perfectly normal. "Ralph told me you're the fun sister."

"Well, he should have told you that I'm also the most violent family member, and I'm not afraid to use physical force on you. Get your ass moving, buddy. Guests will be arriving in less than an hour."

He glanced at each of us, winking awkwardly as he moved to his feet. We all turned our backs to him, even though we'd already seen all there was to see. But it seemed like the right thing to do.

We slowly turned to see a tall, freckled Robby walking toward the main house with his white ass covered in a very large tattoo out on display.

"It's a full moon tonight," Blakely whispered. "What the hell did he write on his butt cheek?"

A loud laugh escaped my lips. "Huntington told me that Robby got a tattoo at Ralph's bachelor party."

"What does it say?"

"'Sparkle,'" I said dryly, waiting for them to look at me. "That was the stripper's name, and our Robby boy fell hard and fast for Sparkle Moonlight that night."

"Nooooooo," they both said in unison.

"He said it was love at first sight. And she came back to the hotel with them and spent the night with Robby."

"Really? And they're dating now?" Blakely asked.

"Nope. She robbed several of the guys. She stole their credit cards, a couple watches, and she even took Ralph's cell phone and tried to blackmail them with the photos on his phone from the bachelor party."

I'd gotten the whole rundown from my brothers last night.

"That's so savage," Montana said.

"Well, they caught her, because she didn't turn her location off on Ralph's cell phone, so he was able to track her down."

"Where'd they find her?" Blakely asked.

"The strip club she works at. The jackasses never thought to try that first." I rolled my eyes. "They got everything back, aside from the money she'd spent on bagels and Starbucks with the cash from Robby's wallet, along with his dignity."

More laughter.

"Okay. One crisis averted. Let's go get ready for this wedding," Montana said as thunder boomed in the distance.

"She's really not moving the ceremony into the tented area?" Blakely asked, shaking her head. "The rain is coming."

"Nope. I've tried to convince her, but she's stubborn. I'll go try again, and I'll call you if I can persuade her to do it. We'd just need to get all the chairs moved inside the tented area."

"Got it," they said in unison, and we all went our separate ways.

Duty called.

The last hour before a wedding was always filled with challenges.

But this wedding would go down in the books as the most eventful.

The guests started arriving. They were led to their seats outside, since Velveteen had refused to move it inside. Never mind the fact that a black cloud hung above the chairs; she was determined to have the wedding outside.

"We cannot have this outdoors, Vi," Montana said into my headset.

"Listen, I tried. This is her day. She refused to have the chairs moved into the tented area. She said she'd take her chances." I kept my tone down as I stopped at the bride's suite to get the wedding party ready to line up, while Montana went to get the groomsmen.

"It's game time, ladies," I said.

Paris gave me a look that let me know the shit was about to hit the fan.

Literally and figuratively.

"Violet, I need you!" Missy shouted from the bathroom. "Grandma Helen has the shits."

Grandma Helen was Missy's mother, and she was far too sweet to have given birth to Satan's spawn. I'd spent several holidays with her, and she was always kind to me.

"Get lined up and ready to go," I said, directing Velveteen and her bridesmaids to the door as I hurried to the bathroom.

Sweet Grandma Helen was sitting on the shitter smiling, like she was enjoying this, which only made me laugh.

"Is this comical to you?" Missy hissed at me.

"I mean. Everything seems okay, aside from you appearing unhinged," I said before turning my attention to the elderly woman on the toilet. "Are you all done?"

"I think it was that mac and cheese I had for lunch. Everybody poops. My daughter is such an overreactor," Grandma Helen said as she struggled to stand.

"I'm sorry, Mother," Missy said, her voice dripping with sarcasm. "They need you to be seated now, and I do not have time to deal with this. You should have used the restroom hours ago. Not right when it was time to go."

"I didn't have to go hours ago," she said, shaking her head. I reached for her arm to help her up.

"Move. She needs to be lifted this way." Missy shoved me out of the way and bent down, like she was going to grab her mother's ankles.

That's when I heard the tear.

Followed by a glass-shattering shriek.

Missy's dress split across her ass, the expensive satin fabric making a perfect line.

Grandma Helen pushed to stand on her own and held on to the counter. I grabbed her walker and tried to scoot Missy out of the way as she turned to look in the mirror at the damage.

"My dress is ruined. It's ruined!" she screamed.

"Well, you shouldn't have gotten down on the ground. What was the plan? Were you going to hoist me over your shoulder?" Grandma Helen asked.

"Get her out of here!" Missy yelled, and I pulled the bathroom door open and used my headset to ask Blakely to come pick up Grandma Helen, Velveteen, and the bridesmaids.

I spent the next ten minutes sewing Missy's dress back together with the needle and thread I kept in my belt bag while she complained about her mother. I didn't respond. I just got the job done.

"This will have to do. You have your wrap, and you can just keep that around you tonight. You'd have to look close to see it."

"I can see it when I look in the mirror." She frowned as she glanced over her shoulder at her ass.

But can you see what a raging bitch you are?

I ignored her and listened as Montana said that it was time for the MOB, or mother of the bride, to be escorted down the aisle.

"They're asking for you, Missy." I led her out the door, and she quickly hurried toward the ushers who would walk her down the aisle with Peggy Parker, Ralph's mother.

"I need you to walk with me and stay behind me, Violet," Missy said, her voice softer now. "Just in case anyone can see the rip."

I nodded. My job was to make this as smooth as possible.

Montana had the bridesmaids, Velveteen, and my father in a room around the corner.

I let her know I'd be there soon.

I followed behind Missy and Peggy, who barely acknowledged one another.

We made our way outside, where the rain clouds were so dark that it appeared much later than it actually was.

I said a silent prayer to the nature gods to hold the rain for forty more minutes.

My gaze moved toward the crowd and found Charlie and Harper, sitting in the back. He wore a navy suit, and I swear my breath hitched in my throat.

My gaze locked with his.

And that's when all hell broke loose.

"Let go of my arm," Missy grumped under her breath to the woman beside her, who was suddenly clinging to Missy to keep from falling.

"I've been stung."

I've. Been. Stung.

A motherfucking bee had just beaten the rain and stung the MOG under the clouds of doom and gloom.

I watched as she clutched her throat and started to fall.

I grabbed her arms as I braced her fall, and I moved to the ground with her.

"She's allergic to bees!" Ralph shouted.

Of course she's allergic to bees.

And what kind of bee hangs out when there is no sunlight whatsoever?

"Does she carry an EpiPen?" I called out, trying to hide the panic from my voice as the woman struggled for air.

"Yes." Robby ran over, hysterical, and was soon on the ground beside his mother.

She was coughing and grabbing her throat.

"She keeps it in her undercarriage if she doesn't have a purse," Robby said.

Did he seriously just say "undercarriage"?

It didn't matter. The woman was not okay. I had to think quickly.

I shouted for someone to call 911, and I slipped my hand up her dress, and sure enough, she'd tucked an EpiPen in her pantyhose.

This wasn't my first rodeo, or my first allergic reaction.

I knew the drill.

I stabbed her in the leg with the pen, and we all hovered around her.

Waiting.

Her hand dropped from her neck, and she blinked up at me, her voice hoarse. "Thank you."

"Of course."

The wedding might be a shit show, but I'd basically just saved a woman's life.

Montana was on one side of me, while Charlie moved behind me.

"I'm on the phone with 911. They're pulling up now," he said.

Velveteen came running out to check on Peggy Parker, who was now sitting up, but her dress was still bunched around her thighs.

"Ralph just saw you in your dress before the wedding song played," Missy shouted. "The marriage is doomed now."

I sighed and was reassuring my sister that everything was fine when the paramedics came running toward us.

And that's the moment when the nature gods decided to flash us all the middle finger, and the clouds released the rainstorm from hell.

I wasn't sure if the marriage was doomed, but the wedding had certainly hit rock bottom.

CHAPTER TWENTY-EIGHT

Charlie

I'd never seen anything quite like the scene in front of me.

Violet was kneeling down beside the groom's mother, who'd had an allergic reaction to a beesting.

I couldn't remember the last time I'd seen a bee, but one had made its way through this dark, cloudy afternoon, and the woman had dropped to the ground.

And then the downpour of all downpours had unleashed on the ceremony.

The rain fell hard and fast.

People were frantically running as they hauled ass to the tent. But I stayed right here with Violet, and Harper had one arm wrapped around my leg and the other in Violet's hand.

Like the three of us were unbreakable.

That's how it felt lately.

The rain poured down on us as Thomas, a medic I'd grown up with, led the gurney away. Blakely had agreed to ride in the ambulance with the mother of the groom, who'd insisted that they move forward with the wedding.

Once they'd stepped away, Violet turned to look at me and shook her head. Her hair was soaked, her dress clinging to her body, drenched from the rain.

"You saved that woman's life, Firefly," I said.

She started laughing, and once she started, she couldn't stop.

And of course that made Harper laugh hysterically as I pulled Violet up on her feet, knowing I needed to get them both inside the tent and out of this rain.

"You okay?" I asked as I wrapped my arms around her before lifting Harper and settling her on my hip.

"She wouldn't move the ceremony inside the tent. Knowing it was going to rain, she still wouldn't do it." She shook her head, tipping it back again and letting the rain fall on her beautiful face. "And then the mother of the groom goes into anaphylactic shock. I can't make this up."

"If I didn't see it with my own eyes, I probably wouldn't have believed it. Let's get you both in the tent, yeah?"

"Race you there," Violet said as she took off toward the tent. Harper erupted in giggles when we chased after her.

Montana was there with a few of the waitstaff they'd hired for service, and they passed out towels so the guests could dry off. I had no idea where she'd found this many towels, but these women were full of surprises when they threw weddings.

They chatted briefly before Violet went to speak to Velveteen and Ralph, along with both families. It was decided that the wedding would take place immediately, since Ralph's father wanted to get to the hospital to check on his wife. They didn't want to take the time to move the chairs over; they just wanted to quickly say their vows and make it official.

Everyone stood in the covered space, the rain beating down on the heavy canvas above as they said the fastest vows I'd ever heard. I was far from a pro when it came to wedding etiquette, but this seemed unusually quick.

This was my kind of wedding.

Violet and Montana were thrilled that the rain let up briefly as they moved the guests over to the other side of the property where the reception had been set up.

Harper gasped when we stepped inside, because there were several crystal chandeliers hanging above, as well as tables covered in white linens with flowers and candles every which way you looked.

The ceremony may not have been what the bride wanted, but this room looked like something you'd see in a magazine.

"Daddy, someday when I get married, can I have sparkly lights like this?" Harper asked. "Oh, and all the flowers. But I want all the pink flowers. Light pink. And dark pink."

"Sounds like you want to have a Pinkalicious wedding?" I teased. "And yes, you can have whatever you want, Harps."

Violet had gone back inside to help her sister get her hair and makeup fixed from the rain, as they'd be making their grand entrance soon.

We made our way over to where Benji was manning the bar. He made Harper a Coke filled with more cherries than any one little girl needed, which made her smile. He cracked a beer open for me and passed it over.

"That was a whole lot of drama for one ceremony, huh?" he chuckled.

"Yep. But from what Violet tells me, it's par for the course."

He nodded. "I can tell. Let's hope the reception is drama-free."

"Yeah, that would be nice. I'll come check on you in a little bit. We're going to go find our table." I knocked my knuckles against the wood bar top and led my daughter over to where our name tags were.

I was surprised to see we were seated at the family table, but happy because Huntington and Brenton were there, and they were cool dudes.

"I guess we're sitting with you," I said, my gaze moving to their father, sitting beside them. I hadn't met him yet, but he'd walked Velveteen down the makeshift aisle in the tent, so I'd figured out who he was.

"Yeah. Thankfully Velveteen didn't make us sit with the wedding party," Huntington said, and his father shot him a look.

I laughed as we took our seats.

Her father reached his hand out. "I'm William Beaumont. You're Violet's boyfriend?"

Harper moved over to where Violet's brothers were sitting when they pulled out a deck of cards and asked her if she wanted to see their magic trick.

"Yep. I'm Charlie Huxley. This is my daughter, Harper." I shook his hand. It was on the tip of my tongue to tell him it was nice to meet him, but I wasn't going to lie to the man.

He'd treated the woman I love like shit, and I wasn't on board with that.

"How long have you two been together?" he asked me, like he and Violet were casual acquaintances.

"Long enough to be in love with her, which was as easy as breathing," I said, my tone coming out harsh.

This guy didn't deserve any details.

If Violet wanted to share more with him, that would come from her.

He hadn't even taken a few minutes to go see her new home.

The man was a selfish bastard in my book, and I wasn't looking for a new buddy.

He nodded. "Have you met her mother? She's a real piece of work."

The fucking nerve of this guy.

"I guess you have a type," I said, leaving him to dissect those words all on his own.

He gave me a questioning look just as his wife came walking over in a huff. She glanced from me to Harper and then looked at her husband. "This is Violet's date?"

"Yes. It's her boyfriend and his daughter."

"Well," she said, turning to look at me. "Your girlfriend promised a smooth wedding, and this has been anything but. We've had beestings and rain. I don't think anyone would call this wedding smooth."

I narrowed my gaze. "I don't know any wedding planner who can control the rain. Perhaps if you'd listened to her advice about moving the ceremony inside the tent earlier on, you would have avoided the mass chaos of the downpour. And as far as the beesting, I hope you thanked your daughter for saving your new son-in-law's mother's life. She should be commended for how quickly she reacted."

Missy's eyes widened, as if she wasn't used to anyone standing up to her.

Her husband nodded. "It was impressive the way she administered that EpiPen without hesitation."

"Yeah, Vi's a badass." Huntington pulled a card from his sleeve and slapped it down on the table as Harper gasped.

"She's always been someone who just gets the job done," Brenton said. "Remember when she came to my college dorm room after Mom and Dad left, and she turned my room into the coolest room on campus?" Huntington said, glancing at his parents.

Missy's shoulders stiffened, and she glanced at me.

I nodded. "Sounds like my girl."

She cleared her throat as the DJ, who already appeared to be several cocktails deep, by the way his words were slurring, made an announcement through the speaker system.

"It's DJ Daddy O, bitches!" he shouted, and I glanced at my daughter, who thankfully was hyperfocused on the magic trick. "We're getting ready to introduce the wedding party, and let me tell you, there are some *hot-tayyyyys* in the house."

"What did he just say?" Missy gaped at her husband. "Who allowed this man to be here? Did Violet choose him? He must be a local?"

"He's your son-in-law's old fraternity brother," I said before Violet's father could say he didn't know, because that appeared to be his go-to. A shrug with a clueless look. "Violet didn't approve, but it's ultimately up to the bride and groom."

Violet had shared her concerns about this jackass having a microphone after her Zoom call with him.

"Oh," Missy sniffed and then turned her chin up as he started announcing the wedding party.

The music blared, and he asked everyone to get on their feet. Harper came to stand beside me, and I picked her up and settled her on my hip so she could see.

Violet and Montana stood off to the side watching as each couple strode onto the dance floor once their names were announced.

"Daddy, that music is loud," Harper shouted in my ear.

I chuckled. "Yep. I think the party has started."

Missy had her arms folded over her chest with a giant frown on her face.

"We've got a nice surprise for you all," DJ Drinks a Lot shouted. "Look who made it back in time for the party. Mama Parker is back in the *hiz-zayyyy*!"

"Oh, she should have just gone to her room after that scene she caused," Missy snipped loud enough for everyone at our table to hear.

But her sons were jumping up and down with their hands in the air, just like the rest of the people watching.

The groom's mother and father came into the tent dancing and cheering, and the crowd went wild.

Maybe things were turning around, because everyone appeared to be having a good time now.

They'd dried off, and they were now sipping cocktails and smiling.

Violet glanced my way, relief on her face, and I winked, holding up my beer bottle in toast to her.

My girl was a rock star.

She smiled, just as the DJ told everyone to put their hands in the air for the big moment. My daughter had her hands in the air, and Huntington and Brenton both high-fived her.

"It's time for the stars of the evening. Ralph 'Mad Dog' Parker and his bride, Smooth as Velveteen Parker!" he shouted.

Ralph practically knocked his bride on her ass as he stormed past her with two bottles of champagne in his hands. His tuxedo coat was off, and his dress shirt was unbuttoned halfway down his stomach, and he shook his head like he was a frat boy on spring break.

Velveteen looked highly annoyed as she moved up beside him, just as he bent down on the dance floor and slammed both bottles against the wood, like that was a brilliant idea.

Unfortunately, the bottles both shattered, and the liquid spewed all over the floor.

Velveteen slipped and shrieked as she went down. A few of her bridesmaids hurried to assist her, and they all fell right along with her.

Ralph didn't miss a beat, just jumping up and down with two broken pieces of the bottles in his hands. The crowd stopped cheering and dancing once everyone realized the women on the ground were crying and clearly upset.

Violet and Montana were on the move. I saw Violet shout at the DJ, and the volume was turned down.

Missy hurried toward her daughter and then turned around and shouted at her husband to come help her.

I watched in shock as Violet pulled Velveteen to her feet, then wrapped her hands in a napkin and hurried her out of the tent.

Montana helped two other women to their feet and took them out as well.

Harper had gone back over to watch Huntington and Brenton's magic tricks again, and this time she got to pick a card and slide it into the middle of the deck.

The waitstaff was already getting the floor cleaned up, and Ralph and his jackass brother hadn't missed a beat. They were making a scene at the bar, cheering loudly with their shot glasses in hand.

Missy, William, and Paris came back to the table, and Violet's sister took the seat beside me, keeping her voice low. "What a disaster, huh?"

"What happened out there? I saw a lot of broken glass," I asked.

"Velveteen cut her hand and her calf. Her husband is out of control tonight," she said, shaking her head and smiling. "But per usual, Violet saved the day. She wrapped the cut so it wouldn't get on her dress, and she got her out of there before she was completely hysterical."

"Is she crying because she's hurt?"

"I think she's probably embarrassed. I don't know," Paris said as she sipped her wine. "Maybe the realization that she has to spend the rest of her life with a man-child is setting in."

"Violet shouldn't have let Ralph carry those bottles into the reception." Missy glanced at us over her shoulder, letting us know she was listening to the conversation.

"You know what, Mother?" Paris said as Missy turned around to look at her daughter. "Aren't you tired of blaming Violet for everything? Because I know I'm tired of hearing it. She's the only reason this wedding has been salvaged. Ralph's mom is lucky to be alive, and that's all thanks to Vi. And Velveteen ignored Violet when she begged her to move the ceremony into the tent. You did too. So stop blaming someone who has stepped up for your daughter on her special day. We all know you don't like her because Dad had a child with another woman before he met you, but come on, enough is enough. It's appalling, actually."

The table was silent, and William squirmed in his seat.

Such a weak man.

"I agree. Vi's the best," Huntington said.

"Yeah, Mom. We all talk about it. It's pretty awful the way you've treated her," Brenton chimed in, and then he looked back down at the table quickly as if he was terrified of his mother's wrath.

"What is with this attitude. And now you've got your brothers brainwashed. William, say something to your children." She glared at her husband.

"I think your mom wishes Velveteen was my first child too." He shrugged. "It's hard on her that I had a life before her."

Missy gaped at him. "That is not true."

Everyone just stared at her. Me included.

The jig is up, Pissy Missy.

CHAPTER TWENTY-NINE

Violet

"You all right?" I asked Velveteen after I'd cleaned her hands and put some clear bandages on her palms so they wouldn't show in the photos people would be taking tonight.

Montana had already taken the bridesmaids back to the reception, but Velveteen had several cuts on her hands and two on her left leg where she'd slipped.

That fucker Ralph was going to get a piece of my mind.

She nodded. "I'm sorry."

"Hey, this wasn't your fault," I said, pushing to stand and setting the box of bandages on the desk beside the chair.

"I'm sorry for being such a bitch to you all the time." She shrugged. "When you were talking about that hotel room in New York, I didn't know that's what happened, Vi. Mom had told us that you didn't want to stay in a room with us."

"Listen, that's not on you, and this is your wedding day. We don't need to deep dive into why your mother doesn't like me." I chuckled.

"Please, my husband hasn't even come to check on me. I'm in no rush to get back. He's living his fraternity days out tonight, and I knew who I was marrying when he proposed. He's a good guy when it's just us. When the party is going, that's another story." She smiled and then pointed at the bottle of tequila sitting on the desk beside the box of bandages. "Can I have a sip?"

My eyes widened. My sister was always a little uptight, and this was out of character. I handed her the bottle, and she took a long pull before handing it to me.

I shook my head. "I've got a wedding to oversee. And believe it or not, it's one that's important to me. It's my sister's special day."

I sat in the chair beside her as she took another pull. "Why'd you keep coming around when my mother was so cruel to you?"

"Because I wanted to know my siblings. I don't have a lot of family. My mom is no walk in the park," I chuckled. "I guess I just wanted to fit somewhere."

"Shit. I've been such a jerk to you." She took another swig from the bottle, and I couldn't believe that we were actually having this conversation.

On her wedding day.

"We were kids, Velveteen. We were pitted against one another at a very young age." I shrugged.

The truth is, she was pitted against me.

I was always just flying solo.

"I want you to feel like you fit." She reached for my hand.

"You know, I finally do. I mean, I fit here, in Blushing. I fit with Charlie and Harper. I fit with Montana and Blakely. This is my home. I've spent most of my life trying to force something that was never going to work. I don't have to do that anymore. I didn't have to try when I finally found my home. Found my people," I said as a single tear rolled down my cheek.

It wasn't falling because I was sad.

This tear was falling because I was happy.

"Mom and Dad are such dicks sometimes. They could have united us." She shook her head with disgust. "I always resented you for being so cool. Like you didn't care what anyone thought, and I cared so much."

I chuckled. "I cared. I'm just better at hiding it."

"Maybe it's not too late for us," she said.

"Crazier things have happened."

She laughed. "Yeah, like my jackass husband smashing two bottles of champagne on the dance floor and bringing a raging lunatic to DJ at our wedding?"

"I mean, your mother-in-law also went into anaphylactic shock before you walked down the aisle."

"There was that, followed by a downpour of rain," she said as the door cracked open and Paris peeked her head in.

"Oh. What's happening here?" She strolled into the room and grabbed the bottle before taking a long pull.

"Just some sisterly bonding," Velveteen said.

"It's about damn time." She smiled. "And everyone wants to eat, but Mom insisted that they wait for the bride. Ralph is getting shit-faced, so I think you'd be wise to get him fed."

Velveteen nodded. "Okay. Sisters' dance on the dance floor after dinner?"

"Count on it," I said as we made our way out of the house and back to the tent.

They both walked inside, and I said I'd meet them at the table, but I needed to talk to Montana and Blakely first.

"This goes down as the craziest wedding we've ever thrown," Montana said, keeping her voice low as we huddled beside the entrance of the tent.

"Well, I did ride in the ambulance with a hot medic, and he asked for my number. So this is my favorite wedding to date." Blakely chuckled.

"It's been a lot. Are you sure you guys can handle this on your own? I feel bad bailing on you, but I sort of hate to leave Charles and Harps alone with my family." I glanced across the room to see Charlie laughing at whatever Paris had just said. Harper was sitting between my brothers now, and they looked perfectly comfortable.

"The only people who look awkward at that table are your stepmother and your father. They've looked out of place the entire time," Montana said.

"Missy had the balls to try to stop me from riding in the ambulance," Blakely huffed. "She told me I should stay back and manage the weather. That woman is completely unhinged."

"Yes. She scolded me about the rain, as if it were my fault the clouds finally gave in." Montana laughed.

"What did she say?" I asked.

"She said, 'Shame on you ladies for botching this ceremony with this ridiculous rain.'" Montana rolled her eyes. "I was like, 'Take a seat, Pissy Missy.' That woman is the biggest rain cloud I've ever met."

We all three shared a laugh, and then they insisted that I get to my table, since the food was being served.

"Love you guys," I said.

"Love you big." Montana kissed my cheek. "Go eat dinner with that sexy man of yours."

"Yeah. He's looking awfully sexy in that suit of his," Blakely added with a grin.

I made my way over to the table and took the seat on the other side of Charlie. He tugged my chair closer and kissed me, right there in front of everyone. "I missed you, Firefly."

I moved closer so only he could hear me. "Missed you too."

Fillets were set down in front of Harper and me, and Charlie had the salmon. Everyone was raving about how good the food looked.

DJ Crazy Ass had quieted down for dinner, thankfully, and we could actually have a conversation.

My brothers were asking Charlie all about his business, and Paris was going on and on about what a great job he'd done over at my house.

"That was all your sister. She tortured me with all the changes," he said with a laugh. "But in the end, her eye for design has made that place look like something out of a magazine."

"I'd like to come see it tomorrow," my father said, surprising everyone, as it was the first time he'd spoken since I sat down.

"We're doing gifts in the morning, and then we've got plans for lunch in the afternoon," Missy said as she cut into her steak.

"I don't mind skipping lunch. I'd like to see Violet's new home. Is there a time that works best for you?" he asked, turning his attention to me, as Missy's eyes widened.

"I'm around in the afternoon, and you're all welcome."

"Well, we're staying over there, and I have no desire to watch Velveteen and Ralph open toaster ovens, so I'll be there when you come over," Huntington said as he winked at Harper.

"Yeah, Mom, Ralph is not going to be waking up and opening gifts in the morning," Paris said. "I'll be sleeping in at Vi's house, and we can all go have breakfast at the diner. I love downtown Blushing. It's so cute."

Missy's gaze locked with mine, and I could see the panic.

Why did I care that she was upset? She'd always been terrible to me.

"Count me in. I promised Charlie and Harper I'd sleep over there tonight, but we'll meet you guys at the diner in the morning. And you're welcome to join us," I said as I looked at Missy and my father.

"Yes!" Harper pumped her fist. "The Brown Bear Diner has the best pancakes. And then we can all go to Vi's house after. Maybe we'll see Chompers. He lives in her trees."

"I'd like that. I'll meet you there," my father said. "And then we'll go see your house."

"What's a Chompers?" Missy asked, her shoulders relaxing as if she wasn't going to fight anyone about their plans for tomorrow.

"He's a groundhog," Charlie told her, and then he filled them in about all the damage he'd done to my house during the renovations.

We laughed and talked, and for the first time, I didn't feel like the outsider.

I felt like I was exactly where I should be.

We finished up dinner, and Harper was having the time of her life with my siblings. They'd taken her out to the dance floor, and she kept waving at us. Charlie and I had danced a few times, but we'd spent some time moving around and chatting with people as well. He'd followed my lead, and every time I'd ask if he was okay, he'd say the same thing.

"I'm exactly where I want to be, Firefly."

We came back to the table once the cake was served. Ralph actually surprised me by not slamming the cake into Velveteen's face, as I'd expected him to do. Instead, I noticed the way he'd inspected her bandaged palm and planted a kiss there. It was the most tender thing I'd ever seen that man do. He then pulled her onto his lap and shared a piece of cake with her.

It gave me hope that maybe they'd be okay.

Because even when Velveteen had been unkind to me, which was most of my life, I still loved her.

And tonight it felt like we'd made progress. Like we might find a new normal that worked for us.

But either way, I'd be fine.

Charlie carried an exhausted Harper out of the reception, and we dropped Paris, Huntington, and Brenton at my house before we drove the short distance to his.

Sweet Harper fell asleep in the back of the truck, and we got her inside and changed her into her jammies before tucking her into bed. We made our way out of her room as her little voice called out.

"Daddy, Vi," she whispered, and we both turned around as we stood in the doorway.

"Yeah, baby girl," Charlie said as I made my way back to her bed and sat beside her.

"I had fun tonight," she said.

"I did too." I leaned down and kissed her forehead.

"I love Daddy and I love you. But most of all, I love that we feel like a family. A real family," she said as her eyes fell closed.

I placed a hand on my heart, because I felt her words so deeply, it was difficult to speak.

Because we were a real family.

CHAPTER THIRTY

Charlie

I laughed as Harper filled Violet in on some school gossip that I had zero interest in, but damn, I loved the way these two just got one another.

Violet had been staying over at our house most nights, and now when she didn't sleep here, I had a hard time sleeping without her.

I never thought I'd be dependent on another human, but here I was.

Violet Beaumont had brought me back to life in a way.

I'd been living for my little girl, and that would never change, but I looked at the future differently now. I wanted things that I never thought I'd want.

"Davey definitely has a crush on you if he's giving you half his cookie every day at lunch," Violet said as she reached for her orange juice.

"Whoa, whoa, whoa . . . She's seven years old. Davey needs to take a hike," I said, and they both laughed.

"Denise Quigley has a boyfriend," Harper said.

"Well, good for her. You're not dating until college."

"Oh boy." Violet shook her head and used her hand to cover her laughter. "Good luck with that."

"Daddy." Harper looked at me like she was seven going on thirty.

"Harps." I mimicked her tone.

"I don't want a boyfriend. The boys in my class are annoying."

"Attagirl. Boys are bad news."

Violet rolled her eyes. "You were a boy once."

"Correct. And I was bad news."

More laughter.

This was our new normal, and I fucking loved it.

"Daddy has so many rules," Harper grumped.

"'Stay away from boys. Don't talk to strangers. Listen to your father.' What else you got, Harps?" I asked.

"'No demon.'" She cocked her head at me like I should have known what she was going to say.

The fucking demon.

I'd been hearing about this slide for the last six months.

"You keep talking about the demon. I don't understand what the big deal is. It's a slide?" Violet asked as she looked between us.

"The coolest slide in Blushing. And Denise Quigley's mom let her do it."

I was getting really tired of hearing about Denise Quigley. Her mother gave into her every whim, and I wasn't going to let a seven-year-old decide if something was age-appropriate.

"Is there an age or weight requirement?" my girlfriend asked.

"No. No one monitors it," I said. "But it's been around forever. It's just too steep for a kid, and I've seen kids get real wild on that slide. I'll reconsider when she's ten years old. She's too young."

It was my job to keep her safe.

"So it's just a slide?" Violet chuckled.

"A big slide. A slide for older kids." I looked at each of them.

"He finally let me start riding a two-wheeler," Harper huffed. "Lily has been riding a two-wheeler since she was five years old. And she's asking her mom if she can go on the demon."

"Lose the attitude, Harps. We don't do things just because other people do them," I said.

"I don't want to do it because other people do it, Daddy. I think it's cool, and I know I could do it. You did it when you were a lot younger than me. Mrs. McAffrey even told me so."

I'll be giving Jeanne a piece of my mind next time I see her.

"I didn't have parents looking out for me when I was your age. So yeah, I did things that weren't smart. I got hurt doing dumb things, when it could have been avoided. My job is to keep you safe. End of story."

She frowned, and Violet looked between us before turning her attention to my daughter. "Hey, you're pretty lucky having a daddy who looks out for you. I didn't have anyone watching out for me when I was a kid, and I used to be very jealous of the kids who had parents who cared." Violet took her hand and squeezed it.

Harper sighed. "I know. But I'm not a baby."

"I don't think you're a baby," I said, stopping myself from calling her "baby girl." I added, "I think you're very strong and capable. And you are killing it on your two-wheeler. Come on. We have a deal that we never stay mad at one another. Give me a hug."

So maybe I'm a little irrational sometimes when it comes to safety.

A wide grin spread across my daughter's face, and she moved to her feet and climbed on my lap. "I love you more than all the blueberry pancakes."

"I love you more than all the birds in the sky," I said.

Violet moved to her feet and wrapped her arms around us. "I love you more than all the pink balloons."

Harper laughed hysterically, and I winked at Violet as I set my daughter down on her feet.

"All right, I've got to drop you at school early, Harps. I need to meet the landscaper over at the hotel." I stood up and reached for their breakfast plates.

"Oh man, I don't want to go early today because Lily has a dentist appointment, so she won't be there to play before school."

"I can take you. I don't have to be at work for an hour," Violet said. She'd gone with me to drop off and pick up Harper from school a couple of times before. But she'd never done it solo.

"Yay!" Harper held her hand up to high-five my girlfriend.

"Are you sure?" I asked.

"Yes, of course. It's on the way. And that way I can scope out Davey," she said, and I rolled my eyes.

"Sounds good. I'll see you both later." I kissed Harper on the cheek, and then I dipped Violet back and kissed her.

She smacked me on the ass after I grabbed my keys and my sunglasses and made my way out the door.

Once I was in my truck, I adjusted my rearview mirror, catching my reflection.

I had a goofy smile on my face.

This new normal was definitely working for me.

"Well, look who it is? I didn't think you'd show," Myles said as Benji laughed loudly.

I'd met him for a drink at the Moose Brew, and I knew he was going to give me shit because it had been a while.

"Hey, you don't always show up either."

"I'm just giving you a hard time. I'm happy for you, brother." He clapped me on the shoulder.

"Well, fuck you both for being ridiculously happy." Benji set a beer down in front of me with a wicked grin on his face before walking off when a customer waved him over.

"So, how's it going? I hear Violet practically lives at your place." He took a sip of his whiskey.

"Yeah, she's over a lot. She likes us to come to her place, too, but it's easier at my place with all Harper's things there. So we stay at her place on the weekends, when Harper doesn't have school."

"I'm glad it's working out. I was worried you two would kill each other when she first moved into your guesthouse." He smirked.

"Yeah. There were some close calls. And she loves to challenge me and give me shit, but it works, you know?"

"Yeah. I know. I get it," he said. "So will you make it official and ask her to move in?"

"Hell, I'd make it official today," I said. "But Violet needs to do things on her time. She's pretty guarded and cautious, so I don't want to scare her off."

"I don't know about that. She's different with you. Montana notices it too. You're different with her as well. Sometimes it's just right, and you have to stop questioning it."

"How are we different?" I asked.

"Well, for one, I thought you didn't know how to smile before, but it turns out you were just a miserable fucker." He chuckled. "And Violet is always looking all goofy around you and Harper, which is rare for her. It's a good thing. I'm happy for both of you. You're not going to scare her off. She's in just as deep as you are."

"It's not something I ever expected, you know? I didn't ever expect to find someone I'd want to be in a relationship with." I shrugged. "I mean, she and Harper practically booted me out of the house tonight. They're doing some sort of face-mask, skin-care bullshit together, and it's fucking adorable. Violet just fits—like she was always meant to be here."

Myles smiled. "I'm happy for you, man. It's scary as shit when it first happens, but once you let yourself enjoy it, it's not scary at all."

"So you've got the wedding to look forward to. I take it she's doing all the planning?"

"Yeah, that's her thing. You know me, I'd marry her today at the courthouse and just make it official. But she wants to have our friends and family there, and I'm fine with it. I don't give a shit who's there as long as she's happy."

"You are one pussy-whipped motherfucker." My head tipped back in laughter.

"I'm not denying it. But she's talking about kids, and I know I want that, I'm just—"

"You're worried you won't be good at it?" I asked, knowing exactly what Myles was feeling.

"Yeah. I mean, any kid is going to be lucky to have Montana for a mother. I know that. But I had a pretty fucked-up father, and I don't want to fuck up anyone, you know?"

I chuckled. "Dude, your dad is an asshole."

"I can be an asshole too."

"You're a different kind of asshole." I held up a hand to stop him from blasting me before I continued. "You can be an overbearing, overprotective asshole. That's different. You love deeply. You aren't a selfish prick like your father. Hell, I struggled with all of this when Harper was born. I doubted myself every single day those first few months. But let me tell you the secret I've learned so far that has served me well. As long as you show up and you love that child, you're going to be fine. The only way you fuck it up is by not being there. If you show up every damn day, and you love them the best way you can, you're going to be fine."

"I can handle that. I just don't like to suck at anything. I like to win. I want to be a rock star dad," he said, holding up his glass for another one when Benji looked over.

I laughed. "Of course you want to be a rock star dad. You don't even have a kid yet, and you're already competing to be the best."

"You're pretty damn impressive, especially when you wear those little pigtails." He used his hand to cover his mouth to keep from laughing. "And that was blue glitter, right?"

"Damn straight, asshole. And you'll do the same thing. In fact, I'm going to wish three daughters on you now."

He chuckled before he straightened his face. "If I had a little girl like Harper, I'd let her do whatever she wanted to do to me. You're the standard, Charlie. If I'm half the dad that you are, I'll be winning."

My eyes widened just as Benji set our drinks down. "What's going on here? It looks serious."

"I think this broody bastard just complimented me, and I'm processing it." I smirked.

"I don't think anyone in town would argue with the fact that Charlie's a damn good dad," Myles said.

"I have to agree with that one. And now he's practically married, and he's living the dream," Benji said.

I rolled my eyes and acted annoyed, but I couldn't hide the smile spreading across my face.

Because I *was* living the dream. I'd become a big sappy bastard, and I wasn't even denying it.

And I couldn't wait to get home to my girls.

CHAPTER THIRTY-ONE

Violet

Charlie was working late, and I'd gotten off work early today, so I was happy to go get Harper from school. Jeanne had texted me, and we were going to take the girls for ice cream, since the weather was so nice.

When I arrived at Rosewood River Elementary School, Jeanne was already there, and she didn't look happy.

"What's wrong?" I whispered. The girls were still getting their backpacks from the classroom.

"Denise Quigley is the problem. She's calling the girls 'babies' because a few kids in the class went down the demon this week." She shook her head and rolled her eyes at the same time.

"What is the deal with this slide?" I chuckled. "I keep hearing about it. And Charlie said she needs to be ten years old to go down it. Is it that big?"

A loud laugh escaped her mouth. "No. Charlie and I went down that damn thing when we were in kindergarten. It's just old and the sides aren't super high, but I was thinking of going down with Lily, so I could hold on to her."

Denise's mom stood a few feet away from us as her son ran in and out of the classroom, and she just talked on her phone. Mrs. Wharton did not look happy as she escorted him out for the second time since I'd arrived.

Harper and Lily came walking out with frowns on their faces, and Denise hurried out after them.

"You two really can't go? I can't believe you're afraid of a slide," she said, and my hands fisted at my side.

"I'm not afraid, it's just my dad's rule that I can't do it," Harper said, hands on her hips, head high.

Attagirl.

"My mom said I could go if I want to, and I'm not afraid at all." Lily glared at Denise.

"I bet you're too much of a baby to go down, even if you go over there."

"How about you take care of yourself and mind your own business?" Jeanne said to Denise as she took Lily's backpack from her.

"Poor Harper is the only one who isn't going," Denise said before sticking her tongue out and then laughing. "Maybe we should call you 'scaredy-cat baby Huxley.'"

"Denise, why don't you go help your brother. He's licking the pavement again." I bent down and hugged Harper. I was definitely going to ask Charlie to speak to the school about this. Denise was clearly bullying Harper at this point, and the school needed to get involved. "Hey, Harps. How was your day?"

"It was fine. Can we go with Lily and Jeanne to the demon and watch Lily go down before we get ice cream?" She blinked a few times, and I could tell she was fighting back tears.

Harper didn't get upset often, so I knew she'd had a rough day.

"Of course we can. Let's go check this slide out and cheer Lily on," I said, slipping her backpack on my shoulder and taking her hand.

Lily and Harper were filling us in on all the drama from the day. The way Denise had made fun of several kids, and Bianca had gone home with a stomachache after Denise had told everyone that Bianca had gone up the ladder on the slide and then come back down the ladder because she'd been too nervous to go down.

Denise Quigley was a bully, and I had a problem with bullies.

I would assume the teacher was aware at this point, but I was going to insist that Charlie make an appointment to discuss this situation to see how they were going to handle things.

"Harper told Denise to leave Bianca alone, so Denise got real mean to Harps," Lily said. "And Denise had to pull a red card, which means she sat out recess for being a meanie."

"What did she say to you?" I asked.

I didn't miss the way Harper shook her head ever so slightly at her best friend, as if she didn't want her to repeat it.

"It wasn't a big deal. She just called me a baby," Harper said.

When we turned the corner, I laughed at the sight before me. It was just an older playground slide like I used to go down when I was a kid. It wasn't like the new fancy slides with the high walls on the sides and the spongy padding on the bottom. It was certainly not anything I hadn't seen before. The park had some older swings with chain-link sides and black rubber bottoms, like the kind I used to do flips off of. There was a merry-go-round and a wooden seesaw that looked like it had seen better days. I watched a few kids go down the slide, and it was a bit steep and the sides were lower than on the slides you saw at newly remodeled parks, but if you came down carefully, it wouldn't be a big deal at all.

Several kids stared up at it like it was some sort of mythical beast they'd been told about. A kid was up at the top shouting at his mom to take a picture before he came down. It was definitely steep, and the kid came flying down, then tucked into a ball and rolled on the ground before coming to a stop.

"Oh, look who came to watch me," Denise said as she walked up behind us. "I've done this so many times. It's so easy for me."

She marched past us and climbed the stairs, and I glanced over to see her brother attempting to get on the seesaw, which looked like it would be impossible to ride without getting several splinters.

I waved at his mom and then pointed to the seesaw to make sure she knew he was on it, but she just turned her back to me and continued talking on her phone.

"Who is she talking to all the time?" I huffed.

"I have no idea. But she's got one on the demon and one on the death-saw," Jeanne said.

I laughed. This park had quite the reputation from the locals who'd grown up here.

"Harper! Lily! Look at me! I'm not a big baby!" Denise shouted from the top before sitting down and pushing off. She came down faster than the last kid, and my instincts had me running toward the bottom of the slide to break her fall.

She crashed into me, and I fell back and wrapped my arms around her to keep her from hitting the ground hard.

She got up and laughed. "You didn't need to do that. Maybe Harper needs help, but I don't."

"You're welcome," I hissed, scrambling to my feet and brushing off my jeans.

"Come on, Mom," Lily said, and she took Jeanne's hand and walked toward the back of the slide.

"Lily's going down and you're not," the little hellion taunted as she moved to stand in front of us and laughed. "Poor Harper Huxley."

"Hey, walk away, Quigley," I said.

"You can't even take her down because you're not even a real mama. You're just her friend. Only a real mama could go down the slide with her." She smirked.

This kid was like seven going on seventeen.

She could write the mean girl manual all on her own.

And this slide had been ridiculously built up, as it wasn't even the tallest I'd seen—not that I was a slide connoisseur by any stretch, but this was not that big of a deal.

"How about you go find your own mom?" I grumped, wrapping an arm around Harper's shoulder.

I leaned down and whispered in her ear, "She's just jealous."

Harper nodded as she stared up at the demon, where Lily and Jeanne stood at the top.

I squinted, trying to make them out, and Lily was definitely hesitating. She sat between her mother's legs, and they pushed off. Harper squeezed my hand as we watched them come down. With Jeanne behind Lily, she wasn't moving quite as fast, and they stumbled a little at the bottom, but Jeanne was able to right them easily.

A few more kids arrived and made their way to the top.

"How was it?" Harper asked Lily.

"It was fine. It wasn't even that fun," her best friend said, keeping her voice low.

A few kids from their class showed up and came over to congratulate Lily.

"Are you going down?" Davey asked Harper.

"My dad won't let me," she said.

"And Violet isn't her real mother, so she can't even take her down. She's just like a babysitter," Denise said as she moved right in Harper's space, the little stalker she was.

Harper shoved her back, which shocked me.

I'd never seen Harper get physical with anyone.

"Go away. Violet is a real mother. She's not on the phone like your mom always is!" she shouted.

"Hey, hey, hey." I took her hand and walked her away. "Harps, you can't react to her. That's what she wants."

Tears ran down her face, and I bent down to get eye level with her and wrapped my arms around her.

"She's been saying that all day. That you're not a real mama. That I'm just a big, sad baby." She sniffed.

I had the sudden urge to drop-kick Denise Quigley, even though I knew I couldn't do that. It didn't stop me from wanting to.

"She's just unhappy. You're not sad and you're not a baby."

"You feel like a real mama sometimes, Vi," Harper said, her voice cracking as the words left her mouth.

I feel like a real mama when it comes to this little girl.

"I love you the way a mama does, Harps. And that's all that matters. So Denise Quigley can suck a lemon," I said, and Harper's body shook with laughter as she sniffed a few more times.

I looked up at the slide as two more kids came down, one by one, without incident.

Jeanne had just done it with Lily.

"I know you do."

"And we don't care what Denise Quigley thinks, Harps. We know how we feel. We know who we are. She's got her own issues. So let's just have some fun today and ignore Denise, okay?"

"Okay. I like that idea." She smiled after wiping the last of her tears away.

"Maybe me and Harper could go down the slide together," Lily said. "It's not really even bigger than the one at Blushing Park by your house that we go down all the time. It's just not yellow and pretty." Lily chuckled.

"Do you think I could go down with Lily, Vi?" Harper asked me, with all the trust in the world.

"Let me ask you something," I said, tucking the hair behind her ear. "Do you want to go down the demon because it's something you want to do, or because you don't want Denise to tease you about it?"

Because we are not going to let a seven-year-old bully decide what we do.

"I don't care what Denise thinks. She's a meanie anyway." Harper smiled this crooked little smile that almost killed me. "I just want to show Daddy that I'm a big girl."

Jeanne shook her head and chuckled. "It wasn't bad at all. I'd tell you if I was concerned about it."

"Give me a minute, okay?" I said, pulling out my cell phone. I dialed Charlie's number. I needed him to let me do this with her. He didn't pick up, and I knew he was in a meeting this afternoon. I sent a text.

Me: Hey. I love you and I'm at the park with Harps, Lily, and Jeanne. Jeanne just went down the demon with Lily. Harper really wants to do this. What if I go down with her?

Charles: I hate that fucking slide. It's dangerous.

Me: She'll be with me, and I'm a grown woman. I promise I'll keep her safe. Do you trust me?

Charles: You know I trust you, Firefly. It's the fucking slide I don't trust.

Me: What could possibly happen on a slide with me holding her? Come on, Charles. You're being irrational. Let me do this with her.

Charles: Fine. But I'd much prefer you both just go get ice cream and stay off tall slides.

Me: I'll take that as a yes. Thank you for knowing that she's safe with me. Love you.

Charles: Love you. Keep my little girl safe, Violet.

I tucked my phone in my purse and handed it to Jeanne.

"What if I go down with you?" I asked Harper.

"Yes!" She clapped in excitement.

"Come on, Harps. We're doing this." I glanced over at Denise, who was watching us like a hawk.

"Go, Harper!" Lily shouted.

We marched hand in hand toward the back of the ladder.

Of course, Denise jogged up behind us, because she had nothing better to do than taunt everyone around her.

I turned around and glared at her. I didn't speak a word. I just gave her that look.

Not today, Satan.

Harper went first, and I followed behind her.

Denise stayed right on my ass, and I heard a few boys behind us now as well.

She had a way of drawing a crowd with all her big talk.

"Don't pay them any attention. I've got you," I said so only Harper could hear me.

"I'm not even scared, Vi," she said.

When we got to the top, Harper and I both chuckled, because it wasn't that big of a deal. It was just like any other slide, minus the low sides and the hard ground beneath it.

"You ready?" I asked as she reached for the pole to hold on as she moved to sit.

"You can still change your mind, Harper!" Denise shouted. "That's what all the babies do!"

I turned around and glared at her.

My God, this kid is working my nerves.

"Let's do this, Vi." Harper smiled up at me, her eyes dancing with excitement.

I dropped to sit, and as I was getting her settled between my legs, a hard kick hit my back, and we slipped forward.

Denise landed on my back—she'd clearly kicked me and lost her balance—and I fell forward.

I did everything I could to adjust Harper. Both of my arms wrapped around her as one of her legs hung off the slide, and I frantically tried to pull it in. I was partly turned sideways. Denise had all her weight pressed against my back, and we were moving fast. Harper had her back pressed against my chest as she giggled and squealed as if this was the best thing she'd ever done.

I could hear a boy laughing behind me, and I realized more kids had jumped on behind Denise.

I wrapped myself around Harper the best I could as we approached the bottom, and we hit the ground on a hard whoosh.

I tried like hell to protect my girl.

My girl.

Jeanne and two other mothers were there trying to pull us all apart as Denise and two older boys tumbled on top of us. We got everyone off, and Harper let out a loud cry.

She was lying on her back, holding her arm and wailing.

"Are you okay?" I frantically touched her face and her head.

She nodded as tears ran down her face. "My arm hurts, and my neck hurts, Vi."

I could see the way her arm was bent, and she wasn't moving her neck at all, and I knew she wasn't okay. Her arm was clearly broken.

"Call an ambulance," I said to Jeanne, and she already had the phone in her hand.

I didn't have a car here, and I was afraid to move her.

"Sorry, I fell on top of you guys," Denise said with a sniff as the two older boys ran off.

I looked up to see her mother watching us, and I'd never felt so much rage in that moment. "Come get your damn kid, Quigley!"

She actually ended her call and jogged over.

I just sat over Harper, stroking her face and keeping her still as I told her she was going to be okay over and over. Luckily the ambulance showed up within minutes, and I told them what happened, and I was crying now too. They assessed her and quickly got her on a gurney, stabilizing her neck. I held her hand as we loaded her up in the ambulance. Jeanne said she'd meet us there, and I asked her to call Charlie.

"I'm so sorry," I whispered to Harper as we made our way to the hospital.

"It's okay, Vi. We did it. We did the demon." She winced, and it was clear that she was in pain.

"Is she going to be okay?" I asked, and the paramedic's gaze softened.

"Yes, she'll be okay. I think she probably broke her arm and maybe her wrist, but they'll get her all fixed up at the hospital," he assured me. "They'll just want to check her neck and make sure it's all okay. I've got her stabilized for now."

I nodded, the panic coursing through my veins. Her arm was probably broken. Maybe in two places.

And what if her neck was broken?

I tried hard to keep it together as we hurried inside.

The nurse suggested I wait out in the lobby, but I was hysterical, and Harper got upset, so they allowed me to stay with her.

She whimpered as she lay in the hospital bed, my hand in hers.

"I'm right here, Harps. Daddy's on his way, okay?" I said, my voice shaking.

I knew that Jeanne had called Charlie, and she was probably out in the waiting room now with Lily as well.

"You'll stay with me?" she croaked.

"I'm not going anywhere."

"Where is she?" The sound of Charlie's voice, angry and gruff, came from behind me.

He stormed into the room, and the look on his face had my heart sinking.

He'd never forgive me for this.

He rushed over to the side of her bed, and I could actually see his heart breaking as he took in her tear-streaked face. "You're okay, baby girl."

"My arm hurts, Daddy." Her voice was soft and shaky.

"I know it does. But you're tough as nails, Harps. We're going to get you all fixed up."

He hadn't looked at me yet, and the doctor walked in and introduced himself. Dr. Jenkins asked what happened, and I gave him a brief breakdown about how she went down the slide awkwardly as I tried to secure her, and we crashed at the bottom of the slide with several kids behind us who piled on top.

"I tried to shield her," I said, my voice quaking. "I didn't press down on her when we hit the ground, but a larger boy who'd been behind me went over my back and landed on her."

"All right. Accidents happen. She's going to be okay. We're going to get some x-rays of her arm and her wrist, and we'll do a CT scan and check out the neck and spine. She'll most likely be going home today if everything looks okay."

Two nurses walked in the room and said they were ready to take her for x-rays.

"Can they come with me?" Harper whimpered.

"We can let one person come back with us," the nurse said, looking between Charlie and me.

"I'm her father. I'm going with her," he said, still not looking at me.

I nodded. "I'll just wait out in the waiting room."

I kissed Harper on the forehead and glanced up to see Charlie watching me. Our eyes locked for the first time since he'd walked in, and I wished I hadn't looked up.

Because the disappointment I saw there shattered me.

And I knew nothing would ever be the same again.

CHAPTER THIRTY-TWO

Charlie

I'd calmed down over the last few hours, but the fear that my baby girl had been badly hurt was almost paralyzing.

Jeanne had called and told me that Harper had been taken by ambulance to the hospital.

I swear, I felt like I couldn't breathe.

I'd never felt panic like that.

It was all because of that damn demon slide.

The one I'd known Harper wasn't old enough to go down.

And now we were here, and she was getting a cast put on her broken arm.

Her radius bone had been fractured, which is the bone that connects from the elbow to the hand.

Thankfully her neck was okay, and her wrist was just sprained, not broken.

We'd been here for hours.

Harper had fallen asleep for a while in between the x-rays and getting the cast on. I'd stayed right here with her.

Violet had texted a few times, and I'd let her know that Harper was okay and she was welcome to come back in the room, but she'd stayed out in the waiting room.

We were both obviously processing a horrible situation.

I knew Harper was too small to go down that fucking death slide, and I was pissed at myself for saying yes, and even pissed at Violet for asking.

Hell, maybe I was just pissed at everyone and everything because seeing Harper cry in pain made me feel helpless.

My job was to protect her, and I hadn't done that today.

"Okay, we're all finished up. Looks pretty cool, doesn't it?" the orthopedic technician asked my daughter.

Harper was all smiles now. She had a hot-pink cast on her arm and pain meds running through her little body to manage her discomfort.

"It's so cool. Wait till Violet sees it. And it's pink, Daddy. Pinkalicious would get a pink cast," Harper said with a big smile on her face.

Her eyes were still swollen from all the tears she'd shed earlier, but she was feeling much better now, that much was obvious.

"Yep. It's pretty cool, Harps. But no more going down slides for a while," I said, my voice coming out harsher than I meant it to.

"From what I heard about the incident, I don't think you can blame the slide," the technician said. "It sounds like the problem was the kids landing on top of her."

I nodded, but none of it would have happened if she hadn't gone down in the first place.

The nurse came in and gave me some paperwork to sign, and they insisted on taking her out in a wheelchair, even though I offered to carry her.

Once we made our way out to the lobby, Violet was there in a chair, with Montana and Myles beside her. Jeanne, Tim, and Lily were there as well, and even Benji and Will had shown up. How the hell did they all know to come to the hospital?

My gaze found Violet's, and I realized it was her.

She'd called all my people. The people who felt more like family.

Everyone hurried to their feet and came to check out her cast.

"Oh man, Denise Quigley is going to lose her mind that you got a pink cast." Lily stared down at her best friend's arm.

"And we both went down the demon today," my daughter said.

I got the short version from Jeanne when I'd lost my shit about how a group of kids had jumped on behind Violet, which was exactly what I hated about that damn park.

Everyone took turns giving Harper hugs and telling her how brave she was.

My gaze locked with Violet's. Her eyes were swollen, and her cheeks were streaked from hours of falling tears.

I wanted to comfort her, but she could barely look at me.

"We did it, Violet. We went down the demon," Harper said, her voice filled with pride.

"Is her neck okay?" Violet asked, her voice small and shaky.

"Yes, her neck is okay. She broke her radius bone on her arm, and her wrist is sprained," I said, my voice flat, because I was fucking exhausted.

I glanced over at the nurse, patiently waiting to take us out to the car.

"Can you pull my truck up to the front, Will?" I asked, tossing him the keys. He nodded and jogged out the door. "You all need to go home and get some rest. I'm going to take Harper home and get her cleaned up and fed, and hopefully she can sleep for a few hours."

Everyone said their goodbyes, and Violet leaned down and kissed my daughter's cheek.

"I love you so much, Harper Huxley." Her words broke on a sob. "I'm so sorry."

"Thanks for being a real mama, Vi. We were both brave today."

What the hell did any of this have to do with being a real mama?

It hit me that it was a big deal to my daughter that she'd gone down that slide. And the tech who'd put on her cast was right—the slide wasn't the cause of the accident. She'd been hurt because the other kids were irresponsible, but that's what kids do, right?

I used to be one. I should've known that.

Violet looked up at me, her pretty green gaze holding mine.

"I'm sorry," she whispered.

"I know you are. This wasn't your fault," I said, not wanting to have this discussion with an audience around. "Let's talk about it at the house."

She took a few steps back. "It's been a long day. I'm going to catch a ride with Montana and Myles tonight. Text me if you need anything, okay?"

Her voice wobbled, and I knew she was on the verge of losing it.

A part of me wanted to pull her into my arms right there. Tell her it would be okay.

But Will jogged in and said the truck was out front, and the nurse started pushing the wheelchair.

So I just nodded and walked out the door, because right now I needed to be a dad.

I'd already failed my daughter once today, and she had the cast to prove it.

We carefully got Harper in her car seat, and I drove the short distance home.

"Isn't Violet coming over tonight?" Harper asked as I got her out of the car.

"Not tonight. I think everyone needs to get some sleep."

I carried her inside the house, took her right to the bathroom, and turned on the water to the bathtub. She was filthy from her fall, and I wanted to get her cleaned up.

I racked my mind about what I had in the freezer that I could toss in the oven for dinner, because I didn't have it in me to do more than that right now. We didn't use as much water as usual, and I quickly got her cleaned up and washed, all while she held her casted arm up and out of the way. I dried her off and got her into her jammies before combing through her long hair.

The doorbell rang, and I padded out to the front door and pulled it open.

"Hey, Charlie," Freddy Taylor said. He was a high school kid who worked over at the Brown Bear Diner as a busboy. "Violet ordered some dinner for you and Harper, and she asked us to drop it off. We're all sorry to hear about Harper's accident. Is she doing all right?" he asked as he handed me the bag of food.

Damn. Violet knew what I needed. She knew what we needed.

She hadn't brought it herself, though, which surprised me.

She wasn't one to stand on ceremony.

But today was heavy, and I knew she was already retreating. Beating herself up for something that wasn't her fault.

But she'd still thought of us. She'd sent dinner over because that was her way of being here for us.

I unpacked the food as my daughter came around the corner, and she climbed onto her chair.

"Violet sent dinner over," I said.

I should have talked to her at the hospital. I should have told her I'd had my share of accidents with my daughter. I should have made it clear that this wasn't her fault. That some things were out of our control with kids.

"I love Violet. You know she's a real mama, right?" Harper asked, her long hair still wet as it hung over her shoulders.

I set chicken fingers on a plate with some french fries, and I chuckled at the separate container of brussels sprouts and broccoli, because Violet was always trying to get Harper to eat more veggies. I added those to her plate and set it down in front of her.

She'd sent a steak for me, with some onion rings and a salad.

My girl was thoughtful.

I sat down across from my daughter. "What do you mean by that? What is a real mama, and why does that keep coming up?"

"Jeanne took Lily down the slide, and me and Violet were just going to watch Lily. And Denise Quigley kept on calling me a baby, and

Violet told her to leave me alone." She paused and bit into a chicken finger, and I cut a piece of steak and waited for her to finish. "Then Denise said that Violet wasn't a real mama—she was just a babysitter, and she couldn't take me on the slide. But she is a real mama. She loves me and I love her. We're a family, right, Daddy?"

I nodded. I could imagine how tough it was for Violet to have to stand by and hear that little shit ridicule Harper.

Violet loved my daughter.

I knew that.

"So you and Violet went down that slide because Denise didn't think you could?" I asked.

"No. I wouldn't go down a slide because of Denise. I don't even like her, Daddy. And I told Vi that. I wanted to go down the slide to show you that I wasn't a baby. And Lily asked me to go down with her. But Violet wanted to be there with me. And it was fun, Daddy. I mean, until all those kids fell on top of me." She giggled. "But Violet had them all on her back, and she did everything she could to keep me safe. When Violet's with us, we feel like a family, don't we?"

"We are a family, baby girl." I took a sip of my water. "So it was fun, huh? You weren't scared up on that slide?"

"No. Because I was with Vi. She held on to me the whole way. Those kids jumped on the slide behind her. They were supposed to wait, but they jumped on Vi's back. But she held me and made me feel safe, Daddy. That's why she's a real mama. She makes me feel safe."

Fuck me.

My seven-year-old was smarter than me.

"Being with Vi is just like being with you, Daddy."

I nodded but didn't reply. Because she trusted Violet, and so did I.

We finished dinner and I read *Pinkalicious* to her, and luckily she was exhausted from the day. I told her I'd sleep on her bedroom floor, because I was worried she'd wake up in the middle of the night in pain, and I wanted to be close.

Once she was sleeping, I made my way out to lock up the house.

I grabbed my phone, wanting to text Violet to thank her for sending over dinner.

There were quite a few texts from her.

Firefly: I'm so sorry, Charlie. I messed up.
Firefly: How is Harper feeling? Is she in pain? How will she bathe with the cast on?
Firefly: How long will she have the cast for?
Firefly: I understand if you never want to speak to me again.
Firefly: I love you. I told you I wasn't good at this. I knew I'd mess it up. It's what I do. But I'd never want to do anything to endanger Harper, and I don't know if I'll ever forgive myself.
Me: You have nothing to apologize for. I should have said it at the hospital, but I was just freaked out. We can't stop kids from getting hurt, Violet. You did everything you could to protect her. It would have been much worse if you hadn't been there. You used your body to shield her.
Firefly: No. This is on me. I asked you to trust me. I promised to keep her safe. And I didn't do that.

I reached for my phone and dialed. She picked up on the first ring, and I heard the sobs before she spoke.

"I-I'm so sorry," she cried.

"Violet, you need to relax. She's okay. We're okay. She's a kid, and she's going to get hurt sometimes," I said.

"No, Charlie. I'm just not good at this stuff. This is why everyone always leaves. Because I mess up. And now your daughter has a broken arm and is wearing a cast." She was gasping as if she couldn't catch her breath.

It killed me to hear her like this.

I couldn't wake Harper up and take her over there.

"Come over here, baby," I said. "I am not upset with you. This could have happened to anyone. Come home."

"Charlie, this is on me," she cried. "I think we need some time to figure things out."

I closed my eyes and rubbed the back of my head.

This was her MO. She felt like she'd messed up, and she was going to retreat.

"Don't run, Firefly. Everyone's okay," I said, desperate to soothe her.

"Harper is not okay. You're not okay. I'm not okay."

"This is love, Violet. It's not perfect. It's messy. And we're going to have our ups and downs. We're going to make mistakes. But we're a family, and we don't run," I said. "I'm not leaving you. I'm not going anywhere."

"How is Harper?" she croaked.

"Harper is fine. She loves her cast. She took a bath, and she loved the dinner you sent over. She's sound asleep."

"Is she mad at me?" she asked, and her words wobbled.

"No. She actually told me that you're a real mama. You make her feel safe, and that's why she went down that slide. Because she was with you. You're what she's been missing, Firefly."

She sniffed several times, and I heard her trying to catch her breath again.

"Can you send me a text in the morning and let me know how she's doing?"

"Of course. Why don't you just come over and sleep here? This is your home," I said. "I love you."

"I love you more than all the stars in the sky, Charlie Huxley. Good night."

She ended the call, and I felt my chest squeeze.

Because it felt final.

Like she wasn't saying goodbye for the night—it felt like she was saying goodbye to us.

CHAPTER THIRTY-THREE

Violet

Montana had come over late last night after calling to check on me, and she found I was spiraling with worry. She'd spent the night with me, and I was grateful she was here.

"Did you finally sleep?" she asked when I padded out to the kitchen. She poured me a cup of coffee and handed it to me.

"Yes. I got some sleep. I'm so sorry for keeping you up so late."

"Stop, Vi. This is what friends do for each other. You've always been there for me. I know it's hard for you to ask for help, but I want to be there for you." She came to sit on the barstool beside me.

"Well, thank you. You helped me a lot. I wanted to pack my bags and leave the country last night." I chuckled. "I don't know why I always want to leave when I mess up."

"First of all. You're being too hard on yourself. You didn't mess up. You took her down a slide. You were with her. You can't help that some lunatic children jumped on behind you and rolled on top of her," she said, shaking her head in disbelief.

"Charlie knew she was too small to go down that slide, and I'm the one who promised to keep her safe," I reminded her.

"You wanted to do this for her, because she wanted to go down that damn slide so badly. And honestly, the demon is getting a bad rap. This accident has nothing to do with the slide. It was caused by a bunch of wild kids who fell on top of her. You couldn't have stopped that, and neither could Charlie." She paused to sip her coffee. "If you're going to be in a relationship with a man who has a child, you're going to be very involved in Harper's life. So sometimes things are going to happen. They will happen with Charlie too. No one is perfect, Vi."

A tear ran down my cheek, and I swiped it away. "Look at me. I cry all the time now. This is why I'm not good at relationships. It's too much for me. Too much room for error, you know? Harper is in a freaking cast, Monny. Because of me."

"Harper is in a freaking cast because she's a kid and sometimes kids get hurt. You shielded her the best you could. You hung on to her all the way down that slide, and you've got bruises on your back from where you had a pile of kids on top of you. You called 911. You got her to the hospital. You did everything you could to keep her safe. Because you love her." She reached for my hands. "And you cry more now because you're actually feeling things. You just think you aren't good at relationships because you're so used to being let down by the people in your life. They've made you feel like you did something wrong. And that's deeply ingrained in your mind, but it's not true, Vi. You're amazing. Charlie knows it. Harper knows it. Everyone who loves you knows it. It's only you who doesn't know it."

I sighed. I was exhausted.

Knowing I'd allowed the little girl I loved more than life itself to get hurt, as well as letting down the man who felt like forever—it was heavy and exhausting.

"I just think I'm doomed when it comes to love." I shrugged. "I mean, my own father left me before I was born. He hadn't even met me yet, and he was one foot out the door. And then my mother's blamed me my whole life for running off the only man she ever loved. And don't even get me started about Missy." I shook my head as the tears continued to fall.

"Okay, let's dissect this a bit, yeah?" She gave me a knowing look. "Your father left his pregnant wife. That had nothing to do with you. He had an affair and fell in love with another woman. He ditched his unborn baby and never looked back. That says a whole lot about his character and nothing about yours."

"He really is a selfish bastard, isn't he?" I sipped my coffee and waited for her to continue.

"Your mother suffered a broken heart. We've all been there. But she then gives birth to her only child, and she blames her baby for her own unhappiness. Clearly there were some issues in their relationship long before you arrived if he was willing to leave her while she was pregnant. And her making the choice to turn to the bottle and be a complete asshole most of your life is, again, her choice, her character. It has nothing to do with you." She swiped at the tear rolling down her cheek now. "You know what your character says?"

"'Let's go on the slide that your father said you weren't old enough to go down'?" I said, my tone laced with sarcasm.

"No, Vi. It says that you care. You stick by people that don't even deserve you. You showed up for Velveteen on her wedding day, even though she's been a complete dick to you your whole life. You help your mother financially, even though she's completely ungrateful. Because your heart is so big." She sniffed several times.

"Great. Now I've made you cry. I'm such a downer right now," I croaked.

She chuckled. "Stop it. Listen to me. You love Charlie and Harper. Don't run from that. It's a good thing. I've watched you fall so hard for both of them, and it's been so beautiful to see. The way he looks at you. The way she looks at you. The way you look at them. It's rare and it's special. But it's also fragile, and sure, you're going to make mistakes. Everyone does. My God, Myles left me and went back home. Do you know how much that hurt? But he figured it out. And I love him even more for realizing that we belong together. Don't run, Vi. Just keep showing up, okay?"

"I'm scared," I whispered. And that was what was at the crux of all of this.

Fear.

"What are you afraid of?"

"Letting down the two people that I love most. What if it had been worse yesterday? What if she'd broken her neck?"

"But it wasn't. Put it in perspective. It was a playground accident. I went down that slide when I was five years old. Charlie was being overprotective, building it up into this big thing. He knows that. He doesn't blame you. He asked you to come over last night. He told you that he loves you. He's not going anywhere. You're the only one running."

"Why wouldn't he leave me after this? People have left me for much less." I shrugged because it was the truth.

"Because that's not Charlie. It was an accident. People don't leave when things are challenging. That's not how love works, Vi. Not real love. What you have with him is real. And you have to trust that."

"I don't know if I can," I said, the tears falling once again.

Because fear could be all-consuming sometimes.

And when you loved as fiercely as I loved Charlie and Harper, the fear of losing them was just as fierce.

Fear and love weren't all that different.

They were both powerful. Both extreme.

"Well, that's what you're going to have to figure out. But I'm here to tell you that it's going to be a lonely life if you're too afraid to love and to be loved."

"I love you," I said, arching a brow.

"Do you know how many times I had to chase after you the first year after we met? Every time we had a spat, you'd go MIA," she said over her laughter.

"I have a hard time getting close to people sometimes." I groaned. "Why is life so hard for me?"

"You're making it harder than you have to. Just stop jumping to the worst conclusions. When you make a mistake, just say sorry. You're human," she said.

"Don't insult me. You make me sound so average." I smiled for the first time since I picked Harper up from school yesterday.

My best friend had a way of calming me down.

She laughed and moved to her feet before wrapping her arms around me. "There she is. I love you, bestie."

"Love you more."

There was a knock on the door, and I padded over to open it.

"Ditch day!" Blakely said as she walked in with a box of doughnuts and two grocery bags full of treats. "Let's watch chick flicks and eat all the junk food."

These two were my ride or dies.

They knew when I was down, and they always showed up.

"Are we really all not working today?" I asked, unpacking the grocery bags and laughing as I unloaded the giant bag of Skittles, licorice, orange slices, chocolate bars, and three different kinds of chips.

"Damn straight. I told Blakely to put a sign on the door that we're closed." Montana pulled the last thing out of the bag and made a face. "All this crap and then you tossed in string cheese?"

"Hey, I figured we'd need some protein, right? Keep the balance."

"Makes sense to me," I said.

"Charlie stopped by the office during the two minutes I was there to put a sign on the door," Blakely said, arching a brow as she looked at me. "He looked pretty concerned when I told him you weren't coming in."

I glanced down at my phone and saw the text from him. I'd messaged him again at 5:00 a.m., knowing he wasn't up yet, but I'd been worried. I'd asked him to be sure to let me know how Harper was feeling in the morning.

Charles: She slept through the night and said she feels good. She wants to go to school and show off her cast. But we both miss you. Come home, Firefly.

Was he really not angry at me about this?

I deserved to be pushed away after what I'd done.

"What did you tell him?" I asked, my thumb tracing over the screen where I'd read his message.

"I told him that we were having a girls' day. That I'd bought a ton of junk food, and we were going to just hang at your place and watch movies. He nodded and gave me this look like someone ran over his puppy before he left."

"I figured he'd wake up this morning and realize I'd convinced him to trust me when he shouldn't have, and he'd ignore me for the rest of my life. I don't know. Maybe I thought that because I don't forgive myself yet."

"Forgive you? There's nothing to forgive. Now, those little hellion kids are a different story." Montana chuckled. "But Charlie loves you, you big, clueless doofus."

"I love when Monny gets mad and calls you names," Blakely said with a laugh.

"Okay, let's watch a movie so I can forget about my troubles for a little while."

We spent the next six hours watching Bourne movies with Matt Damon, because watching sappy love stories was going to make me more emotional than I already was.

"I can't watch any more action scenes. I'm so on edge." Blakely stood up and stretched.

"Same. And I've eaten so much junk food, my stomach is bloated," Montana said.

"Well, I'm ready to get up. I need to text Charlie to check on Harper. She should be home from school soon." I started cleaning up all the bags of food and carrying them to the kitchen.

"I love you, Vi." Montana wrapped her arms around me and hugged me so tight it was hard to breathe.

Blakely did the same, and I thanked them both for having a ditch day with me.

Once they were gone, I sent a text to Charlie.

Me: How did Harper do at school?

Charles: You should ask her yourself. She wants to know where you are.

Me: Can't you just tell me that she's okay?

Charles: No, Firefly. That's not how this works. You don't get to hide and just check in from a distance. She loves you. That doesn't work for her. I love you. That doesn't work for me either.

Me: Did she stay all day at school?

I chewed on my thumbnail while I waited for a response.

Nothing. Nada. Crickets.

Me: You're a stubborn ass, Charlie Huxley.

Charles: Damn straight, woman. Get used to it. I'm in for the long haul. The question is, are you?

I groaned as I walked to the bedroom and opened the top drawer to get some fuzzy socks, so I could climb back in bed and hide under the covers.

I dug through the drawer, felt something weird, and pulled it out.

I stared down at Clementine Claus Huxley, the Elf on a Shelf who had run me off the first time. There was a note tied to her hand, and I read it.

Next time you want to run . . . remember . . . I'm not a serial killer. I'm just a man who loves a woman, Firefly.

When had he put this in my drawer? Was it the night that he told me he loved me? Sometime after that?

I sat down on my bed and hugged that ridiculous elf against my chest. I realized something then. I was so used to being let down that every time anything went wrong, I was prepared for the worst.

I'd never been loved the way Charlie Huxley loved me. And even though fear seemed to be in the driver's seat of my life sometimes, at the end of the day, I knew one thing to be true.

I am just a woman who loves a man and his little girl. And that is enough.

I quickly tucked Clementine back in my drawer, because the last thing I needed to do was out the Elf on a Shelf and kill Harper's Christmas dreams.

The poor girl already had a cast covering half her arm.

I slipped on my tennis shoes and glanced in the mirror. I was still wearing my flannel jammies, my hair was a wild mess, and my eyes were still puffy from all the tears I'd shed over the last twenty-four hours.

But as I stared at my reflection, I smiled.

Because Charlie Huxley loved me no matter how I looked, or what I wore.

He loved me no matter how irrational I was. The highs and the lows . . . He'd stayed and fought for us.

I was the one who had been too scared to just say sorry and ask for forgiveness.

I was out the door and jogging toward his house. I needed the fresh air.

"Hey, Vi. You all right?" Charlotte from Blushing Blooms called out as she walked down the street toward me, looking at me like I had three heads.

"Yep. Never better!" I shouted and waved as I passed her.

I turned the corner and ran the next two blocks all the way to Charlie's house. I banged on the door, because I'd forgotten my key when I ran out.

He pulled the door open, and his lips turned up in the corners.

"Well, what do we have here?" He smirked. "Why are you panting?"

"I ran all the way here. And after eating junk food all day, that was not a good idea," I said.

"What are you doing here, Firefly?" He leaned against the doorframe, crossing his arms over his chest.

"I'm just a woman who loves a man, Charlie Huxley." I shrugged. "And his little girl."

"Welcome home, baby." He opened his arms, and I lunged at him.

He spun me around with a laugh, and Harper came running over. "I missed you, Vi."

I pushed myself up and gave Charlie a chaste kiss before turning to look at Harper. My eyes welled with tears as I took in her cast. A reminder of what had happened.

"I'm sorry, Harps."

"I'm not. Everyone at school thinks it's so cool. Look at all the people who signed it." Her cast was covered with tons of names written in different colors. But one spot in the center hadn't been touched, right next to where her father had signed. "I saved this spot for you."

"I can't believe you saved me the best spot," I said as I traced my thumb over the edge of the pink cast.

"Well, I love you, silly. I want to look down and see your name right next to Daddy's."

I placed a hand on my heart, because I loved this little girl so much that I felt physical pain at her words.

"I love you too, baby girl."

She wrapped her arms around my neck and hugged me.

I didn't care that she clunked me in the side of the head with her cast.

I was just happy to be here.

With Charlie and Harper.

Home.

CHAPTER THIRTY-FOUR

Charlie

The three of us had fallen back into a rhythm.

Most nights Violet stayed at my place, but she'd also redecorated the guest room at her house and made it a Pinkalicious room, so Harper loved when we'd all stay over there as well.

Today was Harper's last day of school, which meant field day and a family picnic.

My daughter wanted us both there. She'd said it like it was just the norm now.

Because we were a family, and I felt it every single day. In the simple things like making breakfast together and helping Harper with her school projects, to the more difficult things like the night my daughter had the stomach flu, and Violet and I stayed up with her all night trying to comfort her.

Things had calmed down with Denise Quigley after I'd met with both her teacher and an administrator about the bullying. Turned out other parents had made many complaints about her behavior, and Denise and her mother were brought in to discuss the situation. I wasn't privy to what those details were, but she'd left Harper alone ever since, which was all I cared about.

I drove the truck over to pick up Violet before we headed to Rosewood River Elementary for the big day.

"I see we've got a special outfit on today," I said, raising a brow as I opened the passenger door for her outside her office.

"It's field day, right?" She glanced down at her pink tennis skirt and white tee that read TEAM HARPER HUXLEY in large pink letters. I leaned forward and kissed her before helping her into the truck. Her hair was in a high ponytail with a pink ribbon, and her white sneakers had pink laces. She was clearly going all out for field day.

Once I got into the driver's seat, I pulled away from the curb.

"We're going for the picnic. I don't usually participate in the ridiculous grown-up water balloon fight. I save that for the overzealous parents who are too competitive for their own good." I turned down the street where the school sat by an enormous green field.

"Charles, I'm the overzealous, competitive grown-up currently wearing a themed outfit. Harper said the water balloon contest is like dodgeball, and the last man or woman standing gets the prize, which happens to be a rainbow unicorn stuffed animal. And our girl wants it. So guess who is playing dodgeball with water balloons? This girl right here. And I am not above kicking and scratching if it means I get the gold."

I barked out a laugh as I pulled into the parking lot. "God damn, I love you, Firefly."

"You're going to love me more when I walk off the field carrying that unicorn. Buckle up, Charlie Huxley—you haven't seen me in competition mode yet."

I came around and opened her door and helped her out of the truck, interlacing our fingers as we walked toward the field.

Harper waved us over to where the kids were all sitting on the lawn. She came running toward us, her nose and cheeks a little red from all the activity.

"Wow! Vi, I like your outfit."

I couldn't help but chuckle, seeing as they were dressed the same, but Harper's tee said Rosewood River Field Day, which all the kids were wearing. But she had on the skirt and the sneakers, and her hair was in the same high ponytail.

"We're twins," Violet said. "How did it go?"

"My class got first in the tug-of-war and second in the water balloon challenge," my daughter said, beaming.

"A gold and a silver, that's impressive," Violet said.

I didn't have the heart to point out that there were only two classes in the competition, so the only options were gold and silver.

"Yes!" Harper exclaimed. Her cast would finally be coming off in two weeks. "I didn't get to do the tug-of-war, but Mrs. Wharton let me run up and down and cheer for my class."

"Of course you did," my girlfriend said.

Mrs. Wharton walked over with a smile on her face, and I didn't even know the woman was capable of smiling. "Charlie, Violet, nice to see you both."

"Nice to see you," we said at the same time.

"I hope you'll both be staying for the picnic and award ceremony after." The elderly woman smiled down at my daughter.

"We wouldn't miss it," Violet said as she grabbed her foot. She was bending one leg behind her to stretch when she noticed other parents heading out to the field.

"Violet is going to do the water balloon challenge, and me and Daddy will be cheering her on," Harper said.

"Good luck. The competition is steep this year." She chuckled.

Mr. Zambo blew his whistle before shouting for all parents participating in the water balloon competition to make their way over.

Violet high-fived Harper and me before jogging out to the field.

"She's the best, isn't she, Daddy?" my daughter said as we found a good spot to cheer.

"She is. And so are you." I rumpled the top of her hair.

The whistle blew, and the next fifteen minutes were the most entertaining of my entire life. At least thirty parents were out on the field. Half were taken out in the first two minutes of the competition. Violet stood out as she ducked and jived, like dodgeball was her day job. The next group was out fairly quickly as well, as most of the parents just sort of stood there throwing balloons before getting pelted and taken out.

Five people were left standing, and of course, Violet was one of them. I wasn't the least bit surprised. She was determined and driven, and I fucking loved it. The four men competing against her didn't stand a chance. The kids were all cheering, and most of them were shouting Violet's name. They now called her the "demon slayer" in Harper's class.

Violet ran all over the field, with water balloons being hurled in her direction, and she looked like a rock star out there.

The last two men on her team got nailed back to back, and they sulked off the field.

It was down to three. Two against one, and my girl was the only one left on her team.

They were firing off shots, and Violet took her time. She jumped over a balloon that had been launched at her ankle, just as she spiraled one at Steve Peterson, hitting him right in the chest. He chuckled and high-fived her as he jogged off the field.

It was just Violet and Josh Jones. The whistle blew, and Josh rifled a green balloon at Violet, who appeared to be running firefighter-style drills on the field as she zigzagged all over the place.

Harper was squeezing my hand, and Josh chucked his last balloon at her and missed again. Violet caught him as he turned to go get more and nailed him in the back.

The crowd roared, and my daughter and Lily took off running on the field as the three of them celebrated like they'd just won the Super Bowl.

Everyone was smiling as they watched, and Jeanne and Tim stood beside me, laughing hysterically.

"You better put a ring on that one soon," Tim said teasingly.

"Did you just quote Beyoncé?" Jeanne said with a laugh.

And I just smiled.

Because it wasn't the first time the thought had crossed my mind.

The family picnic was a lot better this year from having Violet with me. She was social and funny, and I wasn't in any hurry for it to end. Mrs. Wharton gave all the students an award, and Harper received the best reader award for all the books she'd read this year. I'd thought the party was over when Mrs. Wharton took the microphone to speak again.

"Okay, we finished all the awards, but we have one last one that we always save. It's the most special award I give out each year. It's the citizenship award. This award is for the student who is kind and compassionate to everyone in the classroom. This award is voted on by all the teachers who work with our class, including me, Mr. Zambo in PE, Mrs. Clark in art, and Ms. Scott in music. This year was a unanimous decision, and the citizenship award goes to Miss Harper Huxley. She has a heart of gold, and when I asked her classmates about her, every single one of them said she'd always been kind to them. In this crazy world, it's important to be kind, and I'm proud to give this award to you, Harper Huxley."

My daughter's eyes were wide as she jogged up to the front to get her trophy from Mrs. Wharton. I glanced over at Violet. Tears streamed down her cheeks as she clutched the rainbow unicorn stuffed animal she'd won for Harper and watched with pride.

I guess kindness is contagious.

Because both of my girls have it in spades.

"This was really sweet of you," I said as I took in the tent in the middle of her living room. There were twinkle lights strung across the ceiling, a blanket on the floor, and a pizza on a little tray table sitting on the blanket. She had a bottle of wine and two glasses, along with candles lit on every surface nearby. Violet didn't do anything half assed.

"I like our new plan of surprising one another with date nights each week," she said, leading me over to the tent. "So this is dinner and a movie, and maybe you'll get lucky before we go home."

Abigail had agreed to babysit once a week so we could make this time for one another, and Harper was fine with it. If we did it on a weekend, she'd invite Lily over, and if it was a weeknight, she and Abigail would do her homework and watch a show together.

"This is really great. What are we watching?" I settled on the blanket as she reached for the remote.

"Well, I thought we could watch *The Proposal*. It's one of my favorite movies, and it takes place in Alaska."

"Never heard of it." I placed a slice of pizza on each of our plates and opened the bottle of wine.

"It's a rom-com, Charles."

I groaned. "Nobody gets shot or killed?"

"Nope," she chuckled. "You'll love it, though. They bicker a lot, just like we do."

"Maybe we like bickering." I handed her a glass of wine.

"Yeah, I'd rather bicker with you than have a pleasant conversation with anyone else."

I laughed. "Good to know. It brings us back to the same discussion we had last week."

She reached for her pizza and turned to face me. "The one where we had sex on that boat you rented for date night, and then you said you wanted me in your bed every night?"

"That's the one. And you told me to see if I felt the same way in a week, and I do."

I reached for another slice.

"So what does that mean? You want me to sleep over every night, even though I already do most nights?" She shrugged.

"No. It means we live together. We're together every day. Harper is crazy about you. Why have two homes?" I took a bite of pizza as she gaped at me.

"You want me to move in with you?"

"Yes."

"You've never lived with a woman before," she said, as if that was news to me.

"I've never loved a woman before."

Her gaze softened. "And you have no hesitation?"

"Nope. Do you?"

"I don't have any hesitation when it comes to you or to Harper. I just don't know what it means," she said. "Is it fine to live together when we aren't married? You know, because you have a child, and I just don't want to do anything that would be harmful to her."

I smiled. This was music to my fucking ears.

"Listen, nothing in my little girl's life has been traditional. Harper has a mother who visited her once a year, who felt more like a stranger. She's been raised by a single dad who doesn't have a fucking clue what he's doing, but she knows that she's loved. At the end of the day, that's what matters. Nothing about you loving that little girl is harmful. But if you want to get married, all you have to do is say the word, Firefly. I didn't think that was something you wanted, but I'm all in. I'd marry you right now, right here in this tent, if you wanted that. I have no doubts. I know what I want, and I'm looking at her." I intertwined my hand with hers.

Her chest was rising and falling, and she sighed. "I have no doubts either. I just don't want to do anything that would hurt Harper."

"Take her out of the equation for a minute, because you and I being married or living together won't make a difference to Harper. She knows we're a family, and that's what matters to her. She asks me why you aren't there on the nights you don't sleep at the house. You love her, and she knows it. She loves you, and you know it. So take her out of the equation. Do you want to get married?"

"I mean, that was a lame way to ask me," she said as her teeth sank into her bottom lip.

I shoved the pizza box out of the way, moving the wineglasses aside as well. I pushed up and settled on one knee. "Violet Delphinium Beaumont, I love you. I want to spend my life with you. I want to wake up with you in the morning and go to sleep with you at night. I want to argue with you by day and then have makeup sex with you before we go to sleep. I want to live with you. I want to marry you. I want everything you're willing to give me. Hashtag 'love you, mean it.'"

"Wow. You even tossed in the hashtag. Very impressive. But you didn't ask the question." She smirked.

"You are one stubborn ass of a woman. Will you marry me, Firefly?"

"Yes. I want to marry you, Charlie Huxley. Hashtag 'love you, mean it.'" She lunged at me and wrapped her arms around my neck.

I kissed her hard, tipping her back on the blanket and hovering above her. "I don't have a ring, but we'll go get one, okay?"

"I don't care about the ring, Charles. I've got the guy. And my favorite little girl. I've already won this whole marriage gig."

"So we're doing this?"

"Yep. There's no rush. But we can tell Harps we're getting married before I move in." She smiled up at me.

"I like the sound of that."

"Actually, I do have all this land, and we love this house. What if we do an addition and make this place our forever home? We can stay in your place while we renovate."

I thought it over. Her land was spectacular. We could make this everything we wanted. "You sure you can handle doing a renovation like that with me?" I stroked the hair away from her gorgeous face.

"I've never been more sure about anyone or anything."

"Me either."

"I love you," she said as a tear slipped down her cheek.

"I love you. And soon I'll get to call you my wife."

"Don't even dream of going all caveman on me. We're equal partners in everything."

I laughed. "I wouldn't expect anything less, Firefly."

"You sure you can handle forever with me? I'm a handful."

There was humor in her tone, but I heard the fear beneath it. She grew up with selfish parents who hadn't made her feel safe or secure. I planned to change that. I placed my thumb and pointer finger beneath her chin, waiting for her gaze to lock with mine.

"There are very few things in this world that I'm sure of. But the day Harper was born and they placed her in my arms, I knew I'd walk through fire for my baby girl. I knew I'd spend the rest of my life being the best father I could be to her." I cleared my throat. "And when I look at you, I see forever. I've never felt that before. And you can rant and rave and throw things at my head when you're angry, and I'll still be there every damn day. You can redecorate the house and change your mind five million times, and piss me off to no end, and I'll still be there every damn day, Violet. There are two things in my life that I'm sure about, and that's my two girls. So yes, I'm fucking sure I'm ready for forever with you. You sure you're ready for forever with me? Because I'm a package deal, you know?"

She chuckled as the tears continued to fall down her cheeks. "I think seeing you with Harper has made me fall harder for you. Seeing the way you love that little angel is one of my favorite things about you. And I love Harper in a way I never knew I could. Hell, I didn't even like kids before I met her." She chuckled and sniffed a few times. "And being with you, Charlie Huxley—being with you is the first time I've ever felt like I fit somewhere. You make me feel like I'm home."

"You are, Firefly."

I pulled her onto my lap and wrapped my arms around her as she sniffed a few more times.

Loving someone was a vulnerable thing.

And Violet and I had both spent a lifetime trying not to be vulnerable.

So it was scary to love this deeply.

But it was also the best feeling in the world.

"Is it too soon to say I want to put a baby in you someday?" I whispered in her ear.

She laughed, tipping her head back so she could look at me.

"Too soon, Charles. I've got all I want with you and Harper. That's a conversation for a way later date."

"No hurry. Just thought I'd shoot my shot while you were saying yes to everything," I said.

"Let's go tell our little girl the big news," Violet said.

Our little girl.

"Nothing would make me happier."

And I meant it.

EPILOGUE

Violet

"This is so you," Montana said as she slipped a few flowers in my long French braid before turning and doing the same to Harper's hair.

"Yep. Not many people get married three days after they get engaged." Blakely chuckled. "But it's very on brand for you."

"What's 'on brand' mean?" Harper asked.

I bent down to get eye level with her. "It just sort of means your style and your personality."

"Oh. Then I love your brand, Vi. I want my brand to be just like your brand," Harper said, and my chest nearly exploded.

"I love your style and your personality too, Harps. Are you ready to go get married?"

"I'm ready!" she shouted.

We were wearing matching floral maxi dresses with our boots. We'd decided to get married on the patio at the Moose Brew, overlooking the water. Benji had closed the place down. It was just supposed to be Charlie, Harper, and me, but of course Montana insisted on being a witness, and Myles said he'd officiate, and Blakely and Benji both said they'd be the token guests.

It was small and intimate. No frills or stress.

No invitations or worrying about family squabbles and who would show up.

Harper and I picked wildflowers earlier that day, which we'd hold as Charlie and I said our vows.

We walked hand in hand out of the restroom and headed for the patio.

Country music was playing through the speakers, and I looked up to see Charlie watching me walk toward him, with his daughter's hand in mine.

She felt like our daughter at this point, but that would all come in good time.

Montana, Blakely, and Benji sat in the few chairs we'd placed on the patio, and my best friend already had tears streaming down her face. I leaned down and kissed Harper on the cheek, and Charlie did the same, before she walked off and sat with our friends to watch.

"Hey, Firefly," he said. "You ready to make it official?"

"Absolutely."

Myles read from his script about the bond between a husband and a wife, and we all listened intently, trying not to chuckle at how serious he was being. And then he turned to us and asked if we'd like to read our vows.

I nodded for Charlie to go first.

"You know I'm a man of few words, but I've got some things I'd like to say to you," he said, holding my hands in his. I nodded, encouraging him to continue. "For a long time I thought it would just be me and Harps against the world." He paused and winked at his daughter. "I couldn't imagine room for anyone else. And then you stood on a stool in a pair of panties and high heels in the guesthouse, fighting with a smoke detector, and everything changed."

Everyone chuckled, including me, as I swiped at the single tear rolling down my cheek.

"You light up every room you walk into, Firefly. But you lit something in me that had been snuffed out for a long time. My heart beats for you and Harper. I want to do forever with you. I want to fight with you and laugh with you and maybe even renovate a few homes with you. Because I'd rather argue with you than get along with anyone else. I want to grow old with you. Every part of you. As corny as it sounds—you complete me, baby. Hashtag 'love you.'" He leaned down and whispered in my ear. "Mean it."

For a man of few words, he'd managed to bring me to tears.

I sniffled, and Myles told me to take my time.

I opened my paper as a tear fell from my eye and the ink bled out like a spiderweb. I didn't really need to read what I'd written. I knew what I was going to say, but I held the paper just in case.

"Charles," I said, smiling up at him, "I never thought I'd be standing here, reading my vows to a man. I never thought I'd find someone who I knew was the love of my life. The other half of my soul. A man I'd trust with my heart. A little girl I'd call my own," I said as my voice wobbled, and I glanced over at Harper. "And then I made some pink pancakes and tied a whole lot of balloons, and I couldn't get enough." I sniffed as he chuckled and used the pad of his thumb to swipe the tears on my face away. "I never believed I would fit somewhere. I spent my whole life trying to find my place. My home. My people. I'd been so wounded at a young age that I didn't actually believe in happily ever after. And then I met you. And I couldn't run from it, because you're a part of me now. Thank you for showing me what love looks like. Thank you for making me believe in forever." I kissed his cheek and whispered in his ear. "Hashtag 'love you, mean it.'"

I turned to face Harper. "Harper Penelope Huxley, you are also the love of my life. I promise to show up for you every day, the way that you deserve. I promise to tie pink balloons until my fingers bleed, and to hold your hand when you need me beside you. I promise to never take you on the demon slide again," I said as everyone laughed.

"We did it, Vi. You and me." Harper shook her head as tears streamed down her little face.

"Any slide other than the demon, please," Charlie said with a laugh.

I nodded. "I love you, Harps."

"I love you, Vi. You're the most real mama I ever had."

"Well, let's keep doing that, okay?" I blew her a kiss and turned back to face Myles.

"For fuck's sake," he muttered under his breath so only we could hear him as he blinked several times, and a single tear rolled down his cheek. He shook it off quickly. "Okay. Let's finish this off right."

He continued to read from his script as we nodded and repeated the words he read.

Most of it was a blur to me as I just stared up at Charlie.

I couldn't believe I was here.

I'd found my other half.

I remembered hearing Myles say the words, "I now pronounce you man and wife, you may kiss the bride," just before Charlie scooped me into his arms and kissed me senseless.

Our friends cheered and clapped their hands together, but we just kept on kissing.

Because Charlie and I knew we'd found forever.

We'd never quite fit anywhere else, but together, with Harper—we were a perfect match.

Love you, mean it.

ACKNOWLEDGMENTS

Greg, you inspire every hero I write. Love you!

Chase and Hannah, thank you for always being my biggest cheerleaders. Love you!

Willow, Catherine, and Kandi, I am so grateful to be on this journey with you. Thank you for listening, for cheering me on, for making me laugh on the days I need it most. So thankful for your friendship!

Pathi, thank you for believing in me from the start and giving me the push I needed.

Nat, I am SO INCREDIBLY thankful to have you in my corner. I'd be lost without you.

Lauren Plude and Lindsey Faber, thank you for believing in me and in the Blushing Bride world. Thank you for being so incredibly supportive and kind throughout the process. Cheers to our first book together! I'm so grateful for you both!

Nina, thank you for making my wildest dreams come true. I am forever grateful for YOU!

Kim Cermak, thank you for all that you do for me. I'm endlessly thankful for you!

Christine Miller, Kelley Beckham, Tiffany Bullard, Sarah Norris, Valentine Grinstead, Meagan Reynoso, Amy Dindia, Josette Ochoa, and Ratula Roy, I am endlessly thankful for YOU!

Tatyana (*Bookish Banter*), Logan Chisolm, Kayla Compton, thank you for all that you do for me to support every release and keep me on track!

Abi Mehrholz, thank you for all your support and encouragement. I'm so grateful for you!

Paige, forever grateful for your friendship. You brighten Mother's Days! LOL!

Stephanie Hubenak, thank you for always reading my words early! So grateful for your friendship!

Doo, Annette, Abi, Meagan, Diana, Jennifer, Pathi, Natalie, and Caroline, thank you for being the BEST beta readers EVER! Your feedback means the world to me. I am so thankful for you!

Natasha, Corinne, and Lauren, thank you for pushing me every day and being the best support system! Love you!

Amy, I love sprinting with you so much! So grateful for your friendship! Love you!

Gianna Rose, Rachel Parker, Janelle Pegram, Kelly Yates, Rachel Baldwin, Sarah Sentz, Ashley Anastasio, Kayla Compton, Tiara Cobillas, Tori Ann Harris, and Erin O'Donnell, thank you for your friendship and your support. It means the world to me!

Mom, thank you for being my biggest cheerleader and reading everything I write! Love you!

Dad, you really are the reason that I keep chasing my dreams! Thank you for teaching me to never give up. Love you!

Sandy, thank you for reading and supporting me throughout this journey! Love you!

To all the bloggers, Bookstagrammers, and ARC readers who have posted, shared, and supported me—I can't begin to tell you how much it means to me. I love seeing the graphics you make and the gorgeous posts you share. I am forever grateful for your support!

To all the readers who take the time to pick up my books and take a chance on my words . . . THANK YOU for helping to make my dreams come true!

KEEP UP ON NEW RELEASES

Linktree Laurapavlovauthor

Newsletter Laurapavlov.com

FOLLOW ME

Website laurapavlov.com
Goodreads @laurapavlov
Instagram @laurapavlovauthor
Facebook @laurapavlovauthor
Pav-Love's Readers @pav-love's readers
Amazon @laurapavlov
BookBub @laurapavlov
TikTok @laurapavlovauthor

ABOUT THE AUTHOR

Photo © 2020 Chase Pavlov

Laura Pavlov is best known for writing swoony, emotional stories with a side of angst and a dash of humor. A hopeless romantic at heart, she likes to take her characters on a journey that always leads to happily ever after. Pavlov is happily married to her college sweetheart and devoted to her two amazing kids, who are now adulting. She's also a dog whisperer to one temperamental Yorkie and one wild Bernedoodle. The author resides in Las Vegas, Nevada, where she is currently living her own happily ever after.

Printed in Dunstable, United Kingdom